THE BARON'S DANGEROUS CONTRACT

The Dukes' Pact Series
Book Four

By Kate Archer

ARE YOU SIGNED UP FOR DRAGONBLADE'S BLOG?

You'll get the latest news and information on exclusive giveaways, exclusive excerpts, coming releases, sales, free books, cover reveals and more.

Check out our complete list of authors, too!

No spam, no junk. That's a promise!

Sign Up Here

www.dragonbladepublishing.com

Dearest Reader;

Thank you for your support of a small press. At Dragonblade Publishing, we strive to bring you the highest quality Historical Romance from the some of the best authors in the business. Without your support, there is no 'us', so we sincerely hope you adore these stories and find some new favorite authors along the way.

Happy Reading!

CEO, Dragonblade Publishing

**Additional Dragonblade books by
Author Kate Archer**

The Dukes' Pact Series
The Viscount's Sinful Bargain (Book 1)
The Marquess' Daring Wager (Book 2)
The Lord's Desperate Pledge (Book 3)
The Baron's Dangerous Contract (Book 4)

PROLOGUE

Whites, London 1817

THOUGH THE WEATHER was temperate, the six old dukes had ordered a small fire built in their favored room. To a man, they found the damp had become their mortal enemy—it crept into every bone and joint and settled in like an unwelcome houseguest. The Duke of Wentworth was allowed the chair closest to that welcome drying heat, as it cheered the rest that they were not worse off than that gentleman and his gouty foot.

A few of the dukes were in desperate need of cheer at that moment, as they could not quite comprehend how Dembly had come out in front.

That particular duke, being of relatively sound body but perhaps less sound intellect and judgment, threw back his glass of claret and set it down with a cheerful smile.

"Well, gentlemen," he said. "My son has married Miss Lily Farnsworth. You will know the lady as one who is renowned for her skill at piquet. I did wonder how my duchess would take the news, as she was set on a Miss Hayes or Miss Blaise or something or other, but it has all come out right. The couple have gone to the continent for an extended wedding trip."

The rest of the dukes muttered their congratulations.

"Gad," Dembly continued, "I would not have thought it. My

son is so hardheaded."

"As are the rest of them," the Duke of Wentworth said, staring morosely at his foot.

"No matter," the Duke of Carlisle said. "Three of them are wed, we are halfway to our intention of seeing them all so. I believe cutting their funds in half has had good effect—eliminating them all together will spur on the stragglers. We went into this together and we will go on with it together until every last one of them has tied himself."

"Agreed," The Duke of Wentworth said. "I will see a male grandchild on this earth before the gout kills me off."

"Hear, hear," the dukes said in unison.

CHAPTER ONE

Mᴉss Pᴇɴɴʏ Dᴀʀʟɪɴɢᴛᴏɴ folded the letter she'd just received from Lady Ashworth, née Lily Farnsworth. Her friend sounded as delirious with happiness as she had been on the night of her engagement at Lady Hathaway's Tudor ball. She and her new husband had recently crossed the Jura mountains and made their way to Geneva, where they were merrily making ruinous bets. At least, ruinous for those who dared lay down a pack of cards in front of them.

Penny leaned back on the sofa and sighed, remembering that very strange ball at Lady Hathaway's house.

It had all begun exceedingly jolly. In honor of the Tudor theme, they had danced the pavane. Lord Cabot led her and proved to be a competent student to Lord and Lady Lockwood's instruction of the dance. Lord Cabot then claimed the dance before supper—he'd made a habit of doing so, as he liked to talk to her of horses. At least, he would *claim* that was the reason for his rather persistent attentions. Penny had been certain there was something more between them.

She had been mistaken.

First had come Lord Ashworth, carrying Lily down the corridor. Then, the news that they were engaged spreading like a flame over dry kindling. Regardless of the engagement, some were shocked—one was not accustomed to seeing a lord carrying a lady about at a ball. Lady Montague, in particular, had let all and sundry know she considered the behavior outrageous. Of all that was said on the subject, Lady Montague's outrage probably worked the most in the couple's favor—she was feared, but so very disliked. The couple themselves had not seemed to give a toss for anybody's opinion.

Lord Ashworth and Lily had gone into supper and had eyes only for each other. Their other dinner partners were left to sit alone, staring straight ahead with vague smiles on their faces. That was the moment all of Penny's ideas had begun to crumble.

Amidst the Tudor table spread with spit-turned mutton, spiced jellies, and stewed conger eel, she'd glanced at the happy couple and said, "Now you see, Lord Cabot, there is another of your friends to fall to the Dukes' Pact. That is only three of you left and all ridiculously living as schoolboys in a house together."

She had been in the habit of teasing Lord Cabot, but on reflection, she supposed calling him a schoolboy had been a step too far. No man wished to be reminded that he had once been a child. Or worse, to imply he might be as a child still. That it was true that the Lords Cabot and Grayson were currently camped in Lord Dalton's house on account of their funds being halved was a fact that might have been better left unmentioned.

Lord Cabot had stared determinedly at the roasted peacock centerpiece, the poor bird's feathers having been put back on after cooking, and said, "Ashworth is a fool and will live to rue the day."

Penny had expected him to laugh at his current circumstances. But instead, he'd condemned the idea of marriage so derisively! He did not even say it with his usual good humor—there was a seriousness to his tone that could not be ignored.

All along she'd looked upon the Dukes' Pact as some silly game. The fathers would pressure their sons to marry and the sons would just as vociferously claim they would not do it. But, surely, they all would do it when they met the right lady. Had not Hampton, Lockwood, and Ashworth proved just that?

How foolish she had been to imagine she might be the right lady for Lord Cabot.

As the supper wore on, it had been talk of horses, finally, that would take them to an even darker corner. After Penny had thought the lord had thrown off his ill-humor and she had even begun to believe he'd not meant what he'd said, a great debate had sprung up between them.

She'd claimed the Arabian was built for speed because of its larger windpipe, and if one could discover the breeding mechanism, one might gain the attribute for any sort of horse.

Lord Cabot countered that it was the Arabian's lighter weight that accounted for its speed.

It had begun as one of their usual lively sparrings. The sort they'd had so often. The sort that made dinners fly by and made turning to one's opposite partner a chore.

It had not ended so.

The conversation had grown heated enough to attract attention. Then, in front of all who were nearby, Lord Cabot said, "Miss Darlington, while you may drive a phaeton and have picked up bits of knowledge from your father, do not delude yourself into imagining any real expertise in horse breeding."

It had been a slap. A hard and public slap. She would never forgive him for it.

Nor might she ever forgive herself. She had not seen it coming. She'd not had time to gird herself against it. How could she have? It was not just an offhand comment. It was a refutation of everything she'd thought he considered her. He'd spent two seasons pretending to respect her opinions, and in one brief moment, he showed her that he never had.

It had been so unexpected that the sting had leapt into her eyes and she'd had to excuse herself before she wept in front of all. She'd been so mortified that she'd rushed to the ladies' retiring room. She'd sent a maid to retrieve her aunt and then claimed an illness. Mrs. Wellburton had made their excuses and the carriage was called.

Penny had donned her cloak and hurried across the hall to the front doors, refusing to look toward the dining room. She had been humiliated. Publicly humiliated.

She had told her aunt nothing of it, and only insisted that she had developed a terrible headache. She had held back her tears until she was in her bedchamber and then allowed herself to give vent to her feelings. She had cried for hours while her maid, Dora, fussed over her. Dear Dora had started life as a housemaid and had been consoling Penny over various hurts for as long as she could remember. Where once she would have brought Penny warmed milk to soothe, that night she'd been so alarmed she'd brought brandy borrowed from her father's decanter in the library.

Penny was not ignorant of why she had cried so many hours into the night. Though she presented a gay façade to the world, the truth was her feelings had always been easily stung. *Very* easily stung. She'd grown up surrounded by those who loved her, and yet had spent half her childhood weeping over some imagined slight. As she grew older, she grew more adept at hiding that awful flaw. Oh, how she'd worked to mask it! It would not do for one as cheerful as Miss Darlington, it would not do for one bold enough to drive her own Hooper High Flyer.

Her worst fear had occurred—she had been unable to mask her hurt while in public. Then, there was her humiliation at being so wrong about Lord Cabot! She had really thought he favored her. As it was, he only saw her as a vague amusement at supper, until she was no longer amusing and he thought to put her in her place.

He had embarrassed her in so many ways with one curt sentence. All along he'd pretended to admire her knowledge of horses, but it seemed he'd just been indulging her. Further, his ongoing attentions over the course of two seasons could not have failed to stir up talk of something developing. Now, all would understand it had only been a game, with her the gullible mark.

Since that weepy night, she had dried her eyes and those

feelings, once so bruised, had become encased in a hardened shell. Hurt had flown off and brought back antipathy to roost.

Many had witnessed her mortification that night. They would never do so again.

As she had done so often since that night, she was just now staring at the pianoforte and mulling over what scathing thing she might say when she saw Lord Cabot for the first time since that awful dinner. The drawing room, where she was no doubt meant to be sewing, had become the scene of an imaginary theater of reprisal and retribution.

Her father, Lord Mendbridge, interrupted her thoughts.

"There you are, Penny," he said in his usual *hail fellow, well met* cheer. "I suppose my sister has got the packing well in hand?"

Penny nodded. They were to set off for Mendbridge Cottage on the morrow in preparation for the races at Newmarket.

"You know she has, Papa," Penny said, working hard to sound cheerful. "My aunt is not one to leave things to the last minute. She has been harassing Montrose for a week over the arrangements."

"Very good. Excellent," the lord said. "By the by, we are to have a houseguest this year. I suppose that will not surprise, as we tend to have at least one every year."

"Yes, I know all about it," she said, laughing. Penny could not help but to laugh. Her father was so taken up with horses that he often could not recall what had been told him or who had told him it. It had been arranged for months that her childhood friend, Kitty Dell, would come to them.

"You do recall, Papa, that I invited the lady myself," Penny said.

"A lady is to come? What lady?" the viscount asked, looking as confused as he generally did when the arrangement did not involve the stable.

"Kitty," Penny said. "Remember? Kitty Dell is to come to us."

"Oh, yes, Miss Dell. Charming girl," the lord said. "Not who I meant, however. I've got to know a young man who's rather keen, seems to know what he's talking about. Refreshing, actually."

Penny waited for her father to name the gentleman. She was certain it was some young buck who'd taken to following her father around and asking questions. It was likely Mr. Preston, a gentleman just past his callow youth who had made it a point to know and revere the famed Lord Mendbridge. Her dear papa was forever taking on somebody green and attempting to season them up.

"Pleasant fellow. You'll know him, in any case," the viscount said. "Lord Cabot."

HENRY ROLAND, VISCOUNT Cabot and son of the Duke of Wentworth, surveyed Lord Dalton's library. Along with Lord Grayson, he'd been a houseguest in that particular residence ever since his funds had been cut in half.

His friend's library, never very orderly, had become a bedlam of books, empty glasses, discarded neckcloths and kicked off boots. Dalton's butler, Bellamy, tried to tidy it from time to time, but with three lords in the house, Henry knew it was a hopeless operation. How was the man to know to whom a particular neckcloth belonged?

Henry had once walked into the room, only to come upon the scene of three valets debating who owned what. Grayson's valet, a French fellow named LaRue, appeared ready to come to blows over the suggestion that a particular cloth belonged to his master. Between a string of French oaths and threats of violence, he pronounced the material "largement inféreiur."

For days, Henry had been thinking carefully on how to broach a subject that he knew would not find favor with his friends. In truth, when he thought of communicating the idea, he also thought of being near the door—lest Dalton have some idea of locking him up.

Both Grayson and Dalton had been complaining, yet again, about Ashworth. Out of the six of them, three had gone off and got married. Ashworth, they said, was particularly egregious. He had not even been supposed to *like* the lady!

That idea rankled them the most. None of them could understand how it had happened.

"Do you suppose he married her just because she's so good at cards?" Grayson asked, examining his cuffs.

"I do not see why he should," Dalton said. "He was good enough at cards on his own."

"And then, I still cannot fathom what *she* saw in *him*," Grayson said.

"That is only because she saw nothing in you," Dalton said drily.

"As to that, it is no matter," Grayson said cheerfully. "I am entirely recovered from my infatuation with Miss Farnsworth. I've set my sights on Miss Danworth, she of the remarkable blond curls."

Dalton snorted. "Miss Danworth is as cold as ice."

"Do not say so!" Grayson cried. "She laughs charmingly at all my jokes."

"Underneath the laughter is a deep freeze," Dalton said, finishing a letter and sanding it.

Henry had been silent for the past half hour. His friends turned to him.

"Why are you so quiet?" Dalton asked him.

"Oh, no reason," Henry said hurriedly. "I am only thinking of my filly. I ordered my groom to give her extra oats before I take her up to Newmarket."

"When do you go?" Grayson asked.

"Wednesday, I think," Lord Cabot said.

"Wednesday? Why so early?" Lord Dalton asked. "Grayson and I do not go up until Saturday."

"You do not have a horse in the race," Cabot pointed out.

Lord Dalton shrugged. "As you prefer. We'll see you at the club."

Cabot had only nodded. Though he'd had every intention of telling his friends he would not stay at the club, he had not quite got the idea out. His rooms there would be empty, while he would be ensconced in Lord Mendbridge's house a quarter mile away. He knew his friends were deeply suspicious of Miss Darlington, though they had been momentarily soothed after hearing of his contretemps with the lady at the Hathaways' Tudor ball.

In any case, he had very mixed feelings about the whole thing. On the one hand, he both dreaded and looked eagerly forward to seeing Miss Darlington again. He had been rather brutish at their last meeting. He did not even know why! She had teased him, and it had rankled. Then she'd challenged his knowledge of a horse's physiology and it had rankled even more. He had offered a set down.

Too much of a set down, as it turned out. The lady had left in near tears and all had witnessed it. He had been given a cool reception by everybody that had overheard him after the lady had departed. Even Lady Hathaway had shaken her head sadly at him as he left the house.

The very next day, he'd run into Lord Mendbridge at White's. He'd approached the lord with trepidation, but Mendbridge had been as friendly as ever. They'd had a lively debate concerning the talent likely to turn up at the upcoming races. They'd had many such conversations before, as they were both equally keen on horses. The lord had suddenly offered Cabot hospitality while he was in Newmarket. It was a singular honor—everybody wished to ensconce themselves in the lord's comfortable house and have access to his vast knowledge. For all that, Cabot had almost declined. But then, what was he to say?

My lord, thank you, but I best not as I have recently insulted your daughter at supper?

Of course he could not say such a thing. He could not break

with Lord Mendbridge. It was Mendbridge, for God's sake. The man knew horses like he knew the back of his hand.

So, he must face Miss Darlington. In her own house. He could not say what his reception would be. Might they laugh it off? He was hopeful of it. Miss Darlington *was* exceedingly good-humored. And if she did not laugh it off? Well, he supposed he'd clear that fence when he got to it.

But surely, she must laugh it off. He had not been himself on that blasted evening. It had been such a shock to see Ashworth carrying Miss Farnsworth into the ballroom. Ashworth had positively disliked the lady. How was it that he would choose to marry a lady he disliked, when he did not even wish to marry at all?

The spectacle of it, and how bewitched Ashworth had looked at supper, had begun to give Henry the feeling that women were as his uncle had always said. He claimed they were full of trickery and witchcraft. If they meant to wind you round in circles like a sailor's rope on a ship's deck, he'd said, they could do it in a blinking of an eye.

He'd vaguely wondered if Miss Farnsworth had done that to Ashworth, and if Miss Darlington were not doing that to himself. After all, what reason had he to think of her when she was not before him? What else could account for his visions of her jauntily making her way down an avenue, expertly driving her phaeton? Or her upturned face at dinner? Or her copper curls, the like of which he'd never seen? Or that these same curls had a different hue in daylight versus candlelight? For that matter, what compelled him to seek her out so often at a ball, when another lady would do perfectly well?

Somehow, from those ideas, had come an urgent need to prove she had no effect upon him whatsoever. Her charms would not defeat him. He had done so—spectacularly, rudely, and even ungentlemanly.

He'd since seen the nonsense of such flights of fancy. For one, he did not believe in any supernatural forces. For another, if women could wind all men round their finger, they would have far more power in the world than they had. And for another, his uncle was married to a shrew and so had very particular ideas on how that had befallen him.

Whatever the cause of Ashworth's marriage, Henry had no doubt he'd get the whole story from his friend when he returned from his wedding trip. He suspected it would be the most commonplace explanation in the world and have not a thing to do with being bewitched.

Meanwhile, in his sulk, or whatever it had been, he'd acted cruel. And to Miss Darlington, of all people! He had been stupid to deride her expertise in horses, as he very well knew she was educated beyond most men. She might even be more educated than himself. He'd often learned something in their conversations, though he'd be loath to admit it publicly. For all he knew, she was entirely correct about the Arabian's wider windpipe. Over the course of two seasons, he'd found he did not like to have any other as a dinner partner—other ladies generally understood so little.

Just the evening before, he'd suffered through an interminable supper with Miss Juniper. She'd not had the least interest in horses and claimed she almost trembled when even finding herself in a carriage pulled by the beasts. He supposed he was meant to be struck by the lady's delicacy. He also supposed he ought not have said, *I presume, then, that you do not get out much.* She had given him rather short shrift after that particular comment.

What was wrong with him? Why should he care that Ashworth had tied himself? It had no consequence to himself. And why should he take out that irritation on Miss Darlington?

Well, he would just trust to her good nature to carry them past the scuffle. In any case, he ought not to be dwelling on it. He had a far bigger problem at hand. He'd entered his filly into the thousand guinea stakes, though he did not currently have the stake. He'd have to borrow it from somebody, and likely somebodies were beginning to run thin on the ground.

Dalton and Grayson had none to spare and Hampton had not even answered his letter. Burke claimed he'd lost too heavily at hazard these past weeks. Ashworth would have been a likely source. The fellow always had money lying around from his gambling and he was remarkably free with loans. But that was not to be. Just now, Ashworth and his bride would be sliding down an Alp or singing folk songs in a Spanish taberna or whatever one did on the continent.

Despite the difficulties, the money must be found. All of his efforts must be concentrated on that. To turn up at Newmarket, in full view of Mendbridge, and be found lacking the stake would ruin his reputation forever.

CHAPTER TWO

PENNY HAD DONE her utmost to appear unfazed by the idea of Lord Cabot as a houseguest. After her father left the drawing room, she rose and went to the window that overlooked the stables in the back of the house. The sight of grooms rubbing down horses just back from exercise usually cheered her, but now it had little effect.

How could he? How dare he accept an invitation from her father and push into her own house?

Since the awful exchange at the ball, she'd only attended smaller affairs. She had not seen Lord Cabot, nor had she expected to. She had prepared herself to see him at the races. That, she had known she could not avoid. And, most likely, he would turn up at some of her engagements while she stayed in Newmarket. But she need not have any prolonged conversations with him. She intended to be cool, to let him know their interesting discussions were at an end. Then, she would sail off to some more friendly acquaintances and leave him standing alone like a fool.

What was she to do with him in her own house?

Though she had not told her aunt any of what had occurred at Lady Hathaway's ball, she thought she might do so now. She would need reinforcements and Mrs. Wellburton was as fierce a defender as a badger of her cub.

Her aunt had come to live with them when Penny was just five years old. Penny's mother had died and when her aunt became widowed before having children of her own, it seemed a likely arrangement. She'd acted as mother, advisor, and friend, and commiserated with Penny through all the little heartbreaks of childhood. As Penny had been a sensitive child, those heartbreaks were plentiful. Mrs. Wellburton suffered through them all with great patience. Despite her ridiculousness, Penny always had the comforting feeling that her aunt entirely approved of her.

Though, Mrs. Wellburton did not wholly agree with her brother's habit of encouraging his daughter so much when it came to horses, and *really* did not approve of the new phaeton or the tiger that went with it. Still, she was an agreeable lady who did not fight battles she could not win. Rather, she had early turned her attention to seeing that her niece was always suitably dressed and had all the pretty manners of a well-bred young lady.

Her aunt had the further benefit of being generally suspicious of men outside of her brother and her late husband, and particularly suspicious of the gentlemen of the Dukes' Pact. She had already cautioned her niece regarding Lord Cabot's continued attentions. Penny supposed she would be delighted to discover that the lord was no longer favored.

Montrose softly knocked on the door and entered. "Petit and Doom would wish Miss Darlington to know they are in the stable meeting room at your convenience."

Penny turned and straightened her skirts. She had quite forgot about the appointment. "Very well," she said, forcing her thoughts to the matter at hand. "I shall come presently."

⋙✦⋘

THE LORDS DALTON and Grayson contemplated one another. Lord Cabot had made some hurried excuse and rushed from the house not a minute before.

As Lord Dalton pulled aside a curtain and watched his friend leap on his horse, he said, "Do you suppose we trust him? Does Cabot really need to go to Newmarket so early?"

"I know what you think of," Grayson said. "I heard Lord Mendbridge goes up on the morrow. Does our friend follow his daughter, Miss Darlington?"

"Precisely."

"I shouldn't worry about it," Grayson said. "They've had a falling out. I was told by one who was nearby at the supper that Cabot was beastly to the lady. One cannot be beastly to a lady one admires."

"Speak for yourself," Dalton said. "Considering our recent experience, I've given up attempting to guess at how attachments may form."

"You do not think he goes to attempt to heal the rift?" Grayson asked.

Dalton tented his fingers. "I do not know. But perhaps we should repair to Newmarket early ourselves so we might find out. It is you and I who have the strongest reasons to avoid marrying, and I do not like to think of us being the last holdouts."

"Ah, you think the old dukes realize we have ever been the hardest two to crack?"

"I do."

"And so we must hold fast to Cabot," Grayson said. "He will be forever the shield we raise in front of ourselves."

"Such as he is."

"I cannot say I mind setting off early," Grayson said. "Though I will make a visit to old Crackwilder before I go. The man is perennially buried in his books and would starve if one did not remind him to eat."

"Why do you go on with the fellow?" Dalton asked. "It's all well and good that he was your lieutenant, but he's an odd sort of person."

"Precisely why," Grayson said. "He cares nothing for the *ton* or my title. I might be a baker as soon as a marquess. I find it does me good to sometimes be treated as a nobody."

"Yes," Dalton said drily. "I suppose it makes the regular fawning seem as new."

"Just so."

⟫⟪

LORD MENDBRIDGE'S LONDON stables were like no other. He'd long ago bought the three houses that sat behind his own and the one directly next door, tore them all down, and built his own equine utopia.

There were stalls for forty horses, an enormous carriage house, and a roomy yard to walk the horses as a cool down after they'd taken exercise. The stablemaster had his own cottage, the senior grooms each commanded their own apartment, and the junior grooms were doubled up in spacious rooms. The stable staff's meals were prepared in the lord's own kitchen and were of the same quality that were served to the family, though for practical reasons perhaps not as many courses. A fair ration of ale was given each hand, along with a small glass of port for after their dinner.

This assured the lord that he would attract and retain the best talent in the country—who of them would leave for another stable, only to sleep in what amounted to a hayloft? Who of them would suffer stale bread and meat nearly gone off after having feasted on Lord Mendbridge's largesse? Who of them would settle for a late-night cup of tea when they might regard each other over glasses of port like any swell? His staff was loyal, and they had every reason to be.

The tack room was unrivaled. It contained everything a groom might wish to have at hand, and all the first quality. There was a relatively constant influx of new conveyances to admire, each new design that emerged to market quickly snatched up by the lord. Most recently, Miss Darlington's Hooper High Flyer had been the subject of much admiration and debate amongst them.

Especially unique to the lord's plans, there was a meeting room replete with comfortably worn-in furniture and a housekeeper to keep things in order. Any member of the stables might come in for tea and a biscuit when they chose, or arrive with a scratch that needed dressing, and be cossetted by the doting Mrs. Payne. The walls of the dwelling were covered in various genealogies, going back to the Byerley Turk. It was in that room that all plans regarding their horses were made, and Penny had been one of its regular visitors since she was a young girl.

Penny hurried out the back of the house and down the well-worn path to the meeting room. She slipped in the door and found Mrs. Payne fussing over Petit and Doom.

Mrs. Payne was always a wonder to her. She was a very motherly sort of person and was not put off by the roughness of the stable hands. In truth, Mrs. Payne seemed to have little comprehension of rank or manners and looked upon all the world as her own children. She had never called Penny *Miss Darlington* in her life, though she *had* called her a variety of pet names. She was just now ruffling Doom's hair, though he seemed irate about it.

At the sight of their mistress, Petit and Doom leapt up from their chairs. Mrs. Payne said, "Ah, there you are, dove—you'll want tea." The good lady hurried off to fetch it.

Petit, Lord Mendbridge's stablemaster ever since they had both been young men, was a slight and grizzled individual. He lived for horses and anybody not talking about horses was just wasting his time.

"Miss," he said, tugging his cap.

"Yes, hello Mr. Petit, Doom," Penny said, knowing full well they'd all like to be done with the niceties as quickly as possible, "let us sit down and talk about Newmarket."

Doom, though he was but a boy and his real name was in fact Daniel, looked fiercely at Penny and crumbled a biscuit in his hand. This did not put Penny off—Doom acted as her tiger when she took out the phaeton and he was in the habit of appearing threatening. When he'd come to them a year ago, he'd been forced to reveal his real name. It was all for naught, as he'd leap upon anybody that dared to call him Daniel and once bruised up another hand who'd had the bad luck to call him Danny.

After Doom had assured himself that he'd laid waste to the biscuit, he said, "I say I'm ready, Petit say I ain't."

Penny was aware that this eloquent speech was meant to point out that she must decide if Doom were to ride Zephyrus, or whether it would once again be Billy.

Petit knocked Doom on the head. "I didn't say nothin' against ya, I said there's facts to consider."

"The facts is only one fact—Billy is gone and run to fat," Doom said derisively. "Too many potatoes, he shoves 'im in like he was stokin' a fire. How's Zephyrus supposed to carry that lumpy lug?"

Doom had made a salient point. The boy was small and thin; he would weigh no more than Penny herself, they both being slight and of a narrow frame. Billy was experienced, but he'd seemed to have encountered a growth spurt that had gone both vertically and horizontally.

"Nobody questions your riding ability, Doom," Penny said. "It is only that Mr. Petit knows the pressures of Newmarket. Many a boy before you has felt it and failed to hold up against it."

As soon as she'd said it, Penny knew she'd chosen the wrong words to soothe the temperamental Doom. He did not consider himself a boy and could not imagine what he could not hold up against.

His tanned face deepened in color, his hand reached for another biscuit and crushed it. Petit laid a hand on Doom's arm and said in a low voice, "I'll not have any of your outbursts in front of the miss."

Doom relented and opened his fist, allowing the crumbs of the biscuit to fall on his plate.

Mrs. Payne bustled back in with the tea. She looked upon the scene with a discerning eye. As she set the cups down, she said soothing words to Doom. "I can see your hackles are up, love. Do be a dear and put them back down again. Calm yourself and, after you've had your dinner, I'll tell you the story of my great-grandfather what sailed the ocean blue."

Penny thought it was only Mrs. Payne that could settle Doom like a snake charmer calming his viper. The lady was a fearless sort and approached every matter with practicality dosed with firmness and topped off with honey. Not even Doom could hold out against it. The boy breathed out slowly and nodded.

"Mr. Petit," Penny said, "it would of course be ideal if Doom had another twelvemonth to train, but that is not the case. And, I am afraid he is right—Billy has grown too big. We would put ourselves at a severe disadvantage if we saddle Zephyrus with more weight than necessary."

Doom balled up his fist and pounded the table in agreement.

"Let us look at our competitors and see what we're up against," Penny said.

She walked over to the wall at the far end of the room and traced with her finger the most recent genealogies of those horses that would race in the four-year olds' on the Rowley Mile. She then began to trace the bloodlines back in time.

"You see here," Penny said, "Mephistopheles belongs to Lord Burke. He goes all the way back to Jigg and then the Byerley Turk. I suspect him to be swift. Artemis, we cannot be so sure of, he's changed hands under some odd circumstances, though I have heard he bears a remarkable resemblance to Highflyer. Dover's lineage comes down from Eclipse—Lord Mendbridge has seen him and thinks him exceptional. I believe those three will be our fiercest competitors and I'll wager none of them will carry much weight on their back."

Petit nodded thoughtfully while Doom stared him down. "Tis all true," Petit said, "and the boy's got skill. I only don't want to push the lad too fast." He raised his hand threateningly toward Doom in case he would have something to say over that opinion.

Penny walked back to the table and sat next to the boy. "Doom, now I want you to put aside all your pride. It will be Newmarket. There will be crowds, there will be enormous sums laid on the race. Can you imagine yourself there without trembling? And remember, no pride in your answer!"

"I was born for Newmarket," Doom said gravely.

Penny was convinced. "Very well," she said. "Doom rides Zephyrus."

Doom, to signal his approval of this plan, picked up a biscuit and ate it with gusto.

Petit cleared his throat and said, "We might consider Bella for the three-year-old fillies' thousand guinea race?"

"We might," Penny said, laughing, "if we had not already considered it."

Bella was a jewel. Penny had bought her last year—her pedigree was good, going back as far as Selim. What Bella was not, though, was ready for Newmarket.

"I know she could use more experience," Petit said. "But here's your only chance with her for the high stakes. She won't be three next year."

Penny knew that was true, but she also knew a horse like Bella should not be pushed too hard. Bella had her own mind and went at her own pace. She did a thing when she was ready to do a thing. Penny had discovered it when she'd pressed Bella to jump a fence higher than the horse was accustomed to. Though Bella could jump such fences now, she'd not been ready on that particular day. Penny had felt it and pushed her forward anyway. She'd landed in a field for her trouble. Many a horseman would have insisted on keeping her running at the fence until she complied, but Penny had felt in Bella an iron will—she might be pushed over it, but she'd never forgive her rider for the insult. Penny had let it go for that day, and eventually, Bella decided on her own that it was time to take the high fence.

"I cannot consider it, tempting though it may be," she said with finality. "One such as Bella needs to be ready. Running a disastrous race will ruin her. We will bring her, though, as it would be well to expose her to the atmosphere of such places."

Petit nodded, knowing that was to be the final word on the subject.

"Do be of cheer, Petit," Penny said. "I understand my father is running four of his horses and you shall have your hands full."

Both Petit and Doom did cheer up at the notion. There was nothing the stable hands liked more than to be off to the races.

LORD CABOT HAD searched his mind for a source of money for the stakes. He had studiously avoided thinking of one who definitely *did* have the money to spare, but who could be difficult to approach.

His grandmother, the Dowager Duchess of Wentworth, had made London her home and kept an elegant house on Grosvenor Square. The lady's dowry had been enormous and her jointure allowed her to maintain the house, as she preferred not to reside in the dower house on the estate. Or, to *rot away* in the dower house, as she termed it. Her Grace had plenty of money in her pocket, but she was never enthusiastic about doling it out. His only hope was to appeal to his grandmother's soft spot—family honor. Surely, he could convince her that having entered the stakes he must pay for it as a matter of honor. At least, he hoped so.

The dowager was a stern lady, one of the old guard that peered down their noses at modern goings-on. She hosted no end of card parties with the rest of the old guard in which they delighted in talking about how it had been in *their* day. Cabot had last seen her at Christmas and had studiously avoided being alone with her. He did not know what she thought of the Dukes' Pact and had not been anxious to find out.

Yet, here he was out of options and being led into number

forty-two of the square. Bancroft showed him in with a frown. The butler was as old as the hills and apparently not afraid, at this late date in his history, to let his opinion be known. He'd glared at the prodigal grandson, no doubt wondering what one who never called was now up to.

The dowager's drawing room looked as if it had not been redecorated since Queen Anne's time—decidedly baroque, with all curved lines and cabriole legs. It had the faint powdery smell that he remembered from his youth. Those were terrifying visits when he was marched in front of the dowager in his best clothes for a sizing up. The visit only lasted minutes, as then his governess would march him back out again, but he had always likened it to creeping into the dragon's lair and somehow getting back out again unscorched.

The dowager swept in, seeming all energy. He'd thought she'd slow down at some point, but it seemed that as the men died off, their wives only increased their vigor. She looked at him as skeptically as Bancroft had.

"Well?" she said.

The dowager was dressed in a heavy brocade and tightly corseted. Her wig was high and powdered and Cabot was amused to note a silk butterfly lurking in the complicated twists and turns of the thing.

He bowed low and said, "Ma'am."

"Hardly an answer," the dowager said. "I suppose we'd better sit down. Bancroft will anticipate me and bring in tea. Both of us know what a winding path you may take to your purpose."

It was not an auspicious beginning, but Henry comforted himself that interviews with his grandmother never were.

"Out with it," the dowager said. "I have not seen you since Christmas, where you avoided me as if I carried the plague. Now, you've turned up on my doorstep. What do you want?"

Henry clasped his hands together lest they give away his nerves. "As always, I appreciate your directness."

"I have no time to be *indirect*—I'm on the far side of seventy," the dowager said with some aspersion. "Get on with it."

Cabot had hoped to smooth the path in front of him. Perhaps engage in some pleasantries. Clearly, that was not to be.

"I've encountered a small difficulty, ma'am," Cabot said cautiously. "I turn to you for guidance."

"Do you?"

"Indeed, I do," Cabot said, feeling he'd better get right to the point. "I've engaged to run a horse at Newmarket. The difficulty is I do not have the stake for it. It seems to me a matter of family honor that I come up with the sum."

"Does it?"

"Just so, ma'am. After all, were I to fail, it would be spoken of. Spoken of derisively, I might add. I do not like to think of our name so muddied."

"And that is your problem?"

"Yes," Henry said, beginning to become even more wary than he had been. His grandmother's piercing eyes, those eyes which one might hope to be dimmed with age, bored into him.

"That is *not* your problem," the dowager said curtly.

"But truly, it is," Henry said, flummoxed over how she could not understand it was his problem when he'd just said so.

The dowager folded her hands and looked over his head, as if admiring the line of ancestors that hung on the far wall.

"Do you know," she said quietly, "that Lord Rariton and his lady were here for cards the other evening? And do you know they had been present at Lady Hathaway's absurd Tudor ball? And do you know that they spoke of *my grandson?*"

Cabot swallowed. Wherever this was going, it was nowhere he cared to be.

"It seems," the dowager continued, "that *my grandson* was rude to a lady. To Lord Mendbridge's daughter, to be specific. A lord I have known since he was a young man. A lord whose mother was a dear friend of mine. And you come here claiming that your problem is a horse race?"

"That was an unfortunate circumstance," Henry said hurriedly. "Which I intend to repair at Newmarket. Lord Mendbridge has invited me to stay at his house."

"Has he?" the dowager asked. "In my day, a father would take a stripling like you to task for such an affront. Severely to task. I can only claim to be surprised by the lord's liberality."

Henry ignored the idea that he was to be characterized as a stripling, he towered over his grandmother and was certain he could pick her up with one hand. "Uh, I do not believe Lord Mendbridge is aware of the…discussion…that took place between myself and Miss Darlington."

"I'll wager he is not," the dowager said, looking satisfied with the prediction.

Bancroft softly knocked and entered, leading in a footman with a tea tray. The dowager rose. "Only one cup, Bancroft. My grandson must depart this instant to discover within himself what are really his problems. I have done him the courtesy of assuring him it has nothing to do with a horse race."

Bancroft only nodded, but Henry was certain the old fellow was delighted to see him thrown from the house.

He would need to find the money somewhere else.

THE TRIP TO Newmarket would take them two days, with an overnight at an inn at Bishop's Stortford. Penny would have liked to drive her phaeton, but her aunt was vociferously against the idea. According to Mrs. Wellburton, it was one thing to be seen galivanting about town atop the contraption, but quite another to drive it like any coachman on a route. Penny had negotiated that the phaeton must be brought for her use, though she would forbear to drive it there herself. Her aunt had relented on that point, satisfied enough.

Once the arrangements had been made, Penny began to see that it might be for the best, after all. Her father would be on horseback for most of the journey and it would give her ample opportunity to have a confidential conversation with her aunt.

They had left the town far behind and just now briskly trotted through pleasant countryside. Petit, Mrs. Payne, Doom, the housemaids, and the rest of the stable staff had set out the day before with the preponderance of the trunks, horses, and carriages. Now, it was only the family and three carriages following behind carrying Montrose, the lord's valet, Mrs. Wiggins, and the lady's maids, that comprised their current caravan. Penny said, "Aunt, I would wish you to know of something that occurred at the Hathaways' ball."

Mrs. Wellburton had been fussing with various baskets stocked with edibles for the journey. She glanced up and said, "Lord Cabot, I presume?"

"Indeed, Lord Cabot," Penny said, surprised. "How can you know it?"

Mrs. Wellburton smiled and looked indulgently at her niece. "I suppose you think your old aunt too feeble to engage in the social realm these days? Do you think nobody talks to me?"

"Goodness, no, certainly I did not think so," Penny said. "Though, I did not know my conversation with Lord Cabot was widely spoken of."

"Of course it was spoken of," Mrs. Wellburton said. "There were several people nearby who overheard Lord Cabot's rudeness. I must say, though I do not favor the fellow, I would have thought he'd have better manners than that."

"As I feel, too," Penny said, at once relieved that she would not have to repeat the vile circumstance and irritated that it should have been bandied about in conversation so widely.

"I was surprised when you wished to leave Lady Hathaway's ball so precipitously, as you are rarely ill. Though, when I understood the cause I comprehended well enough. Of course, your father knows nothing of it, as far as I can gather," her aunt said. "Else he would not have invited the man to stay. I cannot say I am surprised at his ignorance of the matter, the only gossip your father would ever hear is if it came riding up on a horse and whinnied at him."

Penny laughed at the idea, as it was all too true.

"Now you wonder," her aunt said, "what are we to do with the loathsome fellow while he lurks around the breakfast table and hangs about the drawing room?"

"That is it, exactly," Penny said. "Of course, I had imagined I must see him at some party or other. I'd planned to be decidedly cool toward him and engage in nothing more than the shortest of pleasantries."

"Quite right, my dear," her aunt said. "And that is precisely what you shall do. He will understand your meaning quick enough and not bother you further. It is all for the best, in my mind. Lord Cabot can move on to dispense his attentions elsewhere and God help the girl who falls for it. He strikes me as a determined bachelor and I think him very like his father—his duke was nearly forty when he married and had the gout before he was five years into it. I imagine his duchess to be a long-suffering sort of person."

Penny could not ignore that she felt a tinge of regret at her aunt's assessment of how Lord Cabot would react when he understood their previous good-natured exchanges were to be at an end. While she had worked to imagine her scathing attitude toward Lord Cabot upon their first meeting, she had less examined what his response to it might be. Or, if she *had* thought of it, she had envisioned him to be very struck by it. Perhaps in her wildest moments she had thought he'd be devastated by it. Now, she was to understand he would pack his attentions in his panniers and ride elsewhere with nary a look back.

Her aunt, seeming to sense her disappointment, said, "Now, then, Penny. It does no good to wish it was anything other than a trifle. Further, Lord Cabot's attentions may have crowded out some other more suitable gentlemen. I know your head was turned because he has your own keen interest in horses, but hobbies do not a marriage make. You are coming to the end of your second season and it is time you put your eye toward your future."

Penny nodded, certain her aunt was right. After all, it *was* only horses that had been between them, it *was* only horses that had ever piqued her interest. That was right, was it not?

Mostly right, in any case. She could not claim to be entirely immune to his tall frame and the broad shoulders that towered over her when they danced. Nor his deep brown eyes or the way they crinkled at the corners when he laughed. Or the particular timbre of his voice. She supposed no lady was immune to those attractions and so she was as any other in that regard.

So she hoped, anyway. Further, her aunt was right. She could not go on from season to season without settling herself. Her father would allow it, of that she had no doubt. But that was only because her father would hardly notice it. She must rely on her aunt for good sense and her aunt was right. She had wiled away two seasons as she watched one lady after the next become betrothed. It was time she ought to be thinking of her own future. She had never envisioned herself a spinster and could not do so now. It was time to turn her attention to somebody she could have a real future with. Even if that fellow had the galling attribute of only a middling interest in horseflesh.

CHAPTER THREE

HENRY COULD NOT quite believe he found himself in Cheapside, standing in front of a dusty door that had nothing to recommend it but for the sign nailed to it that helpfully announced its occupants. It was the final effort to secure the money for the stake at Newmarket. Like most problems not easily solved, he'd taken on progressive remedies, running from the easiest to increasingly more difficult. As one idea fell by the wayside, he picked up an even more rash solution.

He'd tried Dalton, Grayson, and Hampton. He'd tried Burke. Ashworth was out of his reach. He'd gone to his club and opportuned anybody he was on remotely intimate terms with. He'd even approached Mackery—a dissolute young man fond of gambling and too much wine. One never knew if Mackery had recently been on a winning streak. As it turned out, Mackery was worse off than he was. Thoroughly in his cups, the man had explained that he'd gone so far as to see a moneylender and had lost that money too. He was currently considering if he ought to shoot himself or remove to the continent. He was leaning toward a flight to the continent as he knew an old Contessa there who was likely to take him in.

Though Mackery had claimed it was likely he would flee, rather than do a violence to himself, Henry had gone to his apartments to warn his valet to hide all the pistols.

He had been disgusted to find Mackery in such a shape, but he had not forgotten his words. He'd got funds from a money-lender and Henry had pressed him for the details.

It was a foolish idea, he was well aware. The rate would be ruinous and if one did not pay a moneylender, he had some vague notion that they had their unpleasant methods. He did not understand exactly how they transacted their business, but everybody knew they were not to be trifled with.

Still, what else was he to do? He must have the hundred guineas to pay the stake. In truth, he must have more than a hundred. He'd planned to be so careful with his money when his funds were cut. But then, he'd seen that what he had would not cover his expenses and he'd thought to increase his purse with some careful gambling. After all, Ashworth had made a career out of it, why shouldn't he? Of course, when he lost some of the money, it had become even more imperative to recoup it through another gamble. It was a story as old as time, and just as stupid.

Now, he needed the stake, as well as funds to pay the men who would transport Bucephalus to Newmarket in short, easy stages, and expenses for the groom who would care for her and ride her. He needed funds to hire a carriage, as his own had been sold—he could not turn up without a valet and luggage, after all. Then there were the incidentals that would come up at the races. What if he needed the services of a farrier? He lived on credit in town, but Newmarket tradesmen were not likely to extend it, only to have their quarry decamp after the races. As well, he would need some walking around money. If he ventured into a tavern to meet with likeminded gentlemen, was he not to have the coin in his pocket to buy a round of ale? And when was the last time he'd paid Jarvis? For all he knew, his valet was making plans to ditch him when the next likely gentleman passed by.

There had been no other option. He'd have to see a lender.

He knocked on the door, ignoring the various passerby looking at him curiously and knowing full well why he was there.

He was let into the building by a young boy who had not

seemed to have encountered a washcloth recently. The boy was solemn for his age and had taken his card and examined it carefully, though Henry was in doubt as to whether he could read it. Seeming satisfied with its veracity, the boy led him up the stairs and down a long corridor. He motioned him to wait and slipped through an unmarked door.

A good ten minutes went by before he was shown in. A good ten minutes went by while he wondered if he ought not just leave or was there not some other idea that might come to him. Still, he stayed standing in the corridor like any schoolboy waiting to be let into the headmaster's chamber. Finally, the door opened again.

Henry could not say precisely what he had expected from a moneylender's place of business. He'd had vague ideas of dark corners and threatening visages. He'd supposed the proprietor would be a shifty-looking fellow—the sort one crossed the street to avoid passing after dusk. He was, therefore, surprised to find a light and airy drawing room of sorts. The furniture was of good quality, the carpet fine and recently brushed, and the windows had not a speck of dirt on them. The only aspect of the room that was not so usual was that the bookshelves held stacks of papers rather than books.

The man who rose from the desk was exceedingly well-dressed in fine linen with nary a spot or fray to be seen. He was the sort of fellow who might be found behind the counter in any shop on Bond Street, who'd been hired for his looks and smooth demeanor.

The man laid Henry's card on the desk and bowed. "Lord Cabot, you are most welcome. I am Nathaniel Farthingale. Please take a seat. I venture a man of your importance may have many matters to attend to and so I will be careful of your time."

Henry took the seat in front of the desk. He did not, in fact, have many pressing matters to attend to. This was the only matter he wished to accomplish, though the man's elegant manners went some way to putting him at ease. He'd wondered how he would explain the importance of the filly stakes to one not familiar with the *ton's* way of living. This man seemed as one he could talk to and would understand his current difficulties.

"May I ask," Mr. Farthingale said, folding his elegant white hands, "by what means you came to discover me?"

"Mr. Mackery recommended you," Henry said. In truth, Mackery had not exactly recommended the man, but that seemed not worth mentioning. "We belong to the same club."

"Ah yes, gentlemen and their clubs," Mr. Farthingale said. "May I inquire, how does Mr. Mackery get on? I had hoped to see him this past week and have been blighted by his inattention."

This, Henry thought, was veering into dangerous territory. He could hardly tell Farthingale that Mackery was set to fly to his Italian contessa. "Oh, he seemed well enough," he said, seeking to adopt a breezy tone.

Mr. Farthingale examined his folded his hands. "I see," he said. "Well, one hopes he makes no rash decisions. I believe Italy is exceedingly hot in this season and I understand the malaria to be terribly unpleasant. Or so my friends who occupy those regions tell me."

Henry did his best to keep his face neutral. How on earth would Farthingale know that Mackery was about the fly the coop? He must have paid off Mackery's servants. Despite his polished demeanor, Henry suspected this man of having associates who were not quite as elevated in their appearance and manners. Further, he must have associates spread out everywhere. He wondered if Mackery would find himself entirely out of Mr. Farthingale's reach on those distant shores.

"But enough about our mutual friend, Lord Cabot. I am at your service."

Henry was relieved to get off the subject of Mackery and said, "It's just this, I suppose you know all about Newmarket?"

"Knowing all about it would be too much to claim, I am afraid," Mr. Farthingale said, straightening one of his cuffs. "But one can hardly be ignorant of its renown for horseracing."

"Exactly," Henry said. "I have a fine filly. Bucephalus, descended from Selim."

"A filly? Named Bucephalus?" Mr. Farthingale asked.

Henry was certain he saw the man's lip tremble in mirth. He realized it was an unpleasant sounding name and had no idea why the original owner, Mr. Porter, had named her such, other than he was a foolish man, generally drunk. As much as he might wish for something like Athena or Juno, the filly had been named and he could not undo it. In any case, she'd been named after Alexander the Great's beloved war horse. He really did not know what was so amusing about *that*.

"Never mind the name, long story," he said. "She's a three-year-old and of course, there is the thousand guinea filly stakes. I am certain she can take the win."

"You must be both delighted and proud, Lord Cabot," Mr. Farthingale said.

"Yes, I suppose," Henry said, wondering if he heard a touch of condescension in the man's voice. "It's just that, I don't have the stake for it. At this moment. Naturally, there are some other expenses I will incur. So you see, it's vital that I take out a loan. Two hundred guineas ought to cover it. When I win, I'll have a thousand guineas in ready money."

"And if you do not win?" Mr. Farthingale asked.

"She'll win," Henry said in all confidence. Really, there was no chance she would not. He'd never owned a horse so swift, and one who enjoyed it so much. One had only to point her in the right direction and she was off like a shot. Further, his groom had been brought in from his father's estate—Rupert was a light and lithe man who had a remarkable way with horses. They could not lose.

"Indulge me, though, my lord. What is to be done if you do not win?" Mr. Farthingale asked, eyeing him critically.

Henry had not really considered that particular outcome and so had to think fast. He said, "Well, I could always apply to my father to cover it."

Mr. Farthingale laughed rich and deep. "You jest, certainly. There cannot be a soul in London who does not understand the intent of the Dukes' Pact. I suspect your father will not cover any of your debts until you are suitably married."

Mr. Farthingale suddenly clapped his hands as if he had remembered something. "But my dear Lord Cabot, are felicitations in order? Can it be that you have secured the lady that is to be by your side for all of your days?"

"No!" Henry said, lest the man become even more enthusiastic over nuptials that did not exist.

"Very sad news, indeed," Mr. Farthingale said gravely. "You see, my lord, what you ask is quite impossible. First, your proposed investment is in a horse race, a notoriously bad risk. Second, you have no means to repay the debt as your father has ranged himself against you. Were I to consider such a loan, it would be at great risk to myself and must be at usurious rates. That, as I consider myself a man of honor, I do not like."

"Is it just the rates, then?" Lord Cabot asked. "Really, I must have the funds, at whatever cost."

Mr. Farthingale did not answer immediately, but rather allowed a silence to fall between them. As Henry shifted uncomfortably in his seat, Mr. Farthingale regarded him.

"Whatever cost, did you say?" Mr. Farthingale said, fingering the corner of a paper that sat in front of him. "If you are certain that is the case, then perhaps something may be arranged."

⋙✦⋘

LIKE ALL LORD Mendbridge's projects, the house in Newmarket had been specially built. The lord had waited with all patience for the right piece of land to come up for sale and then outbid his competitors ruthlessly. The house sat a quarter mile from the town center on a low rise. It was commodious, though not over-elegant. But for the drawing room, there was not a carpet in the whole of the first floor. Lord Mendbridge had been determined that this house be one that a fellow could walk in the front door with muddied boots and not worry about setting off the mistress of the house over it.

Penny adored the place. It lacked fuss and pretension and was solely focused on the task at hand. The floor in her own bed-chamber was covered in a patchwork of smaller carpets that might be easily taken out and beaten to get rid of the dried mud and dust that was inevitably ground into them. Her aunt's bedchamber was the only outlier, that particular room might be found in any elegant house in town and had a charming adjoining sitting room. Mrs. Wellburton had no need of easily-cleaned carpets—the lady had never set foot in a stable, entirely satisfied to meet her carriage at the front doors.

They had arrived to the usual chaos. Though Montrose had sent servants up early to ready the house, it seemed no matter how early they were sent, there was always a last-minute panic. Housemaids ran this way and that, footman bumped into each other, and Montrose stood in the middle of it quietly sighing.

Penny's first priority was to see that Kitty Dell's accommodations were in order before her friend arrived. She had brought a trunk full of things to add to Kitty's bedchamber to make it more suitable for a lady of certain sensibilities—a delicate spread for the bed, a few throws to soften up the rather austere furniture, and a pile of small carpets that might be laid down in some attractive fashion.

Kitty was a second cousin and the two girls had spent every holiday and summer together. Kitty lived nearby in Devon, and Lord Mendbridge and her father had a long connection. Penny adored Kitty, though the girl could not be less like herself. Kitty was bookish and rode a very staid horse at a very staid pace. She was far more educated than most females and often made some remark about a historical event or obscure scientific discovery that Penny was certain she'd never even heard of.

For all that, though, Kitty was thoughtful and had a calmness of spirit that Penny admired. When they had been children, it was often Kitty who would talk Penny round when she was in the throes of some foolish heartbreak. If Penny would lament that her governess was a dragon, Kitty might point out that if the lady *were* a dragon, she was entirely mythical and not worth bothering about.

Mrs. Wellburton bustled into Kitty's assigned room, conveniently next to Penny's own, and looked about at her niece's handiwork.

"Well," she said, "I see you've done what you can with what you've brought. And yet, it is still too severe. Kitty is not one of you horse-mad types and will not understand the advantages of being able to drag mud everywhere with nary a care."

Penny looked critically around the room. It was true, it was nothing like Kitty's own bedchamber, which was a riot of blue and violet silks and velvets, with everything soft and rounded.

"I'll have a footman bring in the peach brocade armchair from my sitting room," her aunt said. "It's well-padded and will be just the thing. As well, a side table next to it where she may stack as many books as she likes. And I believe I have another set of curtains put away somewhere—these look like they belong in a hunting lodge. Last, I am certain we can locate a larger carpet in the attics to soften the whole thing up."

Penny was relieved to have her aunt take charge. If she were to be honest, her various additions had done little to bring the sort of charm that would suit Kitty.

Her aunt laid a hand on her arm. "We will not only have Kitty arriving on the morrow, but Lord Cabot comes too. I do not know why he comes so early, but your father says he has a horse in the thousand guinea and wants her well-settled before time."

Penny raised her chin and said, "I will act the proper hostess and no more. Lord Cabot will find the house rather chilly. I am only sorry that poor Kitty must put up with him."

Mrs. Wellburton laughed. "Poor Kitty, indeed. I would not

worry about Miss Dell," she said. "Though she can seem a retiring sort of person, she is not likely to be run over by a lord. The girl has a deal of sense and it has always been my observation that when she arrives at a considered opinion, she digs in her heels and sticks to it."

Penny nodded, knowing it was true. Kitty did have an enormous amount of sense. She need not even wonder what her friend would advise after hearing she'd wasted two seasons dining with Lord Cabot, only to find herself publicly insulted.

"Now, leave this room to me," her aunt said kindly. "I am certain you wish to be off to the stables to see how everything gets on."

As THE DAWN broke, Henry watched his valet pack up the last of his things. He'd done it, he'd got the money. At what cost was another matter. He'd borrowed two hundred guineas and now he was in debt to Mr. Farthingale for three hundred guineas. It was usurious, though he'd argued for it and the moneylender had argued against it. Mr. Farthingale, if he were to be believed, had never lent funds to a gentleman for a stake in a horse race. He claimed it to be the very worst sort of gamble and far too likely to end in disappointment for everybody.

Henry had taken the man through a history of his horse's genealogy, her habits, her enthusiasm and single-mindedness when she galloped. When that had seemed to have little effect, he'd claimed that his friends would never allow him to fail to pay a debt. It was at the mention of Ashworth being a particular friend that Mr. Farthingale had seemed to relent. Even Cheapside had heard of Ashworth's seeming unlimited ability to win at cards.

Henry could see now how fellows like Mackery got so deep into a ditch. If he were to lose the thousand guinea stakes, just as

Mackery had lost at cards, what then? Borrow from another moneylender to pay the first and so on until the whole scheme eventually collapsed under its own weight?

At least he didn't have to worry about losing. He'd never been so certain of a race in his life. At the end of it, he'd pay Mr. Farthingale and still have seven hundred guineas to spare.

Now that his money problems were at an end, he must turn his attention to the other problem hanging over his head. He would set off for Newmarket this very morning. Miss Darlington awaited him and he could not say what his reception would be. He *could* rightly guess his reception from that old aunt of hers, the lady had been cool enough to him in the past to signal her distaste, now she must be positively livid.

But then, perhaps Miss Darlington had never even told her aunt of their unfortunate conversation at the Hathaways' ball. After all, she was a stalwart sort of girl. Would a lady who drove her own phaeton really go running off to tattle to an aunt? Perhaps not. He knew others had observed what had occurred, but would it have even been mentioned within Mrs. Wellburton's hearing? There was every chance it had not been, after all one never gossips to the people involved in the gossip. Perhaps it would only be Miss Darlington herself that he must smooth things over with.

As he had been thinking through everything that must come, he had been distracted by the near constant sound of feet hurrying up and down the hall. "Jarvis," he said, "what on earth do they do out there?"

Jarvis finished wrapping a neckcloth around a stiff paper roll in his own unique fashion to avoid creases. "It's the other two valets," he said. "Lord Dalton and Lord Grayson have both surprised them with a change of plans. They leave for Newmarket themselves in a few hours and that library downstairs is stacked with gentlemen's items—nobody knows what belongs to who. Never you worry, though, I can't say whether I rescued your own neckcloths from the piles, but I took the best quality.

Let those other two sort out the rest how they might."

Henry felt the faintest flush creep up his cheeks. He had forgotten about his third problem. Dalton and Grayson would expect to find him at the club. He'd not told them he was staying with Lord Mendbridge. And the daughter they were so suspicious of.

Now, he was to understand that particular problem would arrive well ahead of time. In fact, that particular problem would arrive only hours after he did so himself.

⤜⟫⟩⟨⟨⟨⤛

PENNY HAD ORDERED the phaeton brought round. The house had its own modest stables with stalls for their pleasure horses, a roomy carriage house, and accommodations for the stablemaster and the grooms. As did their house in town, there was also a meeting room, though it was housed in Mrs. Payne's tidy cottage.

The horses that would race had been brought to a larger stable that rented out to participants and was far closer to the turf. One did not wish to tire a horse before a race and Lord Mendbridge had early secured stalls in the best situated of them.

Penny was eager to see how Zephyrus settled in. For that matter, she was eager to see how Bella got on with all the noise and frenzy of the environment. The grooms had been directed to exercise her nearby other horses and take her through town on occasion. Though Bella would not race, how she did on her oats and whether she seemed nervous after experiencing so much that was new would tell Penny much about her future.

As they made their way through town, Penny could see that they were not the only people to arrive early. The streets were bustling with activity. She weaved and dodged until they had cleared the center and then trotted the horses toward their destination on the outskirts.

Halting the phaeton, Doom jumped down and gave her a

hand while the attendants employed by the stable raced to the scene. They would lead away her carriage to water the horses and put them in shade. Penny had been there many times before and recognized the grooms. They recognized her too and had speedily come to her aid as she was in the habit of tipping generously at the end of the races.

"Them three seem on their toes," Doom said of the grooms. "Not like some London lads what drag their heels."

Penny nodded, agreeing with the assessment though she had not asked for it.

They made their way into the stables, Doom commenting on everything he saw as if he were the owner come to review his property.

Lord Mendbridge's horses were always kept together at the far end of the stable. Penny picked up her skirts to avoid the worst of the dust and made her way down the aisle.

"Just here," she said. "Moses, High Stepper, Renegade, Falcon. Zephryus, there you are," she said, rubbing Zephryus' muzzle. He bent his head toward her and she rubbed the inside of his ears—he'd had a special fondness for it since he was a foal.

The horse seemed in good spirits and no worse for wear from his journey north. Doom pulled a step stool to the stall gate and climbed atop it to take over the ear rubbing. Zephyrus had a timetable all his own and if one were to shirk their duty in ear rubs, the horse was not opposed to kicking the door to express his displeasure.

Penny moved down to the last stall. Bella shook her mane and seemed happy to see her. The horse cautiously approached the front of the stall. Penny wondered if the filly had been backed up out of nerves or whether it was just happenstance. She would know more as the days wore on.

As she and Doom had talked thoroughly of the steps they would take to prepare for the race, they had no need to converse now. Penny would ride Bella while Doom would get his practice on Zephyrus. They would go for a gallop and see how they went.

Though some of the owners would cosset their animals before a race, overloading them with oats and keeping them quiet, neither Penny nor her father thought it prudent. Those other owners were of the opinion that the horse's energy could be stored and used for one great burst at race time. Penny agreed with her father—leave a horse to do nothing and it would not only decondition, but it would be less mentally prepared when suddenly asked to race.

They saddled the horses.

An hour later, Penny was satisfied that she'd made the right choice in choosing Doom to ride Zephyrus. The boy was both skilled and confident, the confidence perhaps being the most important of the two. Penny had seen many a competent fellow go wrong with a horse when the horse sensed that *it* was in charge and not its rider. Zephyrus would not suffer any such delusions.

Bella, much to Penny's approval, seemed not the least shy of the many new sights and sounds she encountered. Rather, her ears were up and her eyes were bright, taking it all in with interest.

After a long gallop, they had walked the horses back to the stable amidst Doom's commentary on all he saw. Penny listened with one ear to his various opinions, her mind full of the upcoming meets. She was certain her horse would do well at the races this year.

PENNY HAD WOKEN early in anticipation of the arrival of her friend Kitty. She would see to it that Cook prepared an especially lovely tea, though they were not in the habit of such rituals at Newmarket. Here, there was generally so much coming and going that tea, ale, coffee, wine, biscuits, rolls, cheese, and cold meats were made available on the sideboard in the breakfast room, but nothing more formal than that. Kitty adored savarins and almond biscuits and Penny would see that she had them both.

As a usual thing, Penny might have waited in the drawing room, listening for the telltale sound of horses' hooves on the drive. Today was not so usual, though. Lord Cabot would arrive too, and she could not guess which of their guests would be the first through the door. She had repaired to her bedchamber directly after breakfast, as she had no intention of being caught alone in the drawing room when Lord Cabot descended upon them. Since then, she had been pacing the room like a tiger who had become bored of its cage. Pulling a chair near the window that overlooked the drive, she was determined not to leave the room until she saw Kitty's sweet face popping out a carriage window.

Hiding above stairs had seemed a likely plan, but it had given her far too much time to think. When she was out in the stables or driving her phaeton, she did not think too much. But she must be *doing* something to avoid thinking too much. Unlike Kitty, a book would not serve to distract. She had tried a novel once at her friend's suggestion, but she found herself scolding Marianne Dashwood for being a foolish and imprudent ninny. Before she'd even discovered if Marianne was able to rectify her idiocy, Penny had fallen asleep.

Mrs. Wiggins, ever the eyes of the house, had seemed to notice that she'd closeted herself away in her room. The housekeeper had kindly sent up a tea tray. As Penny chewed on buttered toast, her thoughts would keep returning to Lord Cabot.

She wished to see him and did not wish to see him. She wished to cut him, and she wished they could go back to what they had been. She wished there was a way to go back in time and erase what he'd said to her. In particular, the *way* he'd spoken to her. But under all of that, was the sense of humiliation and the anger that went hand in hand with it that still lurked like a pot of water on the edge of a boil.

At Lady Hathaway's ball, she'd failed to steel herself. The

insult had come from such an unexpected quarter that she'd let her hurt feelings show. It still made her face flame to think of it and to know it had been spoken of. She dreaded encountering looks of sympathy from anybody who may have heard of the circumstance, or worse, witnessed it. Sympathy, as she well knew, was just the sort of thing that might cause water to spring to her eyes. Only her aunt, her maid Dora, and Kitty Dell had ever really understood her two temperaments—one for the world and one for the privacy of a bedchamber. Now, others had gained a glimpse of what she had always kept so well hidden. She'd posited to the world that her armor was of silver plate, when in fact it was no sturdier than a French mallow.

She crumbled her toast as if she were Doom himself on the verge of a temper, and then chided herself for being ridiculous.

Carriage wheels and horses' clip-clops interrupted these unpleasant thoughts. Penny peeked out the window to determine if the arrival would bring joy in the form of Kitty Dell, or uneasiness in the form of Lord Cabot.

God be praised, it was Kitty.

CHAPTER FOUR

PENNY HAD LEAPT up from her perch beside the window and flown down the stairs. She had been out on the drive before Kitty's feet had touched the gravel.

The two friends embraced, and Penny took Kitty's hand and led her indoors as the servants unloaded her trunks.

They might have gone into the drawing room, but Penny had come up with another idea. "Montrose," she said, "might we have tea sent up to Kitty's bedchamber? My aunt has made no little effort to make the room comfortable, and there are two very charming chairs grouped in front of the windows."

Montrose raised his eyebrows ever so slightly and Kitty glanced at her friend upon hearing the unusual request, though neither voiced any opposition to it.

While Kitty's maid Martha unpacked her things, Penny and Kitty spoke of casual topics. Kitty told Penny of her parents' liberality in allowing her the trip and permission to attend dinners and local private balls though she was not yet officially out. Her mother had hesitated, but her father had pointed out that the entertainments would be small and well-supervised by Lord Mendbridge and Mrs. Wellburton. It would be good practice, as in the coming year, her brother intended to escort her to London for her season. Her father and mother would come too, of course, but her brother would do most of the squiring. He was being a jolly sport about it, as Kitty was convinced he had his heart set on a certain Miss Crimpleton from their own neighborhood. Miss Crimpleton, at this moment in her life, could only be encountered at a local assembly under the careful eyes of her mother and father.

Finally, Kitty turned to her maid and said, "Martha, it has been a long day of travel and so I think that is sufficient for now. Do go below stairs and avail yourself of a cup of tea and whatever else the cook has on offer."

As the door closed behind Martha, Kitty said, "Now, dear Penny, do tell me why we have closeted ourselves up here in such an odd fashion."

Penny had not imagined that the situation would go unremarked. Kitty Dell was far too astute for that. She had not had the heart to write all that had happened in a letter, so Kitty would not have the first idea of what had occurred. Now, seeing her friend's kind and inquiring eyes looking into her own, she poured out the whole story.

When she had done, Kitty set her teacup down and said, "Goodness. The gentleman was shockingly rude and now he comes to stay."

"Just so," Penny said. "I had fully prepared myself to meet him at some dinner or other, but now…"

"Now he will be underfoot," Kitty said. "You will have no notion of when or where you might encounter him—in the breakfast room, in the drawing room, in the library, or passing by in the corridors."

"Precisely, though I doubt an encounter in the library, you know I am not a very great reader," Penny said. "And so here you find me, hiding above stairs."

"This will not do," Kitty said thoughtfully. "It will not do at all. This is your home and if anybody must be run out, it must be Lord Cabot."

"True," Penny said, "but I cannot run him out. He is a guest of my father."

"Also true," Kitty said, "though you must not be as a rabbit running from a fox. You might take on the demeanor of Olympias, mother of Alexander the Great. She was a fierce warrior afraid of nobody. I believe her stare to have unarmed the boldness of men. I do not find any certain fact of the power of her stare in my studies, but I think it may be surmised based on the evidence. She rode into battle many times."

"Ah," Penny said, this being the first time anybody'd had the notion of her being a warrior. "Did the lady win all of her battles?"

"Most," Kitty said, "except for the last. But then, what was she to do when so many relatives of her victims wished to murder her? Somebody was bound to succeed."

Penny gulped at Kitty's rather cheerful description of Olympias' demise. And yet, she was also heartened by Kitty's confidence in her ability to stand up against Lord Cabot. It was true, she was in her own house. She must hide from nobody.

"I will only caution," Kitty went on, "that it was said that Olympias worshipped snakes. So perhaps do not take the likeness *too* far."

Ever astounded by the bits and pieces of knowledge Kitty had picked up through her travels in her father's library, Penny stifled a giggle.

The distinct sounds of a carriage caused Penny to turn slowly toward the windows. A chill feeling spread over her, as if she'd just stepped out on a winter's day with no overcoat. She leaned forward and looked down to the drive.

A carriage had rolled to a stop, while Lord Cabot sat astride his horse.

"So that's him, is it?" Kitty asked, peering over her shoulder.

"That is him."

"Come, Olympias, let us go down the stairs at just the right moment and get this insufferable first meeting behind you. Chin up and cold stare."

THOUGH HENRY HAD ridden boldly up the drive to Lord Mendbridge's house, he had not felt as bold as he supposed he looked. He'd left London bold enough, but as he traveled, numerous unwelcome ideas had presented themselves. The foremost was the knowledge that he'd never before found himself blithely entering a house that contained a person he had so recently wronged.

Who knew of it? Only Miss Darlington, or everybody down to the servants? What if Miss Darlington had bided her time and only decided to tell her father of it this morning? Would he be thrown out as soon as he got in? Or, if she had told nobody, how was he to enact some sort of apology while others were about?

Whatever was to be his reception, he would soon find it out. A stern-looking butler and two footmen were even now descending the front steps to greet him.

Henry leapt off his horse, handing off the reins to a young footman and leaving his valet to manage the trunks. He followed the butler inside, comforting himself that he would at least have time to collect himself in his room before he was faced with any of the family at dinner. As well, he would remind himself that he was the guest of Lord Mendbridge. It was an invitation much sought after—here, he would be privy to the great man's mind and all the equine knowledge contained in it.

He entered a wide front hall, its floor devoid of carpets and showing signs of having been trod upon by muddy boots. A long bench and boot scrapers had been provided for those wishing to get most of the stable off themselves before proceeding in.

As Henry thought of the remarkably good sense of it, Miss Darlington and another lady descended the stairs. Miss Darlington looked as wonderful as ever. Her copper curls framed her face in that lovely way they had, as if they found her visage charming and would stay close. Miss Dell was taller, dark-haired and pretty, but stern-looking. For that matter, Miss Darlington was looking rather stern too. They appeared as two queens regarding a subject come for alms.

He was certain his face reddened and hoped it could be ascribed to the rigors of his recent journey. Neither of the ladies smiled as they regarded him. They reached the landing and, in a tone as serious as a vicar, Miss Darlington said, "Lord Cabot. Welcome. May I introduce you to my friend, Miss Dell."

As Henry bowed. Miss Dell nodded and said flatly, "Lord Cabot."

The two ladies sailed past him and into the drawing room, promptly closing the door behind them with a decided thud.

It had not been just a cool greeting; it had been a greeting buried under a foot of ice. Henry might not know the status of everybody in the house, but he understood what he had just encountered. Miss Darlington was many miles away from forgiving their last encounter and Miss Dell was staunchly allied with her friend.

It would be a long hike uphill to overcome the ladies' enmity. As he followed the butler up the stairs, he had to finally admit to himself that it had been well-earned. His wishful thinking that Miss Darlington would just laugh off the unpleasantness at Lady Hathaway's ball had been fanciful, indeed.

Still, long road though it might prove to be, he would attempt it. But how to explain himself? He'd not even fully explained himself to *himself.* Ashworth's engagement and his own recent poverty could not excuse cruelty. Perhaps he would just claim he was an idiot and leave it at that. At least it would carry the ring of truth.

But what if she chose not to forgive him, no matter what he attempted? He could not rule the possibility out. After all, Miss Darlington had no need of his acquaintance.

He would not like it, that much he must concede. Henry had never been so engaged by conversation as he had with Miss Darlington. She was jolly. At least, she *had* been. They'd engaged in lively debates. As well, he could not ignore her pretty face and her lively figure. Who could dance as well as she? He did not know. She was pretty and amusing and intelligent and, blast it, why go on with listing her good qualities? He'd found it had become a habit once he'd had an inkling that those qualities might not be available for him to admire in future.

By the time he'd reached his room, Henry's natural optimism began to resurface. Certainly, he would find a way through. After all, it was not as if he'd killed anybody. He'd said something stupid, but hadn't everybody at one time or another? A man could not be condemned forevermore over it.

He began to suspect that his cool reception was only the price that must be paid for his transgression. Certainly, he must be punished and now he had been. He supposed Miss Darlington would even now laugh over it with her friend and all would go back to what it had been.

⇻⇼⇺

PENNY SIGHED IN relief as the door to the drawing room closed behind them. Kitty took her hand and said, "Well done, Olympias. You have got past the first meeting. Every other encounter will be easier from here. Lord Cabot understands you, I think."

"Thank you, Kitty," she said, "for giving me the strength to go right to it, rather than hide in my room until dinner. You are right, Lord Cabot knows my mind and will not trouble me further."

Though Penny thought she might sound as confident as Olympias, inside she had been shaken to see Lord Cabot's handsome face gazing up at her as she descended the stairs.

It was very hard to dismiss all the fun they'd had together! Very hard to dismiss the dances, where he led her expertly, his hand warm through her glove. Very hard to dismiss those deep brown eyes and the way they crinkled at the corners.

He'd smiled at her. He wished to be friends again, no doubt. She would not allow it, though. She would not risk that his cruelty would resurface when she least expected it. She'd put her guard up and it would stay up. Lord Cabot would not make her cry again, she would never give him the power to do it.

"Now," Kitty said, "tell me of our plans for this visit. I know you will be much engaged with your horses and I am well able to amuse myself, but I suppose you will find some time to spend with me?"

"Of course, I will," Penny said, grateful to be pulled away from her brooding. "I have a schedule worked out that I think you will find convenient. I shall go to the stables early in the day to do all those things that must be accomplished before the race. I know you do not care to rise with the sun and so I will be back before you are up an hour."

"And your aunt will be nearby in the event that you run late," Kitty said. "I think I can reliably count upon her to be the only person in the house, other than myself, that is not horse mad."

"Exactly," Penny said. "Further, you have not yet had the chance to explore the library here. My father bought it from a retiring don at Oxford. We cannot make heads or tails of it so I think you will be delighted."

"I know I shall be. And, when I am not devouring a book that is new to me, we might go shopping. I've promised my younger sister a trinket from Newmarket and I will want to find something for my mother too."

"I will drive you myself, in my phaeton," Penny said. "It's a Hooper High Flyer and the most wonderful thing you've ever seen."

"Goodness, a phaeton," Kitty said, not appearing to find the idea as wonderful as her friend.

Before Penny could expound on the wonders of the phaeton, Mrs. Wellburton came through the door. "Kitty, there you are. I missed your arrival as I was in town visiting a friend."

Kitty rose and made her curtsy. Mrs. Wellburton waved her

off. "No need to be so formal dear, I've known you since you were a baby. Now, it seems I missed another arrival as well?"

"Yes," Penny said, "he has come."

"You would have been so proud, Mrs. Wellburton," Kitty said. "Penny was Olympias to his peasant and rained ice down upon his head."

Mrs. Wellburton smiled indulgently at Kitty. "As usual, I have not the first idea of who Olympias might be, though I suspect you found her buried in a book. In any case, it sounds as if the meeting was got through creditably. I am glad of it—dinner will be less awkward, now that the first encounter is over. By the by, Penny, as you might expect, your father has made his way through town and invited as he went. There are to be three extra persons at dinner, a fortunate development given the circumstances, I believe."

Penny smiled at the idea of her father walking through the town issuing invitations. It ever was so when they were in Newmarket. Her father seemed to view the house as more a well-run tavern than a private residence.

"Heavens," Kitty said, "my father's cook would go mad upon hearing of such last-minute changes."

"Fear not for the kitchens, Kitty," Penny said. "They are well used to my father's habits and would have prepared enough for Henry the Eighth's table in anticipation of it."

"For my part," Mrs. Wellburton said, "I will manage the seating arrangements. Penny, I can suppose you wish to be well away from Lord Cabot. The Lords Burke, Dalton and Grayson come. Who should you prefer on either side?"

Penny put her finger to her lip, as she did when she was thinking something through. "The natural choice would be Burke and Dalton. Dalton is a sour sort, but easier to countenance than Lord Grayson's false flattery. Though it would be convenient for *me*, it would place dear Kitty between Lord Cabot and Lord Grayson. That would be too unkind."

"Nonsense," Kitty said. "I am well able to fend off a flatterer and whatever Lord Cabot might have to say for himself."

MONTROSE SAT AT the head of the servant's table, with the housekeeper, Mrs. Wiggins, to his right. As a general thing, he abhorred gossip. Yet, often the only way to get to the bottom of a matter was to invite any gossip floating around to come within his hearing. Only an hour ago, he had witnessed a remarkable scene in the front hall. Miss Darlington and Miss Dell had greeted Lord Cabot as if he were the devil himself.

There had been no mistaking it, though it had been unexpected. As far as he understood it, Miss Darlington favored the gentleman. In fact, if he were to peer into the deepest recesses of his mind, he might find thoughts there that looked approvingly on the idea of Miss Darlington becoming a future duchess. He might be of the opinion that it would reflect well on the house. The house that was under *his* purview.

However, it seemed something had occurred to change what he'd viewed as the inevitable course.

If he *were* to inquire into the cause of this change of course, he ought to do so now, while Lord Cabot's valet was still occupied above stairs. It was true that Martha, Miss Dell's lady's maid, was present and technically an outsider, but she had been with them so often she might be considered nearly of the household.

Montrose cleared his throat, his signal to the rest of the staff that he was on the verge of saying something noteworthy.

The servants round the table silenced.

"I noticed," he said in a grim tone, "that Miss Darlington did not appear enthusiastic upon the arrival of Lord Cabot. I could not help but wonder at it."

The servants looked among themselves as if searching for who would have the explanation for Miss Darlington's attitude toward the gentleman. Montrose let them do it, and he let the silence hang. It had been his experience that sooner or later, given enough silence, somebody would come forward with what they knew. As this matter had to do with Miss Darlington, he suspected that *somebody* would be Dora.

Of course, he had been right.

Dora set her cup down and said, "I don't like to tell tales, but if the miss has gone and let all and sundry see how she feels, I don't suppose there's harm in it."

"Certainly," Montrose said, in the hopes of helping her to elaborate, "there can never be harm for the staff of this house to understand the stance the family takes on any person. I would go so far as to call it a duty."

This idea seemed to strike Dora as quite enough encouragement. She said, "That lord upstairs done insulted Miss Darlington terrible. So terrible, she cried over it. I didn't get the whole ins and outs of the thing, but it was something about him pretendin' to appreciate her and then lettin' on that he don't."

Montrose was nearly felled by this communication. He set his cup down with a clatter. Who on God's green earth would not appreciate Miss Penny? It was unaccountable. It bordered on the unnatural. Who was this heathen that had been let into their midst? What was wrong with this obtuse gentleman that he could not see the value of Miss Darlington? Had the fellow received a knock on the head that he'd failed to recover from? Only a damaged mind failed to see the worthiness of the lady.

And then, if that were not enough to disturb, he was to understand that Miss Penny had cried. The gentleman, if that was what he was to be called, had made the angel above stairs cry. Montrose knew in his heart that had he not been a butler, if he had been a rich lord with no fear of the magistrate, he would march up the stairs and give that lord a pounding. A severe pounding!

The rest of the servants were equally outraged and there was much heated whispering. Montrose pretended not to hear words like swine, worthless, jackanapes, and rotter. He especially avoided hearing any hints that the lord ought to be strung up, though he silently approved of the idea.

Peg, a housemaid who'd never been shy with her opinions, said loudly, "We ought to make the blighter as uncomfortable as possible. Smoky fires, stones in the mattress, and what all."

Montrose nearly shuddered to contemplate the meaning of "what all," and he of course could not agree to Peg's enthusiastic suggestions. Rather, he said, "I would have to reprimand you severely over any such tomfoolery. *If* I were to hear of it."

A quiet descended over the table. A satisfied quiet. Each member of the household understood how they were to carry on. They were to make the blighter as uncomfortable as possible, only careful that it did not come to the notice of their esteemed leader.

HENRY HAD COME down to the drawing room in good time. It was almost a miracle that he did so. Jarvis swore he'd brushed his coat while Henry had been out walking, but when he'd come back there had been pieces of hay clung to it. Neither of them could account for the wood ash smeared on one of his neckcloths or how a pebble made its way into the toe of his shoe. Thankfully, all had been speedily remedied, and he was the first to arrive. He'd brought a book so that he might have somewhere to look if his reception continued uncomfortably frosty. It was not only from Miss Darlington's direction that he expected it, but it seemed Lord Mendbridge's other houseguest, Miss Dell, would not be disposed toward him either.

There was a sideboard at the far end of the drawing room, stocked with ample wines, cordials, and port. He would dearly like to help himself to a hefty glass of claret that might steady him but did not yet know the habits of the house. All he could do was pretend to read while mulling over his valet's various reports.

Jarvis had arrived back from the stables in the late afternoon with the news that Bucephalus had taken to her new stall and Rupert reported her well on her oats. He would see for himself on the morrow—nothing must be allowed to discompose his filly, he had far too much money invested in her success. As far as he could tell, that was about the only good news he would get for today.

As Jarvis had brushed the hay off his coat, he had relayed whatever information was to be had from below stairs. He said the staff of the house were rather cool, as was the tea that had been handed to him. The information that was most alarming, however, was that Dalton, Grayson, and Burke were coming to dine.

He'd known Dalton and Grayson would arrive to town sometime today, but how on earth had they gained an invitation to the house so quickly? Henry had counted on the idea that it would be some days before he would encounter his friends. Those intervening days would wear their outrage on discovering he stayed with Mendbridge down to an irritation.

Though, he did not suppose they'd say anything outrageous at the lord's own table. At least, he hoped not.

He heard the door open and prayed it was one of the few people he might encounter that would regard him with a friendly face.

Mrs. Wellburton sailed into the room, looked about, and frowned at him.

"Lord Cabot," she said. "How do you do?"

Henry rose and bowed. "A pleasure to see you again, Mrs. Wellburton."

"Is it?" she said.

Henry thanked the stars that before he was forced to answer *that* question, the butler entered and begged her attention to some matter. He thanked the stars again when Lord Mendbridge came in with Burke.

"Cabot, there you are," Lord Mendbridge said in his bellowing voice. "What? You sit with a book and nothing to drink? Come now, Cabot, you can do better than that. There is a sideboard just there—help yourself, we go on very casual in Newmarket. I'd best go see how my sister gets on. Burke, show the fellow how it's done, you are no stranger to us here."

Lord Burke nodded and led Henry to the sideboard. As Henry poured himself an ample glass, Burke said, "How do you get on these days?"

"Well enough," Henry said. "You?"

Lord Burke smiled. "I am perfectly well. I was only surprised to see you installed in this house after, well I think you know to what I refer."

Henry should have expected Burke to leap right to the point. They were old school friends and Burke had ever been the practical and direct one of their set.

"Deuced uncomfortable, is what it is," Henry admitted. "But what could I do? One does not turn down an invitation from Mendbridge at Newmarket."

"I presume you've since thrown yourself at Miss Darlington's feet and begged forgiveness?"

"I've not had the chance," Henry admitted. Though, he'd had no notion of throwing himself at anybody's feet. Would it really come to that?

"Why on earth did you do it, man?" Burke asked.

There was the question he'd asked himself more than once. "I do not know," Henry said. "I was aggravated, I suppose. Ashworth, you know. And well, it just came out."

"But aside from the ghastly manners of the thing, what you said was not even true," Burke said, with a note of exasperation in his voice. "Everybody knows the lady has more knowledge in her little finger than most gentlemen."

"Yes, I am aware of it."

"Further, it is ridiculous that you should be aggravated with Ashworth. When will you, Dalton, and Grayson stop acting like boys who've been sent to bed without dinner? Your fathers' pact to push you toward marriage is ill-considered, but it is well meant."

Henry bristled at the comment. "I see," he said. "So am I to presume *you* will marry in the near future?"

Burke looked thoughtful. "It is too soon to say," he said. "Perhaps."

Before Henry could question Burke on who the lady might be who caused him to look so pensive, Dalton and Grayson were shown into the room.

Henry sighed. Let the games begin.

Grayson looked his usual cheerful self, though Dalton had that look about him that signaled he was not particularly amused.

After they both said hello to Burke, Dalton took Henry by the arm and led him to a corner of the room. "What in God's name do you do here and why did you lead us to believe you would be at the club?"

Henry had been ready for the inevitable interrogation. He said, "Do not be ridiculous, Dalton. For one, nobody turns down an invitation from Mendbridge at Newmarket. For another, I have not forgotten that you have a room in your house set aside for guests who wish to go somewhere you are opposed to. Why *would* I tell you where I was going?"

Dalton shrugged at the reminder that he'd once imprisoned Lockwood to keep him away from Lady Sybil.

"In any case," Henry continued, "whatever your fears may be, Miss Darlington and her friend, Miss Dell, have ranged themselves against me."

"And you have not come here to smooth it all over?" Dalton asked.

"Of course I wish to smooth it over," Henry said. "I do not like being glared at. But that is not why I've come. It is Newmarket, Dalton. I have a filly in the thousand guinea stakes. I received an invitation from the leading horseman in England. That is why I am here."

Dalton seemed somewhat mollified by this explanation.

"Very well. By the by, wherever did you finally find the money for the stake? I presume the dowager came through, in the end."

"My grandmother did not, in fact, come through. That visit was as unpleasant as you may imagine."

"Mackery, then?" Dalton asked, laughing.

"No, not Mackery. A moneylender finally was the answer as I had no other choice," Henry said, feeling the slightest cast of a blush over the foolishness of it.

Seeing the look of incredulity on his friend's face, Henry hurried on. "Mackery recommended the fellow, so he is not entirely unknown."

"I would hardly count Mackery's avowal as a recommendation," Dalton said.

"The man was not as you think," Henry said, his defensiveness ringing in his ears. "His name is Farthingale and he is, well he is awfully close to being a gentleman. You would not know otherwise if you saw him on the street and his…office…was very well turned out."

Dalton raised his brows, though what more he might have said on the subject was cut short. Lord Mendbridge escorted his daughter and Miss Dell into the drawing room.

CHAPTER FIVE

PENNY HAD DRESSED with particular care. She might not want to have anything further to do with Lord Cabot, but she was not above wishing to make him sorry over it. If that particular feeling was petty, then so be it. She had chosen a dark green silk, as she knew it to set off her hair rather well. She could not say for certain what color her hair actually was—she'd heard it called copper, auburn, red, and reddish brown. She'd viewed it as a terrible burden until she'd learned which colors to favor. No frothy pinks or pale yellows would suit, she preferred deeper, richer tones. Or rather, her hair preferred them.

She hoped the dark green dress would give her courage, and it had—right up until she reached the drawing room doors.

Kitty, charmingly dressed in a simple white muslin with only a blue ribbon as decoration, squeezed her hand as they made their way in.

Fortunately, Lord Mendbridge being of a type to disallow silence when talk was just as available, took over the proceedings.

"Cabot, Burke, Grayson, Dalton, you all know my daughter, Miss Darlington. Here is come her cousin, Miss Dell. The girl is not yet absolutely out, so no flirting, eh? I'll write her father of it and he'll skin you faster than he'd give you a farthing."

With this unique introduction, Kitty made her curtsy. Any other girl must have blushed furiously to be introduced to four unknown lords and then the idea of flirting thrown out for everybody's consideration, but Kitty was a different sort. She took it in with all equanimity. Penny only wished she had her friend's composure.

Burke greeted the ladies with familiarity. He was already a great friend of the house and had met Miss Dell before on a visit to the Mendbridge estate. Grayson had, to nobody's surprise but Miss Dell's, seemed to attach himself to her side. Penny could only imagine that Kitty's eyes were just now compared to the stars in the sky. She could also imagine that Kitty might just apprise him of what she knew of stars and how little they resembled eyes. Dalton did his best to appear the friendly gentleman, though it always seemed an effort for him.

Penny had purposefully avoided Lord Cabot's eye, though she could not help notice that he seemed to be edging ever closer. Finally, he was by her side. "Miss Darlington, if you would be so kind as to spare me a word."

"Which word?" Penny asked, hoping to confound the gentleman. "There are thousands of words in the English language, you may claim which ones you like."

"No, what I mean is, might we step away for a moment? Perhaps to admire the view?"

"The view is of the gravel drive and the bushes at the far end that hide the road. I can assure you there is nothing remarkable in it."

While Penny resisted Lord Cabot's efforts to seek her out alone, she was torn all the same. He seemed so like his old self just now. Yet, she could not trust him. Never had a fellow changed himself as fast as Lord Cabot had at Lady Hathaway's ball. That man, that cruel man, was still in there somewhere and whoever had the bad luck to be nearby when that cruel man was roused would feel it. It would not, however, be Penny Darlington.

Mrs. Wellburton came into the room and halted any debate about admiring the view by ushering them all into the dining room.

Penny had not been quite certain how her aunt would arrange the seating to her satisfaction. They were always so informal at Newmarket that they paid little attention to rank. Everybody who entered Lord Mendbridge's house understood that the titles that afforded them so much respect elsewhere were so much bits of paper in the gentleman's eyes. If even a duke did not show expertise and deep knowledge of horses, that duke might be given no more consideration than a footman.

As for the table, it was a generally understood thing that if one wished to sit by Lord Mendbridge, one had better be prepared to reveal what understanding of horseflesh one had. In consequence, those two seats were sometimes sought after and sometimes avoided. Like all well-regarded eccentrics, Lord Mendbridge had his own reasons for his vagaries. He considered titles as so many prizes won without effort. It was not the title but what one did with it that mattered. If one did not do something interesting regarding horses with it, then one was pointless.

Penny should have known her aunt would take what she knew of her brother and comprehend precisely what was to be done. "Penny," she said casually, "do take the far middle. Lord Burke, take Penny over and then seat yourself by Lord Mendbridge—he will wish to know how you get on with Mephistopheles. Lord Cabot, do sit to our host's left so he may hear more about Bucephalus. Lord Dalton, if you will take my left? There, I believe we have everybody situated."

Penny suppressed a smile. The thing had been so masterfully done that everybody followed Mrs. Wellburton's direction without pause. Everybody, perhaps, but Lord Cabot, who looked very determinedly at Lord Burke's chair as that gentleman sat down next to her.

As the courses arrived, Penny had a stilted conversation with Lord Dalton. That came as no surprise to her, as conversations with the man *were* generally stilted. She had sometimes wondered about it, as her aunt claimed he had been both a sensitive and jolly little boy. Mrs. Wellburton had resided in the same neighborhood as the family when she had been married and had been often to the house. She said that as a youth he'd been one moment weepy over a dead chick in the yard and the next full of tricks and levity. Penny supposed the war, and the scar he carried on his face, had stolen whatever gaiety there had been in him.

Still, it had come as a relief when she was able to turn to Lord Burke. "I understand you run Mephistopheles this year, my lord."

"I do, and I suspect you have thoroughly researched his genealogy and know all his habits," Lord Burke said, smiling.

"My stablemaster and I have had regular conversations about it," Penny said.

And so began a back and forth between competitors. They had a particularly enlivening exchange regarding whether to rest or exercise a horse on the day before a race—Penny found she was engaged in the conversation almost as much as she had been in the past with Lord Cabot. Debating with Lord Burke had the further benefit of coming at no risk. Lord Burke would never be cruel, she was certain of it. As they were both good-humored competitors, there was much laughter in their diverse opinions.

When Penny was not so engaged with Lord Burke, she had a moment or two to take in the table. Mrs. Wellburton kept Lord Dalton engaged, though it must have been trying. She supposed her aunt did not have much choice, as Lord Grayson was turned to Kitty a shocking amount of time. That left Lord Cabot to mostly engage with her father, which she supposed he would not mind.

On occasion, Lord Mendbridge would engage the whole table, his voice of such a booming nature that he could have reached to the end of the Prince Regent's table at Carlton House if he wished. In one exceedingly awkward moment, he said, "It seems our Lord Cabot here is a dark horse. I was sallying through town today and I encountered Mr. Packlehurst, deuced irritating fellow if you ask me. He wondered who I'd got in my house, angling for an invitation no doubt. I told him Cabot was here and he said, 'Cabot? Lord Cabot? In *your* house?'"

The table had grown silent, as most of the occupants were fully aware of why Mr. Packlehurst might be surprised to hear that a gentleman who had so recently insulted Lord Mendbridge's daughter was also to be found in his house.

Between fits of laughter, Lord Mendbridge said, "Come Cabot, tell us what you've done to the fellow. Whatever it was—I highly approve!"

Penny stared at her plate. Lord Cabot only mumbled something about everybody knowing that Packlehurst liked nobody.

Lord Burke finally came to the rescue. "No doubt it is because Cabot's horse overtook his own at Epsom Downs last year."

Lord Mendbridge seemed to find the idea credible and said, "Packlehurst. A bad sport to the end. Well, he can angle for an invitation all he likes—he'll never get a toe inside of *my* doors."

HENRY HAD WATCHED the dinner unfold as if it were a veil lifting from his eyes. He had thought to place himself by Miss Darlington as it would have been a likely opportunity to profess an apology. However, Mrs. Wellburton had been determined to place Miss Darlington between Burke and Dalton.

Like one of the audience of a stage play, he had watched Miss Darlington and Burke with their heads together, laughing and debating. It was as if he looked upon the very seat he had occupied so many times himself. It was as if it were *he*, but it was Burke. Why should they laugh so much?

As the veil inched ever higher, Henry began to examine various ideas. He'd asked Burke if he planned to marry soon and his answer had been "perhaps." Mrs. Wellburton was determined in her seating arrangements. And how had Burke even managed an invitation to begin? Had he, as Dalton and Grayson had, only happened to run into Lord Mendbridge as he sauntered through town? Was that not coincidental? Was that not *too* coincidental?

Then there was Miss Darlington's refusal to walk to the window with him while they'd been in the drawing room. Of course she'd understood he would apologize. She did not wish to hear it. He'd thought he'd only encountered some initial resistance, that she had punished him upon arrival and would now be amenable to putting it all behind them. By the looks of it, she was not bothered by whether he ever apologized or not.

Lord Mendbridge had talked of encountering Mr. Packlehurst, and that gentleman's surprise at hearing he was in the house. That confirmed his idea that Miss Darlington had not said a word to her father about his behavior on the night of the Tudor ball. He had thought she'd been very upset about it, she had certainly looked so when she'd left in such a hurry. But it seemed the sting had not lingered long. Or if it had, it had been somehow soothed by a willing suitor.

His conclusions were only cemented by his conversation with Miss Dell. He'd thought he might cleverly gain some information. He'd ended up with more information than he'd bargained for.

"It seems Lord Burke finds himself very comfortable at Lord Mendbridge's table," he'd said.

"I suppose he would," Miss Dell answered. "He has often been at the house in Devon. That is how I know him prior."

"Ah, I see. But then, I suppose he finds himself here tonight, just as Lord Dalton and Lord Grayson do, from a lucky chance meeting on the street."

"That I cannot say for certain, my lord. Though I understand Lord Mendbridge and Lord Burke keep up a correspondence. I expect they knew they would encounter one another here and so the invitation may have been prior arranged."

Miss Dell's attention had then been commandeered by Grayson, who would demand to know her opinion on some nonsense or other.

It was all beginning to make sense. Burke was an old family friend, eminently eligible, well-liked, his stable well-regarded—of course Mendbridge and Mrs. Wellburton would favor the alliance. It appeared both Burke and Miss Darlington favored it too. How could he not have seen it over the past season? Did not

Burke always claim a dance? In fact, he'd often claimed supper when Henry did not beat him to it.

Henry paused in his mental ramblings. None of it had anything to do with him. He must not tangle up Miss Darlington's current condemnation of him with whatever her preferences regarding her future might be. The lady was pleasant and he would not deny he missed their encounters. Of course he admired her, everybody did. Who could fail to admire when she jauntily went by in her High Flyer or danced with copper curls bouncing? There was nothing singular in it.

Still, he could not help but be irritated by their laughter. What was so amusing about whether a horse should have extra oats leading up to a race? He would really like *that* explained to him.

HENRY WAS DETERMINED to apologize to Miss Darlington before the night was through. He was certain he'd have the opportunity. Everybody knew Mendbridge did not favor cards. Why would he? Cards had nothing to do with horses. The drawing room would be one of conversation, and that must lead to an opportunity.

First, Miss Darlington had been situated in a cozy alcove with Miss Dell and he had not seen a way to casually insert himself there. Then, Grayson had insisted on calling Miss Dell to look at some painting or other. Miss Dell had not looked particularly enthusiastic over the invitation but had gone to him. Just as fast, as if she would not be caught in a corner, Miss Darlington had moved to the pianoforte and begun to play.

Now, he made his way there.

Miss Darlington played a quiet piece of music, a mournful-sounding Irish air. Henry stood by the side of the instrument, not entirely sure how to begin. He might start with pleasantries, though he did not think that would get him very far.

He decided he'd better just leap in.

"Miss Darlington," he said, watching her hands travel over

the keys, "I would wish to apologize for my behavior on the night of the Tudor ball."

There, he'd said it. Surely, she would not refuse an apology.

"Nobody is stopping you from whatever you wish to do," Miss Darlington said.

"No, what I mean is, I *do* apologize for it," he said, once more confounded by her insistence on taking his words literally and turning them to her own profit.

"Very well," she said coldly. She turned the page of her music and played on.

What was he to say next? He'd not really thought that far. He'd imagined that once she'd accepted his apology, all would be as it had been.

"I would hope," he said, "that we might go back to what we were."

He watched Miss Darlington's head bend over the keys and strike them harder than was strictly necessary.

"*We* were not anything but acquaintance, my lord," she said. "And so we remain."

"But surely," Henry went on, "we might go back to…well, we might go back to talking of horses. I plan on going to the stables first thing—perhaps we might have a look at each other's mounts? I'm certain we should have something to discuss."

Miss Darlington ended the musical piece and stood. She said, "By your own measure, my father would be a more suitable conversationalist on the topic. Let us leave it at that."

She walked away from him with her head held high, deftly rescued Miss Dell from Grayson's clutches, and the two ladies retired. Mrs. Wellburton excused herself soon after.

His first apology had not gone over as he'd expected. In truth, he'd only considered that he might deliver *one* and be done with it. Now it seemed that at least a second would be in order. Considering her cold aspect, he wondered if it might not be three or four.

But why was she so determined to go on with it? She must

know he'd not meant what he said.

Before he could consider the matter further, Grayson joined him at the pianoforte. "What do you do over here?" he asked. "Do you intend to play for us?"

Henry realized he had remained standing by the instrument, staring down at the keys. He laughed and said, "Do not be ridiculous."

"It is you who are ridiculous, friend," Grayson said. "I have the distinct feeling you chased Miss Darlington off, which has led to the marvelous Miss Dell retiring also. Deuced inconvenient."

"I doubt Miss Dell views it inconvenient," Henry said drily.

"Oh, she resists me, naturally. But that is part of her charm. She is bookish, is that not amusing? I haven't the first idea of the meaning of half of what she said. She is out next season and I have a mind to dance with her often."

Dalton had joined them and said, "No lady interested in books could possibly be interested in *you*. You are the least well-read person of my acquaintance and I have yet to see you with literature of any sort in your hand."

"Have you trotted over here only to throw around insults, my friend?" Grayson asked.

"What else am I to do?" Dalton said. "Burke and Mendbridge are delving into equine genealogies to a remarkably tedious degree."

Henry eyed Burke, who was indeed next to Lord Mendbridge with their heads together. "Burke seems very cozy in this house."

Dalton glanced behind him, then smiled. "I suspect him of admiring Miss Darlington, and so he must of course admire the old man too. I'd say a match is in the works."

Henry bristled. "Why should you suspect such a thing?"

"Why should you care?" Dalton asked.

"I certainly do not have a particular interest in the matter," Henry said. "I only think one ought not to go bandying about such ideas unless an engagement has been announced."

"Cabot!" Lord Mendbridge called from the other side of the

drawing room. "Old Burke and I are having a dispute on a fine point, do come and weigh in on the matter."

"Old Burke," Dalton said quietly. "Nothing more familiar than *that*."

⟫⟫⟫✕⟪⟪⟪

THE BOY WHO had once opened the door to Lord Cabot on his visit to Mr. Farthingale's office in Cheapside was just now sitting at that gentleman's desk, looking over accounts. He was Mr. Farthingale's apprentice and had been so for the past six months.

"Freddy," Mr. Farthingale said, propping his feet up on a stool, "I think I have mentioned that your career as a trusted gentleman who might be sought after to lend funds will not get far if you do not make it a habit to wash your face. Even gentlemen in dire financial straits will not be prevailed upon to overlook it."

Freddy shrugged and swiped at the just mentioned dirty face, doing no more than smearing the smudges. "I got time to clean up, don't I? I ain't lendin' nothing yet."

Mr. Farthingale heaved a long and heavy sigh. It was fortunate the boy worked for only bed and board, as he would not have paid him a farthing at this very moment. Freddy was quick-witted and had a head for figures, but the rest of his person was near hopeless.

"The words you sought but failed to find are, I *have* time to clean up, as I am not currently lending," Mr. Farthingale said.

"I *have* time. Got it," Freddy said. "But this here, this loan what says Newmarket/Lord Cabot. You done told me a thousand times we don't do risky ventures, especially to lords as they is so tricky to dun."

"We certainly do not engage in overly risky lending," Mr. Farthingale said. "Many a gentleman in our line of work has found themselves in the Marshalsea from just such recklessness. It is the height of stupidity to fail to pay one's own debts because one has too much capital tied up and cannot get it back."

Freddy picked up the paper and waved it in a threatening fashion. "Newmarket," he said. "You can't tell me it ain't a horse race. Ain't nothin' riskier and you're in for two hundred guineas."

Mr. Farthingale folded his hands. "And Lord Cabot is in to me for three hundred. However, a further tidy profit may be made if one might think to place a hefty bet against Lord Cabot's horse. That person might come away with the three hundred guineas owed plus a delightful amount of winnings. The likelihood of a large gain mitigates the risk."

"What if he don't lose, though?" Freddy asked. "Then you might get your three hundred but you're out whatever you bet."

"He'll lose," Mr. Farthingale said. "You see, Freddy, it is the most precarious thing in the world to count on a horse winning. But losing? That might be made a certainty."

"I don't see how," Freddy said sullenly.

"No, but you will. Now, do go wash your face. I cannot look upon the filth of the town ground into your cheeks for another moment."

THE PHAETON MOVED at a smart trot while Penny watched the sunrise over the line of trees in the distance. The grass on either side of the lane was still wet with dew and glistened in the emerging light. It was her favorite time of day, when all the world was quiet but for her horses' spirited clip-clops.

She could not claim it as Doom's favorite time of day, as he had been inordinately sullen upon climbing on the back of the phaeton. Still, it was not as if they had any choice in the matter. Lord Cabot had made it known that he would go to the stables first thing in the morning. As she had no wish to encounter him, she'd determined to set off long before anybody's understanding of *first thing.*

Penny had been near furious when she'd left the drawing room the night before. As she had expected, Lord Cabot had wished to apologize. What she had not expected, though she no doubt should have, was what a weak tea that apology would be. He wished to apologize and might they just pretend none of it had happened?

The lord did not see that he had allowed her to view a part of his temperament that was, well…it was frightening. Nowhere in his apology did he assure that it would not happen again. Nowhere did he account for it or hint that it was in any way unusual.

Did he really think she would lay herself open to another such exchange? That she would blithely meet him at the stables to discuss their respective horses? That they would go on as they had been? Go on, that was, until the next time she'd unknowingly prodded him and he lashed her for it. She certainly was not such a fool.

She'd sent word to Petit to have the phaeton ready at dawn and she'd dressed herself and crept out of the house as soon as the sky had hinted at lightening. Her aunt would be aggravated that she'd not taken a footman, though her father would not mind it. Lord Mendbridge considered the hired stable, with its cadre of grooms, to be safe enough and he was of the opinion that highwaymen and others of their ilk might be late on the roads, but never early. Those that were too lazy to find proper work were unlikely to leap out of bed to meet the day.

Trotting up to the stables, she'd tied up her horses, not imagining the boys would be up at such an hour. Even the stalls were quiet, the horses sleepy and waiting patiently for the sun to rise higher so they might begin to stamp their hooves in a gentle request for their breakfast.

Doom staggered behind her in a near sleepwalk. As she moved down the line of stalls, she paused. Bella, who should have been in the very last stall of sixteen, was somehow in the third stall.

"Bella," she whispered, "what do you do in this stall that is not your own? Who has moved you here?"

The horse shook out her mane as if she was just as mystified as her mistress.

"That ain't Bella," Doom said sleepily. "She ain't got the three white hairs on her withers. I brushed the girl enough to know every hair on her."

Penny leaned in closer and peered at the horse. Doom was right, this horse did not have Bella's three white hairs. Penny had often noticed the oddity herself, and once joked to her father that Bella had wished to be a grey but had changed her mind.

She stepped back and found a small brass plate nailed to the stall door. *Bucephalus, Cabot*

Reading the plate, she frowned. "Lord Cabot. Why should he have a filly that is so like mine?" she said to herself.

"Is the lord an irritating sort in general?" Doom asked.

"He is," Penny said, though she knew full well she ought not talk about one of her father's houseguests with her groom.

"That's it then, he's gone about findin' another way to irritate."

"Well in any case," she said, rubbing the horse's nose, "it is not your fault, is it? I must only pity you for being burdened with such an unpronounceable name."

The horse whinnied as if she held the same opinion on the matter and Penny continued on to find the *real* Bella. She would shake off her annoyance, it was a glorious morning for a ride across the countryside.

CHAPTER SIX

HENRY AWOKE TO the sounds of horses stamping on the drive. He awoke, that is, if he had even slept at all. The mattress he'd tossed and turned on all night was the lumpiest surface he'd ever laid on short of a particularly rocky field in Belgium. He understood the house was a casual one, but he thought it would not be too much to expect a mattress that did not poke at one as if it were alive and incensed to find a person lying on it. Though it was barely light, he gratefully rolled out of the confounded bed and peered out the window.

To his surprise, Miss Darlington came from the house, mounted her phaeton, and drove off with her surly looking tiger hanging from the back.

He could guess why she left so early. He'd mentioned he would go to the stables first thing in the morning. Of course, he'd known she would go also. He thought it would be an excellent opportunity for a conversation after his apology. It was true that she had not immediately acceded to his proffer of regret, but surely the morning must bring some rationality to the case. Surrounded by horses, she was bound to be in a more cheerful frame of mind.

Now it seemed as if she purposefully left at dawn to avoid him.

He wished she would not go on with it. He'd found the night

before deuced uncomfortable. Why should they not go back to what they had been? Why should Burke have all the conversation?

He leapt up and dressed himself. She would not avoid him so easily.

FORTY-FIVE MINUTES LATER, Henry was finally on his way. He'd meant to make a fast dash out of the house and be on Miss Darlington's heels, but it had been impossible. Dressing himself proved to be a more lengthy operation than he had supposed— where did Jarvis hide his boots and why was it so impossible to locate a neckcloth not smudged with dirt and why could not Jarvis keep the hay off his coats? Then there was Mendbridge's stable hands to contend with—the grooms were awake but moved as if they were walking through knee-deep mud. As if that was not bad enough, they stopped what they were doing when some old woman came out with a tea tray. Who was she? Why was she there? Why was she asking them all how they'd slept? They were all *still* asleep as far as he could gather.

He'd paced and clutched his crop in frustration, that frustration not being allayed by the woman chuckling and saying, "There, love, they've got some tea in them now—you'll be off in a blink."

At being called *love*, he had presumed she confused him with his valet. That theory was disabused when she directed a groom to "hurry it along for the lord."

By the time he'd finally got on the road, the sun was well up in the sky.

Bucephalus was in her stall. She stamped her foot, her own way of saying she would like to be out and galloping. He was somewhat large for the filly, but he knew she would not mind it—she was as strong as she was fast. While a sleepy groom walked her to the yard and saddled her, Henry casually asked which direction Miss Darlington had gone.

None of the stable staff had seen her. She had come and gone before they were even out of bed.

Henry examined the grass in all directions. He could see in a moment that she'd ridden east. Very well, he would ride east too. Then, when he came upon her he would pretend surprise. Surely, she would not gallop away from him. It would give him time to elaborate on his apology of the night before.

He was not certain what it might be that would sway Miss Darlington to give up her anger. How did one go about explaining something that had been so monumentally stupid? He did not suppose he'd insulted anybody to such a degree since he'd been a boy and told his younger brother that he was an orphan who'd been left on the doorstep. He'd felt terrible then and he felt terrible now.

Perhaps that was it. He ought to explain how terrible he felt over it. He had to admit, to himself at least, that he'd not felt *as* terrible about it until last night. But then, he'd had some notion all along that their unfortunate conversation had not led to anything permanent. Miss Darlington would not be over affected by his stupid outburst.

Last night, he'd seen that she might consider their acquaintance as permanently altered. The real damage he'd done had slowly sunk in as he tossed and turned on that lumpy mattress.

Henry mounted Bucephalus. After taking her up to a canter, he gave his filly her head. He must catch up with Miss Darlington.

His filly did not pause for a moment and shot off with him. Despite his misgivings over what he ought to say when he encountered Miss Darlington, Henry could not be wholly unhappy. The cool morning air became wind on his face as Bucephalus went ever faster. It seemed her main interest in life was to reach ever greater speeds.

Though he was on the heavy side for his filly's size, she seemed not to notice it. She *would* notice it, though, when she raced. Then, she would have Rupert on her back and the lighter weight would make her feel as if she could fly. It was a strategy he'd discussed with Miss Darlington and she'd seemed to see the logic in it.

They'd discussed so many things! They really should go back to what they were. Surely, she would see the sense in it. It could not only be *he* that missed the exchanges.

Henry forced his attention back to what he was doing. He was fast approaching a farmer's fence and it would be easily taken.

At the edge of his field of vision, Henry caught sight of a blur of reddish brown with a distinctly bushy tail. The fox darted in front of them. Bucephalus saw the creature moments before they reached the fence. She refused the jump like a carriage hitting the side of a mountain, and then twisted and bucked. Henry lost the reins and felt himself flying through the crisp morning air.

PENNY AND DOOM had gone on a good long gallop and had now been walking their horses back in the direction of the stables for a quarter of an hour. Ahead, the farmer's fence came into view. There was no gate and it was bordered by close growing trees heavy with underbrush. There was only one way through and that was over.

They both spurred their horses and made the approach, easily clearing the low fence. As Penny slowed her horse, a movement at the tree line caught her eye.

"Doom," she said to the groom, "just there."

Doom followed her pointing and said, "That's what looks like Bella but ain't. It's the irritating fella's horse."

It was indeed Lord Cabot's filly standing in the shade of an old oak.

"I bet that irritating fella is gone into the trees to…"

Doom had trailed off. Penny could not imagine why somebody would wander into the trees without even bothering to secure their horse. It was quite irresponsible.

"For what," she said. "Certainly not for berries, it is not the right season."

Doom, much to Penny's surprise, looked away embarrassed. "Well, not berries, I don't think. A man might, he might just decide, considerin' there's nobody about…well, to relieve himself."

Penny turned away in disgust. What sort of man could not complete a ride without stopping for *that*?

As she turned her head, she suddenly saw Lord Cabot. He was not somewhere in the trees, he lay on the grass near the fence they'd just cleared. She must have flown right over him.

"Good Lord," she said, "he's been thrown."

Penny leapt off Bella and threw the reins to Doom. She approached the lord. His face was pale. He breathed but he did not wake. She examined the position of his body. She could not be certain, but there did not seem to be any bones broken. At least, no arm or leg rested in an unnatural position. As for his neck and back, that was another matter. Many a horseman had been thrown and still breathed, until they were moved and the broken neck gave way. Many a horseman's legs did not appear broken, until they were found to be no longer of use.

Penny felt a near overwhelming sense of panic. She had the urge to run from the scene and pretend she'd never viewed it.

She took a deep breath in and forced herself to think rationally. He needed to be moved, but carefully. They needed a doctor and they had none in Newmarket.

"Doom," she said, "tie Bella to a tree, and Lord Cabot's horse too. Ride Zephyrus to the stables for help. We'll need a litter and a cart stacked with blankets or hay to get us over this rough terrain and back to the house. As well, bring at least four of the boys to help move him without unnecessary jarring. Send another of the boys for a doctor to meet us at the house. Tell him to fetch the best man, they are local and will know who to go for."

Doom, ever the cool customer, nodded and leapt down from Zephyrus to secure the other two horses. Lord Cabot's horse shied and looked to make a dash into the woods, but Doom talked to her soothingly until he got hold of her reins. He hopped back on Zephyrus and galloped toward the stables.

Penny kneeled on the grass, looking at Lord Cabot. She watched him breathe in and out, the only sign of life he currently exhibited.

She'd wished all sorts of terrible things to rain down upon his head, but she'd never wished him dead. Or worse, paralyzed—a slower death for a man there could not be. She'd seen it in her own neighborhood. Billy Bates, the son of a tenant farmer, had come home from the war dragging his right leg behind him. There had been the hope that the leg would grow stronger, but not many months later he ended in a wheeled chair. His father pushed him out to the yard on fine days, but what was to happen when the old man passed on? Billy had apparently considered that question too, and set himself afire while his father was out in the fields. There had not been a question of it being an accident— Billy had taken embers in a bucket and crawled far away from the house and the barn before lighting his lard-soaked clothes.

No, Lord Cabot could never carry on in a chair. One who loved to ride as well as he could not bear such a thing.

The minutes ticked by and Penny wished he would wake, and also that he would not wake. She knew that the longer a person was unconscious, the higher the danger. On the other hand, she had no wish to witness a waking where a man realized he could not feel his legs.

It felt like an hour had passed before she caught sight of Doom again. He'd stabled Zephyrus and just now rode postillion on a cart pulled by four horses. The cart was filled with curious grooms straining their necks to get a look at the scene.

Doom expertly turned the vehicle so the open end was as close to her as possible, halted the horses, and leapt down. He turned to the grooms and said, "What ya lollygagging for? Hop to it, we don't got until noon."

The grooms seemed to accept that Doom was to be their leader on this particular excursion and jumped down from the cart.

Penny got to her feet. Before she could even inquire, Doom said, "One of the lads has gone after Doctor Prentiss, he lives not a mile off and is said to be the most experienced in these parts."

Penny nodded and faced the grooms. "Boys, listen carefully. Bring the litter by Lord Cabot's side. Three of you will lift him to one side—under the shoulder, hip, and ankle—the fourth will slide the litter underneath him. It must be done in one smooth motion, no jostling. I will tell you when to lift. Do you understand?"

The boys nodded at her, though she could not ignore the fear on their faces. They knew as well as she what could happen.

Nevertheless, it must be done.

※※※

PENNY PACED THE drawing room while Kitty sat on a nearby sofa. "Do sit down, Penny," Kitty said. "You have done all you could do and now Lord Cabot is in the doctor's hands."

"What sort of hands, though?" Penny asked. "Who is this Doctor Prentiss, anyway? He struck me as a gruff old farmer."

"He is old, indeed," Kitty said. "A mark of a man who knows what he is doing. He cannot have got through thirty years of doctoring and still be recommended as the best in the neighborhood if he were not skilled."

Penny knew Kitty was right. It had just been such a harrowing trip from the fields to the house. After they'd got Lord Cabot in the cart, Penny had put Doom on Bella, while she had ridden Bucephalus. She'd thought the lord's horse might give her trouble, horses often balked when faced with an unknown rider, but the filly had gone on calm enough. She had seemed to prefer to keep an eye on her master and so Penny had ridden her alongside the cart as they made their way back.

Lord Cabot had not fully awakened as he lay on well-padded hay in the back of the cart, though he had shown more signs of life. Those signs had not been very encouraging, as they had mainly consisted of groans.

It had seemed to take forever to reach the house, and they had passed many a curious onlooker. A trio of young boys had followed the cart, jumping up to look inside and gleefully inquiring if the gentleman was dead. It would not be an hour before all of Newmarket understood that Lord Cabot had encountered some sort of accident.

Penny thanked the heavens her father had been at home when they'd arrived. He'd quickly taken over her charge and directed the footmen to carry him up the stairs in the litter. Though her father moved with his usual confidence, Penny could not help but note the worry in his eyes. He understood as well as she did what the real risk was.

The doctor had arrived a half hour later and had been speedily shown up.

Since then, she'd been pacing the drawing room while Kitty attempted to soothe her and encourage her to take tea.

Mrs. Wellburton bustled in, having just come downstairs. "My dear girl," she said, "Montrose has told me all of it. How do you hold up?"

Penny could not say how she was holding up. Was she holding up?

Kitty said, "She would hold up a deal better if she would sit and have some tea. She has had an awful morning, indeed."

Before Penny could repeat that she had no need of tea, Lord Mendbridge came in, followed by the doctor.

Penny stood stock still. Here was the moment they would find out. Had there been permanent damage done? Would he die?

"There now, girl," her father said, "you look white as new-fallen snow. There is no cause for fear. Eh, Doc? Tell them all about it."

Doctor Prentiss, who aside from his respectable clothes did indeed resemble a gruff old farmer, nodded. "He has woken, pupils even, only a mild headache, and screamed like a stuck pig when I put a needle to his feet to check the feeling. No real harm done, I think. He ought to stay quiet for a fortnight, though it's my experience men that age will never do it. At least keep him abed for a few days, until the headache is gone. Then, if he insists on rising, he may run what risks he likes. I'll stop in on the morrow to have another look at him."

Penny felt a wave of relief wash over her. She was certain that part of it was the news Doctor Prentiss relayed, but the other part was Doctor Prentiss himself. He seemed a no-nonsense individual who'd seen this sort of thing a hundred times before and was not about to get excited over it.

The doctor took his leave, and Penny thought he did so with alacrity, as if he had no time to stand around talking to people who did not, in fact, have an illness or injury for him to consider.

"There now," Kitty said cheerfully, "all has come right and there is no cause to worry further."

"Deuced thing, it was," Lord Mendbridge said. "Cabot claims a fox ran in front of his filly right before a fence and she refused and bucked. No horse of *ours* would do such a ridiculous thing, or if they did, I reckon we'd hold on."

With that comforting idea, Lord Mendbridge left the ladies to their drawing room while Mrs. Wellburton hurried after him, determined to get his views on some household matter or other.

"Do sit and have tea now, Penny. The danger is past, and it will do nobody good to starve yourself over it."

Penny sat down and allowed Kitty to pour her a cup and fill a plate with biscuits. After all, she must not be a goose about it. It had been a frightening morning, but as Kitty said, the danger was past.

"I am just very much relieved," she said, "I did think there was a chance of permanent damage. I think you know what I allude to. No man can carry on having lost his vigor."

"You think of poor Billy Bates," Kitty said.

"Yes, that is what I feared."

"And now you may put that fearsome thought from your mind," Kitty said cheerfully. She set her own cup down and said, "I suppose you will forgive Lord Cabot his recent transgression, now that he has come so close to killing himself?"

Penny was silent. She was not at all certain. It was true, during the emergency, she had given no thought to what had passed between her and the lord. She had only wished for his recovery.

"Well, I…"

"There is no harm in it," Kitty said. "Though you might be careful about it. Do not lay yourself open to any further hurtful comments from that quarter. I know how much to heart you take such things and the fact is, an accident does not change a character or cure a temper. I would say be friends, but do not let down your guard."

Kitty was right. Lord Cabot's accident bore no relation to his intemperance on the night of the Tudor ball. This day had found her exceedingly worried, and grateful to see her worry come to naught. *Terribly* grateful, as it happened. She would never forget his pale face, the crinkle gone from his eyes, the smile gone from his lips. It had been horrifying.

But that did not mean he was in any way changed. He'd shown his true character the night of the ball, and that character was still fixed.

Penny found the trial of the past hours had caused the worst of her anger toward the lord to dissipate like fog under bright sun, but caution must still remain by her side.

MONTROSE HAD CONSULTED with Doctor Prentiss before the doctor had got in his carriage. Lord Cabot's condition was not considered serious, though he would remain abed for some days. It was Doctor Prentiss' opinion that there was no particular care required, other than the patient stay quiet with his head on at least two pillows for as long as anybody could keep him there.

As far as the butler was concerned, this was another instance of the lord's unworthiness. First, he upsets Miss Penny, then he foolishly falls off his horse and becomes their patient. Never was one of the lord's houseguests more trouble.

He had conferred with Mrs. Wiggins and they had both agreed that they were not to be put out by the irritating gentleman. He must be cared for, of course he must, else Lord Mendbridge was sure to notice. But that did not mean he must be cared for comfortably.

Between them, they had speedily come to the conclusion that the most uncomfortable way to proceed was to put Peg in charge of the sickroom. Montrose had high hopes that Peg would rain down "what all," whatever that might be, upon the lord's head.

Peg, when informed of this directive, had seemed well-pleased and up to the task. At least, Montrose had assumed so, as she'd rubbed her hands together and said, "We'll just see how we get on, won't we?"

CHAPTER SEVEN

H ENRY HAD OPENED his eyes to find a strange old man holding a candle up to his face. He'd attempted a brief struggle, certain he was being robbed.

Lord Mendbridge had then stepped into his view and Henry had realized he was in his own bedchamber in Mendbridge Cottage in Newmarket. Right on the heels of *that* understanding had come the memory of urging his horse toward a fence and being summarily thrown off by way of a fox.

Though his head pounded, he'd been pleased to hear that it had been Miss Darlington who had discovered him lying in the field. She'd arranged a cart to bring him to the house. Certainly, it was a very good sign that she'd not left him there. It must have been all sorts of trouble to arrange the thing, when she might have trotted by and pretended she'd not even seen him. Certainly, it must show a thawing of ice.

And then, when one comes so close to disaster, others are always more likely to think kindly of them. More than a few of his soldiers had married a girl who'd never looked at them twice, all because they'd risked their neck on a battlefield.

He'd not thought he'd need to nearly kill himself to get back into Miss Darlington's good graces but there it was. He'd since been left alone to rest and, aside from his throbbing head and the diabolically lumpy mattress he lay on, he was rather cheerful.

The door opened and, though he'd fully expected to see Jarvis, a middle-aged housemaid bustled into the room carrying a tray.

He could not say it was an unwelcome interruption, he'd not breakfasted before he'd gone out and found himself ravenous.

"There you are, my lord," the maid said. "I'm Peg and will tend to ya while you be laid low."

Peg set down the tray and grabbed a pillow from the other side of the bed. Before he even knew what she was doing, she'd grabbed his collar, yanked him forward, and stuffed the extra pillow behind his neck. His head swam with the sudden movement and he gripped the bedsheets to steady himself.

Peg seemed to take no notice of it. As his vision settled, he watched her remove the cover from a bowl of something gelatinous and brown.

"What is that? Soup?" he asked, staring down at it. "Might I trouble you for eggs? In fact, I wouldn't mind three fried eggs, four sausages, a rasher of bacon, kidneys, and four rolls. Also, whatever cakes you have on offer. Oh, and coffee. What else? Butter. Lots of butter. And you might as well send up some jam, too."

Peg regarded him with what appeared to be an indulgent eye. "Ain't you the jester? Eggs and sausage after the fall you've had? Goodness no. I've brought you some bone broth, thickened with flour. It'll fill you up and do no harm."

"But I'd really prefer eggs, if you please," Henry said.

Peg stood hands on hips and laughed rather more loudly than he was accustomed to hearing from a servant. "You're a regular goose, is what you are, my lord."

Henry was flummoxed. He was a *goose*? Who was this person? Was the lady really going to refuse him his request?

"Now, do I need to spoon it to ya?" she asked. "Or are ya strong enough to feed yourself?"

"Of course I'm strong enough to feed myself!"

"As you like," Peg said. "Now, I'll just get the fire going."

"Fire?" Henry asked. "I say, though, it's already very warm in this room. I do not see cause for a fire."

"It'll drive out the fever," Peg said matter-of-factly, arranging the wood and kindling.

"I don't have a fever," Henry said, exasperated.

"And you won't get one while old Peg is on the watch. 'Tis my job to see that you don't kick off and I *am* gonna see to it."

Henry was out of all patience with the confounded woman. "Madam, I do not quite comprehend what goes on here. I see no need for a fire and every need for a proper breakfast."

Peg ignored this pronouncement and only said softly, "Delirium. All too common in these cases. Patience is what's required."

"I am not delirious!" Henry said. Never was there such an obtuse person. He shifted uncomfortably on the lumpy bedding. "I do not see how I am to go on lying on this infernal lumpy mattress with only gruel to eat."

"Is the bed that uncomfortable for those young bones?" Peg asked, looking surprised.

"It's deuced uncomfortable, as it happens," Henry said.

"Do ya reckon I ought to tell Lord Mendbridge that the lord don't find his hospitality up to snuff?"

Henry laid back. Certainly, he did not wish any such thing. Why could not Mendbridge's servants just take care of a thing without running to their master about it?

"I'll let him know," Peg said sorrowfully. "He'll be mighty disappointed as he don't like soft gentlemen. He always say, don't let a soft gentleman in through the doors."

"I am not soft," Henry said hurriedly. "The mattress is fine, say nothing of it."

Peg nodded and said, "As you wish. Now, let me get that fire going."

AN HOUR LATER, Henry sweated in his bed, determined to put out that blasted fire. Each time he put his feet on the floor, his vision seemed to turn the room upside down.

Finally, Jarvis knocked and came through the door.

"My lord," he cried, "this room is hell on earth, why do you have a fire?"

"Put it out," Henry said weakly.

Jarvis grabbed a pitcher of water and doused the flames, then opened the windows to let out the ensuing smoke that billowed from the hissing embers.

Henry laid back, grateful for the cool breeze that blew into the room. "A housemaid," he said. "I think she may be trying to kill me."

Jarvis looked about the room with a critical eye, that eye settling on the uneaten bowl of brown sludge.

"What on earth…" the valet said.

"That is breakfast," Henry said, beginning to feel a little better now that he did not feel himself cooking alive. "A diabolical woman named Peg informed me that I cannot have anything else, and that I must have a fire for a fever I don't have, and when I even mentioned this horrible bed she threatened to go to Lord Mendbridge about it. What in the world is wrong that harpy?"

Jarvis appeared thoughtful.

"What is it? What do you know? Out with it," Henry said, well aware that his valet's thoughtful look portended something of import.

"As you know, my lord," Jarvis said slowly, "I am well-liked everywhere I go."

"I did not in fact know that," Henry said.

"It is very true," Jarvis said. "Yet, Lord Mendbridge's staff has so far given me very short shrift. They don't smile, they leave the servant's hall when I come in, and the cook gives me decidedly small portions. In fact, last night the servants were given a roasted beef and I was served the ends. The *ends*, my lord. Naturally, it cannot be anything *I* have done, and so I have assumed it was a reflection upon you."

Henry attempted to parse his valet's speech. As far as he could understand it, Jarvis wished him to know that all the world loved him, he'd never been served ends in his life, and that was to be *his* fault?

"Then," Jarvis went on, "just this morning, I overheard the butler and the housekeeper in conversation. The butler said you were to get "what all." The housekeeper seemed to find it most amusing."

"What is what all?" Henry asked.

Jarvis appeared pensive, then said, "I suppose what all is a fire and gruel. Though, I really cannot imagine what you have done to merit such treatment."

Henry could not either. Until suddenly he did. They knew. Lord Mendbridge might not know of his unfortunate words to his daughter at the Tudor ball. But *they* knew.

Of course they knew! How could he not have seen that they would? Did not Jarvis know far more than he ought? When he considered what a lady's maid might be privy to, and how quickly that lady's maid might regale the servant's table with the knowledge…he'd been a fool not to have considered it. By the looks of it, he had an entire houseful of servants out for revenge.

Henry prodded the lumpy mattress and said, "They've been against me from the start. I'm certain that's why they've put me in a room with the worst bedding in the house. It was deliberate."

Jarvis went to the opposite side of the bed. "I would not suppose they would dare so much. Though, considering the fire and the gruel, perhaps they haven't bothered to turn the mattresses as they should," he said, lifting the cover.

Henry watched his valet examine the mattresses and murmur, "Soft down on top, very regular. Ah, I think I see, there is no feather mattress. The rest of the layers below the down mattress are flock. One might have expected better from a lord's house. I can assure you that your own mattresses follow a very specific order: two down, two feathers, four flock, turned weekly."

"Nevertheless," Henry said, "I do not see why wool is to be as uncomfortable as this. What sort of confounded sheep would produce such a misery?"

Jarvis reached his hand between the down and the flock mattresses. He paused and frowned, then went to the dressing table to retrieve the lord's razor. He slit the top flock mattress at the seam and reached his hand inside.

As Henry watched, Jarvis rose victorious with a small stone in his hand. "Here is the culprit, my lord. The bottom of the second mattress has been stuffed with rocks. They have been set there cleverly—they provide just enough discomfort without giving themselves away."

Henry laid back. He'd been right, the servants *were* out for revenge.

"Never fear, my lord," Jarvis said, a look of resolve settling on his features. "From now on, I will scarce leave your side. I will even go so far as to sleep in the dressing room. Peg, whoever she thinks she is, will find herself ranged against a formidable opponent."

❄❄❄

MR. FARTHINGALE HAD made it his business to understand the ins and outs of the *ton*. In his estimation, to comprehend the whole of it properly one must become the master of two things: who was who, and what they liked to do with their time.

The who was who had been delightfully easy. Debrett's helpfully provided every notable genealogy. The newspapers filled in the rest, with their swooning sketches and verbose descriptions of looks and finery. Who would not recognize Mr. Brummel from his sublimely cut coat? Who would not recognize Mrs. Fitzherbert via her fading looks and too-long nose? Who would not recognize Lord Dalton by the scar that marred his cheek? Who would not recognize Lord Sassbury by way of the birth mark on his chin that was shaped like a clover?

As for what people of that ilk liked to do, he supposed he would sum it up as: frittering away one's time in useless pursuits while sporting a strangely self-congratulatory air.

One of those useless pursuits was held at Newmarket just now and he was far more familiar with it than he'd let on to Lord Cabot. Below the glossed veneer, Newmarket was a scene rife with blacklegs, tricksters and sharpers. One must step carefully through the town to avoid being had. As a precaution, he'd donned the sort of non-descript clothes a pickpocket wouldn't look twice at.

It was well he did so. Just now, as he sat in a tavern and nursed an ale, his ears wide open to pick up the news of the place, a particular well-known gentleman with a particular well-known scar sat down at the next table. Farthingale did not recognize Lord Dalton's friend, he was dressed as an insufferable fop which could be any number of fellows. Farthingale turned his face away from them though he did not think either of the men would recognize him.

"My footman has come back from Mendbridge Cottage to say that Cabot can't have visitors at all today," Lord Dalton said. "Apparently, the butler is formidable and refuses to admit anybody."

"Cabot, though," the other man said. "Of all people, how does *he* fall off his horse and knock his head?"

"Grayson," Lord Dalton said, "anybody might be thrown. I doubt it was serious, what concerns me more is that he's in there without his friends."

Mr. Farthingale sat back and tented his fingers. Cabot had met with an accident. That would not be well for his plan. If the word got about that he would not recover, the bets would flow heavily against the lord's horse. It would not make a lick of sense, as the lord was not the rider and the horse was likely uninjured, but that was the nature of betting. Any little circumstance would spook in the wrong direction. For his plan to work, he needed most of these gambling fools to bet *for* Cabot's horse, not against it. He had confirmed that Cabot had not exaggerated the filly's potential and, if all would go as it should, nobody else would undervalue it either.

"Why should you fear for him in that regard?" Lord Grayson asked. "Certainly, Mendbridge may be relied upon to provide suitable medical care. Especially for a throw, I reckon the old man has been dumped more than once." Grayson paused and it seemed to Mr. Farthingale that a light was dawning upon him. "Ah, I see. Alone in the clutches of Miss Darlington."

"Exactly," Lord Dalton said. "There he'll be, at her mercy, while she acts as sympathetic nurse."

"There's no way to get him out, I suppose," Grayson said.

"No, we cannot get him out. Though, I've already given Cabot the impression that a match between Miss Darlington and Burke is in the works. We might add another layer of protection by turning Miss Darlington herself from any thought of Cabot. I think I know just how to do it via pretty Miss Dell."

"Now, Dalton," Lord Grayson said, "do not tamper with that lady. You know I find Miss Dell charming."

"You find every lady charming," Lord Dalton said. "For my purposes, I would like to know what goes on in that house and have a hand in directing it. We may call on the ladies, I do not suppose that butler will dare an attempt to keep us out of the drawing room. I will also send a servant to gossip with the stable hands or try to catch a footman out of doors."

"Yes! Call on the ladies, of course that is what we should do," Lord Grayson said, appearing instantly cheered by the idea.

Mr. Farthingale rubbed his chin. He would like to see how Lord Cabot got on even more than Lord Dalton wished to, though he had not the least interest in any amorous goings on. He must gain a better understanding into the lord's health. It would greatly affect how he was to proceed during his time here. Dalton might think to send a clumsy servant on a fishing expedition, but he had a rather better resource. He also had, through experience, a more effective strategy to ingratiate oneself into a house to gain information and it was *not* through a stable hand or a footman.

PENNY HAD BEGUN to think that she, Kitty, and Mrs. Wellburton would never see the end of people arriving to call. It seemed the entire town must hear for themselves how Lord Cabot got on.

Some of those who called were known to be the lord's acquaintances. Some others, she was not so certain of. She rather thought the more obscure connections were not particularly concerned with the lord's health, but far more concerned with whether or not he'd be on his feet on race day. Those men had the sort of furtive looks and penetrating gazes that spoke of weighing their bets. Most of the conversations had been tedious, with perhaps the exception of Lord Burke. He had been in, inquired, been satisfactorily answered, and then taken his leave by noting they must be tired of the endless arrivals. Penny wished the rest of the visitors had come with as much sense.

Though all and sundry were told the same thing—Lord Cabot's injury was not serious and he only rested for a few days—Penny was not certain that was altogether true. The doctor had come and gone without speaking to either her or her aunt. Soon after, she had noticed Montrose and Mrs. Wiggins deep in conversation. They had ceased abruptly upon catching sight of her, as if they knew something that she did not. She had asked if they had been told anything of Lord Cabot and they had denied it was so. But they had looked very strangely! Almost as if they harbored a secret.

Had there been a sudden change for the worse? It might be so. Injuries to the head could be unpredictable. One moment the patient appeared recovering and the next his condition grew grave.

But certainly, her father would have informed her of it. Would he not?

Perhaps not, if he thought he would not trouble her with something she could not fix.

Two gentlemen who had claimed to be on intimate terms with Lord Cabot, though Penny was almost certain they were not, had finally been shown out. As Penny began to hope that was the last of them, two more were announced. The Lords Dalton and Grayson.

Penny looked toward Mrs. Wellburton with some hope that they might be turned away. Her aunt understood her meaning, but shook her head. "Do show them in, Montrose," she said.

As if they had been on Montrose's heels, the two men were into the drawing room in a moment. The next minutes were as so many minutes of the day had been—a greeting, an inquiry into Lord Cabot's health, and an assurance that his injury was minor and he would soon recover.

Montrose brought in fresh tea, always willing to show consideration for those individuals who carried with them a title.

"Well!" Lord Grayson said. "We are very much relieved that our friend has not suffered anything serious. Miss Dell, how do you get on?"

Penny bit her lip to stop a smile. Lord Grayson had taken only a moment to dispense with any worry over his friend and turn to the nearest lady. Mrs. Wellburton, seeing this was to be a nonsensical visit on Lord Grayson's part, moved to the other side of the room and picked up her sewing.

"I get on very well, my lord," Kitty said to him.

"I say, you are a very great reader, Miss Dell. Here you are with another book by your side. I quite admire it," Grayson said.

"You admire reading? Or this particular book?" Kitty asked, her eyes seeming all innocence though Penny knew better. Kitty amused herself.

"Ah, both, I expect," Lord Grayson said, coloring ever so slightly. "I suppose you are a great lover of poetry?"

"No more than the usual way, my lord, though I prefer history, biography, geography, and most particularly, science," Kitty said, picking up the book by her side. "This is Malcom's *A History of Persia*. Have you read it?"

Lord Grayson took a sip of tea and Penny thought he very much needed the pause before answering *that* particular inquiry.

He set his cup down and said, "That particular book? Not yet. Though I am certain I should find it fascinating."

Kitty smiled. "As you plan to read it yourself, I would not for the world spoil it for you. I would only hint that the commencement of the Sassanian Dynasty was particularly riveting."

"The Sassanians, yes they would be," Lord Grayson said, appearing completely lost.

"Perhaps you would be interested in some other books in Lord Mendbridge's collection," Kitty said. "There is a small selection of titles I am interested in, just there on that shelf. I am sure my host should not mind if you borrowed one."

Lord Grayson seemed to perk up at this idea. "Those are of particular interest to you? If you would consult with me on the best choice, Miss Dell," he said.

Penny watched in great amusement as Kitty and Lord Grayson made their way to the small bookshelf at the end of the room. She was certain Kitty led the lord on a merry chase by way of his lackluster efforts to appear learned.

Beside Penny, Lord Dalton said softly, "Grayson has not read a book since school, and even then not many."

"As anybody might surmise," Penny said.

"Miss Dell would be better served to compare her ideas of the history of Persia with Cabot, is all I say."

"Lord Cabot?" Penny asked. "That gentleman is no more the scholar than Lord Grayson."

"As he would have people believe. He does a credible job of hiding it, I'll give him that. A holdover from his school days no doubt. He was terribly teased in his first terms, everybody called him the know-all. Since then, he's kept his proclivities under wraps and pretends only to be interested in horses."

"I am surprised, Lord Dalton," Penny said. And, indeed she was. Lord Cabot *had* only seemed interested in horses.

"Most people would be, I suppose," Lord Dalton said.

"Though, if you'd seen his personal library and knew how he spends his evenings when he does not go out, you would not be. Head buried in a book with a glass of claret by his side."

Penny was entirely nonplussed. "But if he is naturally of a scholarly nature, why should he hide it so well?" she asked.

"Habit, I think. All those years ago he was teased mercilessly until he showed a talent for picking horses, and then he became very popular."

A silence fell between them as Penny considered this startling news about Lord Cabot. As much as they had fallen out of late, she had thought she knew him fairly well. How could it be that there was another side of him that the world had never seen? A side that *she* had never seen?

Lord Dalton set down his cup and said, "It is no matter, I suspect. His secret preferences are likely to soon see the light of day. I understand he admires Miss Dell to a great degree and so he will wish her to understand that he is of a similar turn of mind."

Penny noticed the hand that held her cup tremble and she set it down. Lord Cabot admired Kitty? It seemed a most unlikely preference. Impossible, really.

Though, perhaps not so impossible if what Lord Dalton said was true. In general, she would take the lord's words with a grain of salt. But who would make up a tale of a person being a great reader?

In truth, when she examined the idea more closely, she must admit that Lord Cabot was exceedingly well-read when it came to horses. Much more so than the average gentleman. How many times had he waxed on about some dusty tome on horsemanship from the late 1500's by Gervase somebody? What was to say he'd not read books on other subjects?

And then, his terrible put down at the Tudor ball. That began to make much more sense. He'd accused her of thinking she knew more than she actually did. It would follow that he should consider himself superior in knowledge if what Lord Dalton said was fact.

Penny's cheeks grew hot as she imagined the lord to have studied all manner of sciences. Perhaps he had some formulas that proved her theory of the Arabian's wider windpipe accounting for its speed had been only fanciful. Perhaps he pitied her very limited knowledge, so confined to horses as it was.

It might very well be so. The story did carry with it a general ring of truth. Young men *could* be beastly to their own. She could very well see how one might be teased for studying too much, and she could easily imagine the teased boy succumbing to the pressure of it.

And then there was Kitty. She was so lovely. What gentleman would *not* be interested in her friend? Lord Grayson was just now gazing at her as if he were lovelorn.

Before Penny was forced to voice an opinion on the facts recently communicated to her, Kitty and Lord Grayson returned to them.

Lord Grayson held a book. Kitty said, "You will know that Lord Grayson has made an excellent choice—John Galt's *The Life and Administration of Cardinal Wolsey*. I had the pleasure of reading it last year and had thought to go back and revisit some of the more fascinating sections. I very much look forward to a thorough discussion of the subject."

Lord Grayson, for his part, smiled weakly. Penny thought reading an entire book about a long-dead cardinal was more than Lord Grayson was used to do in pursuit of a flirtation.

It would not be too much for Lord Cabot, as it turned out. They were all soon to discover he was a scholar and admiring of Kitty. She supposed Lord Cabot would know all about the cardinal.

Penny brushed a crumb from her dress as if that crumb were the most irritating thing she'd ever encountered. She did not care a fig what the lord's reading preferences were or who he admired. It only rankled that he'd set himself forward as somebody he was not. Or hid being somebody that he was.

She was horse-mad, she knew it. She cared little for books or all those tedious skills women seemed to think so worthwhile. Her efforts at sewing were not real efforts at all and not a thing made by her would ever be of any use. She'd only somewhat mastered the pianoforte to please her aunt. Her primary interest was horseflesh. There was not a thing wrong with it. But for another to pretend he was precisely the same as she was, well she did not know what sort of crime that was. At the least, it was off-putting.

She was most irritated that Lord Cabot had thought he hid his proclivities so well from her. It rankled that he thought himself on the verge of surprising the world with his knowledge.

Perhaps she might apprise him that his ruse no longer deceived. She might send a book up to the sickroom. The most confounded book she could find. *That* would let the lord know he'd been found out. That would educate him that his extensive reading had come as no surprise to Miss Darlington. Then he could be free to spout off any knowledge he liked to Kitty.

She knew just what book she would send up. Last year, Penny had desultorily scanned the books her father had acquired from the Oxford professor and one particularly drab tome had amused her. *Principles of Algebra*, by some fellow in the 1790's. It had not been the title that tickled her, but the note inscribed in ink on the first page by a recent reader of the book. It had said, "Beware, this author rejects negative quantities!"

Penny had not the slightest idea of what it meant, but the outraged scrawl sounded to her the sort of rabbit hole that a puffed-up scholar would delight in. She would not be surprised to hear of two such gentlemen nearly coming to blows over whether one was to accept or reject the negative quantities. There could be nothing more obscure and ridiculous than that book.

This would be an instance where Lord Cabot would fail to take her unawares. He would know the moment he saw it that his great secret was out.

DOOM HAD BEEN raised by nobody and had early on experienced the unpleasant consequences of an empty belly. He had never been lazy, no matter how tempting it might have been. There had been days when he'd been weak in body and the sun had shined and it had seemed almost irresistible to lay oneself on a patch of grass in a park and rest. He had never given in to the feeling and it had served him well.

He'd started his career by holding horses for gents who wished to stop into a shop or a club. Then he'd been hired to muck out stalls for Mister Melvern. Then he'd been tasked with exercising the horses and had shown a proclivity for it. Then he'd ended up racing one of Mr. Melvern's horses in a private bet with another gentleman. Lord Mendbridge had been there and he'd been promptly poached by that fine gentleman. It had not taken much convincing. Once he was apprised of the general situation, he'd only to confirm that he was to be called Doom and not Daniel. His father, wherever the blighter was now, was called Daniel. Doom wouldn't stand for honoring the old criminal's name and preferred a more threatening moniker. Once that was agreed to, he'd packed up his meager belongings and turned in his notice.

Since then, he'd become a connoisseur of two things—horses and food. Both were the finest at Lord Mendbridge's establishment. He'd never eaten so much meat in his life. He'd never drank more fresh milk. He might have tea and a biscuit whenever he liked from Mrs. Payne. When he had the notion of something finer, he might slip into the house kitchens to discover what Mrs. Lowell was up to. There was no end of cakes that lady might whip up, particularly now that a certain Miss Dell was in residence. It was said that Miss Darlington's friend was particular for fairy cakes and savarins and Doom had found a need to confirm the idea himself.

Just now, he sat at the small table in the corner of the kitchen, sampling Mrs. Lowell's seed cakes.

There was a soft knock on the back door leading to the yard and a small boy entered carrying a large wicker basket.

"Is that from Mr. Slincher's?" Mrs. Lowell asked, eyeing the basket. "I've been waiting on lard and flour this past hour."

The boy, who Doom thought had the hard look about him of one used to managing for himself, said, "Slincher? He ain't to be counted on. This here is from Mr. Cumberbald."

Mrs. Lowell put her rag down on the counter. "Well that's interesting," she said. "As I never did order anything from a Mr. Cumberbald, whoever he may be."

"Not yet, my good woman," the boy said. "This here is *compliments* of my master. He's the best grocer in these parts and he knowed that once a 'lustrious person such as yerself done tried his wares, ya give old Slincher the heave ho."

"Did he now?" Mrs. Lowell said, eyeing the basket. "Very well. Never let it be said that I'm opposed to a tradesman vying for business. Let us see."

The boy, who told Mrs. Lowell his name was Freddy, unpacked the contents of the basket, introducing each new item with what Doom considered a particular dramatic aplomb.

Freddy laid a fine-carved wood box on the table. "Tea, from the hand of Mr. Twining himself."

He next pulled out a wood bowl filled with wrinkled brown specimens of something or other. Doom leaned over and examined them, flummoxed by what they might be.

"Turkish dates," Freddy said. "Nothin' sweeter than them from the distant land of Turkish. Good for eatin' alone or in baking. Ya might even stuff 'em into a fowl."

"I know what to do with dates, young man," Mrs. Lowell said sternly, though her features belied her tone. She seemed rather taken with the dates.

"Then we got your more regular items—butter, sugar, salt, flour," Freddy said, laying them out one by one. "And I save the last for your inspection as something that old Slincher never has got a bony hand on in his life."

Doom waited expectantly to discover what this thing was that old Slincher had no hope of acquiring.

Freddy carefully lifted an oblong item wrapped in cloth. He unwrapped it with a flourish.

Doom heard Mrs. Lowell take in a sharp breath. He was certain this thing that lay before them was special, though he could not imagine what it was. It was exotic looking, and nothing he could fathom England grew. It was a pale yellow-brown, dotted with thorny protrusions, and had a great sprout of sharp green spikes on top.

"Now then," Mrs. Lowell said, "wherever did you get your hands on a pineapple?"

Doom was perplexed beyond measure. He would have thought, if there were apple trees that grew a thing called pine apple, somebody would have mentioned it before now. Though it could be from Scotland, he supposed.

Freddy crossed his arms and surveyed the goods laid out on the table. "My master has got connections, while Slincher don't. My master know all sorts in London and at the ports, while Slincher don't. If you just need middlin' eggs and flour, Slincher's your man. If you be lookin' for something finer, Cumberbald's your man. It's that simple."

Doom had thought all these fine things that Freddy had delivered would be relegated to the family. However, Mrs. Lowell had different ideas. She said that nothing went to the family without her trying it out beforehand. That led Doom to his first, and possibly last, experience of pineapple. While he carved up the large slice that Mrs. Lowell had laid before him and tasted something sweet and yet tangy and yet indescribable, Freddy told him of the faraway islands where it was grown.

Doom was secretly relieved that he'd not given his ignorance of the thing away. He'd have sounded like a rube if he'd ventured that it was Scottish. As it was, he only nodded sagely. Privately, he found himself rapt to hear of those unknown places only reached by sailing ship.

The conversation eventually drifted away from Mr. Cumberbald's goods, as Freddy inquired into the latest gossip. Mainly, Freddy was interested to know if Lord Cabot would die, as was being speculated on in the town. He'd even heard there were beginning to be bets laid on it and the odds were leaning toward dead by Tuesday.

Mrs. Lowell, mightily appeased by a pineapple and dates, decided to give Freddy the advantage on the betting. She regaled him with the real case of the thing. The lord was not particularly in danger, but he was not made comfortable either. He was a rude young gentleman who'd offended the miss of the house. On account of it, Mrs. Lowell had been sending up a wretched soup of flour and mutton fat, and one might just find rocks in his bed if one were to look. He wouldn't go out in a coffin, but he'd go out a deal thinner and more sore than he came in.

Freddy appeared fascinated by the tale. This was all of great interest to Doom too. He'd known the lord was not liked and had followed suit in giving his valet the cold shoulder, but he'd not known of an actual organized campaign. It tickled him to hear of it. He was fond of Miss Darlington and if the high and mighty lord had offended her, then he ought to pay heavily for it.

Much to Doom's surprise, they were interrupted in their cozy conversation by Lord Cabot's valet. Jarvis appeared red in the face, as if he'd run a great distance. He stared at Mrs. Lowell and said, "There is to be no more of that wretched gruel sent up to my master. I require proper food to take to him. I require it this instant. Cold meats and rolls will suffice for now."

"Calm yourself," Mrs. Lowell said. "I'm sure the patient is complaining, don't they all? Still, he'll be better off with my bone broth."

"I'll be the judge of what's better, madam. If you do not comply, I shall go directly to Lord Mendbridge about Lord Cabot's treatment in this house."

Doom had expected Mrs. Lowell to give the valet the what for, but Mrs. Lowell had looked distinctly frightened.

"As you wish, then," she said, hurrying to find a plate.

Jarvis looked down upon the spread at the table and said, "And a large slice of that pineapple, if you please."

As HENRY LAID waste to ham, beef, rolls, butter, and a large helping of chopped pineapple, he thought Jarvis had never proved his worth more. At least there was one servant in the house not set on killing him off. And how on earth had the fellow got hold of pineapple? Jarvis would not say and had only given him a knowing nod. The only thing Jarvis *would* say was Mrs. Lowell had been made to understand that her shenanigans on the food side of things would no longer be tolerated.

Whatever had transpired, his plate of real food sent energy through his veins. His headache faded and he felt better than he had since being thrown. That was well, as he must get up and show himself round the town soon. Perhaps as soon as the morrow if he could get his hands on a few more meals like this one. Jarvis had told him there was no end of speculation going round about his condition and he ought to put a stop to it before letters were written and the accident was more widely known. He had no wish to be bombarded by post from anxious family members, or worse, find one of them staring down at him.

There was a knock on the door, followed by the diabolical Peg coming in as officious as a government clerk. She stopped and appeared startled as she took in the scene.

Henry watched her with interest, suspecting Jarvis would make short work of her before she could light the fire or pile more stones in his bed.

"Oh!" she said nervously. "You done gone against doctor's advice and skipped the broth, then? Well, I suppose nobody ain't to tell a lord what to do."

Jarvis glared at her. He went to the side of the bed and picked up from the floor the bag of stones he had removed from the mattress. He held the bag in front of him and said, "This, I believe, is yours."

Peg took the stones and muttered, "I can't say if it is or it ain't as I don't know what it is—"

"Cease your flimsy excuses," Jarvis said. "Furthermore, never enter this apartment again. *I* am in charge now."

Peg's coloring had been growing progressively more pale. Cabot watched in some amusement, but then also with the uncomfortable realization that he, himself, had got nowhere attempting to fight off the woman.

"As you prefer it," Peg said, throwing her chin up in the air, "though I suppose I can be allowed to carry out a thing tasked to me by one of the family? Miss Darlington wished to send a book to the patient."

She held out the book in question. Jarvis took it from her reluctantly, holding it away from his person as if it were a live viper. It appeared his valet looked upon everything in the house with deep suspicion.

Henry, however, was enormously cheered by it. Certainly, Miss Darlington could not still hold any anger against him if she'd sent a book. A lady of the house might be expected to ensure a guest did not actually die on the premises, but there was no cause to send something to read unless the lady particularly wished to. Further, was it not well-known that the very choice of a title must communicate an idea? Much like the choice of a flower, a book would indicate the giver's thoughts on the receiver.

Miss Darlington was sending him a message, he was certain of it. He only hoped it was not some treacly romance or other. After all, a lady's feelings might swing in the opposite direction a bit *too* far, especially toward one who had been injured. Grayson always said that females liked nothing so much as a tragic hero. What could be more tragically heroic than lying unconscious in a field?

"You may go," Jarvis said to Peg, with a finality that left her no choice but to exit.

After the door closed, Henry put aside his tray and held out his hand to take the book. He read the title.

Then he read it again.

Algebra? What on earth did it mean?

He opened the book to see if perhaps a note had been placed inside. There was a message, hastily scrawled on the inside cover. *Beware, this author rejects negative quantities.*

Does she say she rejects something? Was *he* the negative quantity? But then, maybe it was her anger that was negative and to be rejected? He could not fathom what she was trying to tell him.

Henry fanned the book and shook it, but there was no other communication. He held it out to Jarvis. "What do you make of this?" he asked, pointing at the phrase. "Certainly, Miss Darlington has written it. It is a message, but what am I to make of it? What does it mean?"

Jarvis stared at it and rubbed his chin. "Miss Darlington rejects negative quantities. Hmmm. I cannot be sure, my lord, but I am fairly certain I'd reject them too."

"Reject what, though?"

"Who can say? However, I'm certain positive quantities would be a deal more pleasant than negative quantities. It's all in the name."

Henry spent the next hour pondering the message with little success. In truth, if he were to swear to it, he met with *no* success.

MONTROSE STARED DOWN the servant's table. He might not have been at his leisure to have a confidential conversation with his staff, had that confounded valet chosen to sit down to dinner. As it was, Mr. Jarvis was above stairs, having closeted himself in Lord

Cabot's bedchamber like a knight of old guarding a fair maiden.

The servant's table had been quiet, all of them now aware that the stones in the mattress had been discovered and the wretched gruel handily rejected by the irate valet. They were left to consider what might be the consequences if Jarvis ever did what he'd threatened to do—go to Lord Mendbridge.

Montrose was of the opinion that they might carry it off by explaining they'd been made aware of Lord Cabot's vile insult to his daughter, though he was not entirely clear about what that insult was. They had been, as loyal servants, only defending the house.

Still, one could not be certain how Lord Mendbridge would take a thing. Especially when it involved one of his horse cronies.

He cleared his throat and the room grew silent. "It appears that the jig, as they say, is up."

"He can't prove who put those stones in his bed," Peg said defiantly.

"And he can't prove I knew that gruel was awful," Mrs. Lowell added helpfully.

"And maybe I *did* think a fire was in order, on account of an oncoming fever," Peg said. "One can't be condemned for making a simple mistake."

"All I mention is," Montrose interjected before his staff could go any further with their defense, "we must not give that confounded valet any more facts he can point to. I say good luck to him on complaining about perfectly good soup and one small fire. The stones in the mattress would of course be a slightly more difficult matter, but it occurs to me that they may have been *forgotten* stones."

There were murmurings around the table of the word forgotten, as if it were the most obvious thing in the world.

"Perhaps," Montrose went on, "the laying of small stones is an old trick meant to settle the flock and the stones should have been removed. Alas, in the hurry to open the house they were *forgotten*."

"Alas, they were," Peg said softly.

"But nobody wants flock settled," one of the footmen said. "A body wants the flock fluffed up."

Montrose slowly closed his eyes and opened them again. "And who above stairs would know how mattresses are maintained or what flock is meant to do?"

"Nobody, that's who!" Mrs. Lowell's kitchen maid cried. Then she promptly covered her face with a kitchen towel as if to hide her outburst.

"Does this mean we got to go all nice on the valet now?" a daring maid asked.

"This means," Montrose said gravely, "that we must not do anything further that might be pointed to. I hardly think, though, that a valet would get very far in complaining that the house staff was cool toward him. I hardly think a valet would dare *attempt* to complain of it."

"Or complain that he gets the ends of the beef," Mrs. Lowell said, nodding sagely.

"Just so," Montrose said.

⟫⟫⟩⟨⟨⟨

It was a fine morning and Penny had already been to the stables and back again. Doom had entertained her with endless comments on everything he saw and some things she was certain he pulled from his lively imagination. He'd even claimed to have recently eaten a pineapple, which was delightfully absurd.

She had been glad of the company as now that she sat down for breakfast she would have none. Mrs. Wellburton would breakfast in her room and it was still far too early to see Kitty. She'd briefly spoken to her father at the stables and was certain he would be much engaged there for some hours.

She'd waited until the footman left the room and she was only under the watchful eye of Montrose before she spoke the thing that had been much on her mind.

"Montrose," she said, "I did not speak to the doctor the last he was here, though I suppose you must know how Lord Cabot gets on."

"It is my understanding, miss, that he gets on well enough," Montrose said.

"Well enough," Penny said. "I see. And, I did send up a book yesterday. I do not suppose the lord made any particular comments about it?"

From the corner of her eye, she could see that the butler did not appear to know what she spoke of.

"Oh, never mind," Penny said. "I sent it up with Peg and she will not have bothered to mention it to you."

At the mention of Peg, Montrose looked somewhat alarmed, though Penny could not account for it.

"I suppose he talks a great deal of Miss Dell," Penny said, though *why* she said it she could not fathom.

"I could not say what the lord speaks of," Montrose said. "His valet is the only one privy to it as the fellow has practically moved into the chamber."

Penny thought there was a distinctively derisive tone to Montrose's description of the valet, though he provided no cause for it other than the fellow was often in Lord Cabot's room. But then, it was not so unusual that the servants of two different households clashed over some matter. At least, Dora had said that was often the case.

Penny turned toward the sound of the door opening. She took in a breath to see Lord Cabot framed in the doorway. He was meant to be abed, what on earth was he doing downstairs?

Had there been another door, Penny would have dashed out of it. As it was, she was trapped.

The lord seemed equally struck to find *her* there, though she was where she was supposed to be and he was not.

Penny breathed in slowly to regain her composure. "Lord Cabot," she said in a matter-of-fact tone, "I did not realize you were to be up so soon."

"Yes, well, I am perfectly recovered," he said. He then hurried to the sideboard and began piling meat on his plate.

Penny glanced at Montrose and was surprised to see him glaring at the lord. Surprised, but also gratified.

Lord Cabot sat down across from her and looked about.

"Tea or coffee, my lord," Montrose asked.

"Coffee," Lord Cabot said.

Montrose, with all the grandeur he could bring to bear when he had a mind, walked with the coffee pot to Lord Cabot's side.

As neither Penny nor the lord had the first idea of what to say to one another, they stared at the butler as if his every move were of some importance.

Montrose carefully poured coffee into Lord Cabot's cup. He filled it to the very brim.

Penny pressed her lips together to hide a smile. Certainly, that had been purposefully done. Montrose was far too skilled for it to have been an accident. Further, the butler did not apologize or in any way look as if he'd made a mistake.

Lord Cabot stared at his coffee. Cream and sugar were out of the question as either would instantly overflow the cup. For that matter, Penny did not see how the lord would even raise it to his lips without spilling it everywhere.

Rather than attempt it, he looked up and said, "Miss Darlington, I must thank you for sending up a book yesterday."

Penny nodded. "I thought it right, as you were indisposed," she said. "I presume you had the opportunity to read it."

"No," he said, "I am sure it is a worthy subject, but why, what I mean is…algebra."

"There is no need to further dissemble, my lord," Penny said.

"Dissemble what?"

Penny paused to take a sip of tea. She was not certain how to answer such a ruse. Was he really to go on pretending he was not a scholar when he was so soon to reveal it to Kitty? Did he attempt to play her for the fool once more? She was sure he'd understood her meaning by way of book. Perhaps he found it amusing to confound her.

"Do not pretend it is beyond your capabilities, my lord," Penny said sharply. "In any case, Miss Dell shall be gratified to hear your thoughts on the subject."

"I did not say it was beyond my capabilities. At least, I wouldn't know. Wait, why should Miss Dell be gratified to hear my thoughts on it? Is that why you chose that one? Because it is of interest to Miss Dell?"

"Everything of a scholarly nature is of interest to Miss Dell, as I am sure you are very much aware," Penny said.

"I was not particularly aware," Lord Cabot said, "other than she always seems to be reading. But even so, why should I, what I mean is, I am happy to oblige I suppose, though it does not seem a thing I should excel in."

"As you claim," Penny said.

"Claim what?" Lord Cabot said, sounding exasperated. "And also, the note. The negative quantity, what does it mean?"

"I did expect *you* would parse that out by reading the book," Penny said. "There is no reason *I* should know anything about it."

Lord Cabot's forehead wrinkled. "We get nowhere on this subject. Let us not examine the book further. I had much rather, well you see I'd prefer…"

Montrose suddenly appeared by Lord Cabot's side and said, "Is there something wrong with your coffee, my lord?"

"No," Lord Cabot said, his gaze once more directed toward the dangerously overfilled cup.

Montrose remained standing there, staring down at the lord with raised eyebrows.

The lord, seeing the butler did not intend on going away until he was assured of the state of the coffee, reached his hand out for the cup. He drew it toward him in a slow and steady manner as the liquid sloshed back and forth. He managed to get it to his lips and then hastily set it down again, but not before a splash had escaped.

Montrose peered down at the brown streak on the lord's neckcloth, appeared satisfied, and removed to the sideboard.

Lord Cabot ignored it and stared down at his plate for some moments. He looked sharply up and blurted out, "Miss Darlington, all is not right between us. I would wish to make it right. I cannot account for my words at Lady Hathaway's ball. I can only say that I deeply regret them."

Penny had been playing with her fork during this speech. She laid the utensil down and looked across at Lord Cabot.

If only he *could* account for it. He was so handsome, sitting there across from her. They had gotten on so well before that horrible evening. There had even seemed to be something between them until that moment. Something lovely and happy between them.

And yet, he could not account for his words. He could not account for striking out at her so mercilessly. There had been no particular reason, no circumstance that had caused such a terrible and public put down. Did that not confirm to her that his cruelty was something fixed in his temperament? When would be the next time he could not account for it?

And then, here he was, admiring Kitty as if poor Kitty might be expected to put up with such treatment.

Penny rose and said, "Being unable to account for it rather accounts for it, do not you think? As for Miss Dell, you may flout your knowledge as you will, but she is unlikely to be taken in by it."

As she swept from the room, he called after her, "What knowledge?"

CHAPTER EIGHT

H ENRY STOMPED BACK up to his bedchamber for a new
neckcloth. He'd glared at the butler before exiting the
breakfast room, but the man had only smiled and nodded as if all
had gone on satisfactorily.

He found Jarvis sitting on the windowsill with a tray of toast
and tea, ever guarding the room from ambitious housemaids who
might think to trifle with the mattress again. Jarvis looked at his
neckcloth and quietly sighed.

"It was not my own clumsiness," Henry said of the stained
cloth. "That Montrose fellow purposefully filled the cup too high,
it was impossible not to spill."

"I have not the slightest doubt of it, my lord," Jarvis said. He
lifted a piece of toast from his tray. "As you can see, appropriately
brown on this side and burnt black on the underside. I suppose it
was meant as a surprise when I bit into it."

"This cannot be allowed to go on," Henry said. "It is the most
ridiculous thing in the world to be so harassed by these people."

Though he said it could not be allowed to go on, Henry did
not have the least notion of how to stop it. What was he to do?
Complain to Lord Mendbridge that the butler put too much
coffee in his cup? Or worse, that his valet's toast was too well-
done on one side?

"We might think up an excuse and repair to the club," Jarvis said hopefully.

"I could never do that," Henry said. "It is an honor to be invited into Lord Mendbridge's house. An honor much sought after."

"Perhaps it is only sought after by those that have no notion of what awaits them," Jarvis said with asperity.

"I doubt Lord Mendbridge's other guests are treated so wretchedly," Henry said.

"One cannot be certain. They are a mob of cretins and may well torture everybody."

"No matter," Henry said, "we must do our best to struggle on. By the by, have you heard anything of Miss Dell? Anything about her loving algebra?"

Jarvis' narrowed his eyes, as he did when he was thinking over a matter. "I hear little, as none of them wish to speak to me directly. However, of those times when I am at table and they make small talk amongst themselves, I have heard only a few things about Miss Dell. They spoke of dusting all the books in the library, as she was sure to be rummaging through them, and they spoke of her love of savarins. She appears well-regarded, as does her maid."

"I do not understand it at all," Henry said. "That confounded book on algebra that Miss Darlington sent up yesterday is somehow meant to impress Miss Dell. Why should *I* learn anything of algebra to impress Miss Dell?"

"I would not even hazard a guess, my lord," Jarvis said. "This is a most mysterious household."

Henry thought his valet was right on that score. At the heart of the mystery was Miss Darlington. Why should she wish that he impress Miss Dell with algebra? Why should she carry on refusing his apologies?

He thought he'd done rather well this morning. Did he not say he regretted his words? He'd even said he *deeply* regretted them. What else could he do with those words but regret them deeply?

It almost seemed as if she were angry about something else, but he could not for the life of him think what else he'd done to the lady.

"This evening is Lord Beckman's soirée," Jarvis said. "Perhaps the conundrum of the algebra book will be illuminated in some fashion there. You might take Miss Dell into supper and discover more about it."

Henry nodded, though he had no intention of escorting Miss Dell into supper. Still, he was rather cheered by the reminder that they would attend Lord Beckman that evening. Beckman held the party every year at Newmarket. It would be a decidedly small affair, only including those Beckman termed the 'horse set.' Beckman had firm ideas of what constituted his horse set. He held no respect for those who only took a keen interest in horseflesh when there was a race on. He derisively called those particular unfortunates the 'horse tourists.'

Certainly, at Beckman's, Miss Darlington could not refuse a dance. There would not be enough gentlemen there for her to do it.

They had danced so often these past two seasons, perhaps a reminder of those happy days would steer her in a more forgiving direction?

He might even take her into supper, just like old times.

AFTER LEAVING THE breakfast room, Penny had gone up to Kitty's door and knocked softly.

Though Penny herself had been up for some hours, Kitty was still abed though awake. She was propped up with pillows and had an array of books laid on the blanket and one open in her hand.

Penny smiled and said, "As I always expect to find you, near buried in books. It is becoming a veritable library in here."

Kitty laughed and laid down the book in her hand. "There are far too many temptations in this library, I'm afraid. I can hardly settle on one subject. Have I stayed abed shockingly late?"

"No, you have not," Penny said. "I have asked Peg to bring up a tea tray so you may not hurry yourself."

"She will have been shocked by the notion, I'm sure," Kitty said. "Here I am, not even out and yet lying around like a married lady."

"If the truth be told, I think little shocks Peg," Penny said. She picked up a book and examined it. Then laid it down and picked up another.

Peg knocked and came in with the tray. Just as Penny had predicted, the woman did not seem particularly shocked. After she'd laid the tea things and left, Kitty said, "Now Penny, you have examined five of the books I have strewn on the bed though I know you do not have the least interest in any of them. What weighs on your mind?"

Penny had been determined to apprise Kitty of Lord Cabot's interest, and to warn her of his intent to flout his knowledge. Now that it had come to it, though, she did not know how to start.

"I'll venture it has to do with Lord Cabot," Kitty said.

Penny looked up. "How did you know?"

"I did not," Kitty said, "but he is the person who has caused you trouble these past days so it was a reasonable guess."

"Well, you are right, though not for the reasons you might think. I wished to warn you of him. It has been told to me that he has expressed an interest in you."

Kitty sputtered and wiped the resulting spray of tea from her nightdress with a napkin. "You jest, surely," she said.

"I do not," Penny said. "And here is something even more shocking. It turns out that Lord Cabot is secretly a scholar and means to reveal his tendencies to you in order to impress. I merely warn you so you might be on your guard."

Kitty heaved with laughter and set her cup down so she

might not stain her nightdress any more than she had already.

"Lord Cabot? A scholar?" Kitty said. "It cannot be so."

"As I would have thought too," Penny conceded.

"Do you know," Kitty said, "that the horse he's entered in the races is named Bucephalus?"

"Yes, of course," Penny said, unsure of what that had to do with anything.

"And do you know what it means?" Kitty asked.

Penny frowned. "I believe it was the name of Alexander the Great's war horse. Or so I was told by Lord Burke. A stupid name for a filly, though Burke says the horse was named when Lord Cabot bought her."

"Yes," Kitty said, "Alexander's war horse. But the meaning of it is ox head. Is that not amusing? It is precisely what I think of Lord Cabot, he is a bit of an ox head."

Penny had not known the meaning of the name, though she found she was in agreement with Kitty. He *was* an ox head. She also found herself well-pleased that Kitty so clearly meant to give Lord Cabot very short shrift. It was not for her own account that she was gratified, it was just…it would suit, that was all.

"Well," Kitty said, "the ox head may attempt to flout whatever few facts he's managed to store in his mind. It will only be an amusement to *me*. Between him and Lord Grayson I shall be mightily entertained. I intend to examine Lord Grayson mercilessly on his understanding of the life and history of Cardinal Wolsey and I predict that understanding will be decidedly dim."

Penny was cheered by Kitty's speech. In truth, she was cheered by Kitty in general. Never was there a girl with more sense or a sunnier disposition. She must emulate Kitty in that regard.

"I do hope you can enjoy yourself this evening as well," Kitty said. "I would never be allowed to attend such an affair had it not been hosted by Lord Beckman. When Lady Beckman was apprised that I would be in town, she wrote my mother that I ought to come and that she could keep a sharp eye on me. It really is my first venture out in regular society outside of my own neighborhood, even if it is to be a small affair and I am not *officially* out."

"It is a debut of sorts," Penny said, having not considered the matter in that light.

"Just so," Kitty said. "I hope we are both very jolly this evening."

Penny nodded. Kitty was right, as she always was. After all, what had she to be unhappy about? She was at Newmarket with her loving family and her dearest friend in the world. They were to go to Lord Beckman's party this evening which was always a diversion. She would wear her amber silk, a favorite, and she *would* be jolly despite the ox head in their midst. She might find herself even more jolly over Lord Grayson's plight. She would stifle her laughter over the poor lord struggling to keep his head above water while he drowned in Cardinal Wolsey's history.

"You are always right, Kitty," Penny said. "I have been too gloomy of late but I am determined to throw it off. We are young and will be merry, as we are meant to be."

"Quite right, Pen-pen," Kitty said. "Now, you better help me clear off these books. If I am not dressed and downstairs in the next hour, your aunt shall think me a frightful layabout."

PENNY HAD SPENT the rest of the day weaving between Kitty and the stables. It reminded her very much that she lived two lives—one in a drawing room receiving callers and pretending at sewing, and another in the environs of the stables with her beloved horses. She was forever shaking her skirts of hay and dust in one direction and crumbs and threads in the other.

Kitty had insisted that she cease her wanderings and go above stairs at a reasonable time to rest and ready themselves for the ball. Penny had given herself over to it. They had spent a merry early evening over tea and biscuits, running between each other's rooms to consult on this silk or that comb or that pair of gloves.

She had almost been able to cease thinking of Lord Cabot in those pleasant hours. Had he not been an inmate of the house, she might have been able to forget him altogether.

As it was, when Mrs. Wellburton had collected her and Kitty and led them down the stairs, Lord Cabot and her father had awaited them at the bottom.

He was so handsome in his close-cut dark blue coat. His tanned face and brown eyes showed nicely against his white neckcloth. As well, she could not help but notice his powerful legs encased in tight trousers. She very well knew she was not meant to observe such a thing. Her aunt would wave a fan over the idea. And yet, she had often noticed the varying differences in men's legs. Particularly, she had noticed that those men who rode often tended to have more muscular legs than those who preferred transport by carriage.

Though Penny had firmly decided that she must make a match with some pleasant fellow who might not have the same interest in horseflesh that she did, she would never marry a man with toothpick legs. When one of those toothpick-legged individuals eventually did don some riding clothes, their stockings sagged in a hopeless effort to find something to hold on to. It was a shocking thought to have, she knew, but there it was.

Mrs. Wellburton had been determined that there be no awkward standing about in the hall. Once the usual pleasantries about how well everybody looked were got through, she hustled her charges into a waiting carriage while the gentlemen followed on horseback.

Lord Beckman's estate was not a mile further from town than Mendbridge Cottage itself and they arrived there in good time. Kitty had delighted in the long cobblestoned drive, lit by torches and winding gently through old oaks that draped their leaves overhead. Her friend had marveled at the house, it only having been built a few years before and sporting an elegant Palladian style. It was a great white box of a house, its only adornment the carved columns that lined its front.

Penny knew her father considered the design a commonsense answer to the Gothic revival that was currently in vogue. She suppressed her laughter as she peeked out the window. As she had expected, Lord Mendbridge pointed at the house and said loudly, "See there, Cabot, that is what I call a proper house. Not like some other buildings being put up just now that look more suited to ghosts and goblins than people."

As it was to be a small affair, there was no usual crush of carriages lined on the drive and they were speedily disembarked and led inside.

They had been greeted kindly by Lady Beckman. Their hostess took a particular interest in Kitty, having already promised her mother that she would keep a sharp eye on her. After it was satisfactorily settled that Kitty was never to be out of her view, they proceeded on to hand off their coats and receive their cards.

Penny had paused to wait for her father before entering the ballroom. This was a courtesy he would expect, though in this instance it meant waiting for Lord Cabot too. She was certain her father would do as he did at every ball. He would survey "the field" as he called it, pronounce it satisfactory, kiss Penny on the cheek, and make his way to the card room. While he did not look to play whist or piquet at home very often, he always said it looked far more attractive when the choices were to either spend the hours dealing a pack of cards or watching young people hop around a ballroom floor.

Lord Mendbridge had finally ceased his joking with Lord Beckman and led them into the ballroom. Lord Cabot was hot on his heels, though Penny wished he would take himself off elsewhere.

"Well, Cabot," Lord Mendbridge said in his booming voice, "I do not suppose there will be any two prettier ladies here tonight."

"Certainly not," Lord Cabot said gallantly.

"Well? Jump to it, man," Lord Mendbridge said. "I suppose

you'll want the first and supper. Now, my advice, actually my *request*, is that you take Miss Dell into supper. She is not technically out, you see, and I'd have her with somebody I can trust. If you get my meaning."

Penny was not a stranger to her father saying something that made her face flame. The dear man could be quite oblivious to what might embarrass a lady. But *this* was rather more than anything she'd experienced in the past.

To force Lord Cabot to put himself down on their cards! And then, her poor father was so naïve. He would put Kitty into the hands of the very man who wished to flirt with her the most. Well, with perhaps the exception of Lord Grayson, who had seemed to settle his gaze upon Kitty recently. Grayson, however, posed far less of a threat. Kitty would only fall for a highly educated man and Lord Cabot was poised to spring that hidden part of him upon her. Kitty might doubt the lord was such a person, but Penny thought it likely that he was. What might Kitty's thoughts be if Lord Cabot suddenly discussed the negative quantities of algebra? Or even, Cardinal Wolsey's history?

Lord Cabot nodded in acquiescence and held his hand out for the ladies' cards. Mrs. Wellburton stepped into the scene and said, "Goodness, Lord Cabot, very courteous but no need to dance with the girls as you see them so often as it is. You'd best allow other gentlemen to have their chance."

If her father had caused embarrassment by forcing Lord Cabot to put himself down on their cards, her aunt had just trebled the feeling by insisting he did not. Lord Cabot's hand hung in midair, as if he had no notion of which direction it ought to go.

"Nonsense, sister!" Lord Mendbridge said. "It is already settled. Cabot takes the first with my daughter and he takes Miss Dell into supper. We must be careful. Our Kitty is not officially out, you know."

As there was no going against what Lord Mendbridge had so firmly decided, Lord Cabot's hand continued on to reach for Penny's card. He dutifully filled in his name and then did the same on Kitty's card.

As Penny willed the blush to disappear from her cheeks, Lord Mendbridge said, "Ah, here they are—Dalton and Grayson. Well fellows, have you come to beat down the doors of the ladies' cards?"

Any notion of regaining equanimity flew from Penny once more. Despite knowing his habits so thoroughly and being certain he would take himself off to the card room, Lord Mendbridge seemed in no hurry. *This* night, he seemed determined to stay and manage the festivities.

"Indeed, Lord Mendbridge, there can be no other doors worth approaching," Lord Grayson said smoothly, holding out his hand for Kitty's card. His expression became a deal less sanguine when he looked at it.

"That's right, Grayson," Lord Mendbridge said in high good humor, "I've arranged for Cabot to take the little lady into supper. She is not technically out, you know."

Lord Grayson did not seem to follow the logic of the lord's speech, but only smiled weakly and put himself down for Miss Dell's first.

"No need to be so glum, my good fellow," Lord Mendbridge said kindly. "I happen to know, as I have been standing here since the beginning, that my daughter's supper remains free."

If Penny could have opened up a mine shaft below her and fallen through it to some dark reaches of the middle earth, she would have gladly done so. Her father was skilled at so many things, but escorting anybody to a ball was not one of them.

Lord Grayson had nodded and dutifully filled in his name on Penny's card. Lord Dalton had entered his name on both her and Kitty's cards.

Penny would like to stamp her foot in frustration. She was meant to be becoming more acquainted with some gentleman who might be a future husband, and instead her card was being filled with those who certainly would not. Nor would any of them provide much pleasure or entertainment.

"Move along, then," Lord Mendbridge said merrily to the flummoxed gentlemen before him. "You must make room for other fellows who wish to make their daring approach."

The lords Cabot, Grayson and Dalton did as they were directed. Penny looked beseechingly at her aunt.

Mrs. Wellburton said, "Brother, I suggest we make haste to the card room. If we arrive too late, you can be certain we will be left to partner with Mr. and Mrs. Jelton."

"God, they are awful whist players," the lord said, rubbing his chin.

"Just so, but very keen all the same," Mrs. Wellburton said. "You can be certain it will be a game of musical chairs to see who is plagued with them."

Lord Mendbridge nodded. He was perhaps not as keen on cards as Mr. and Mrs. Jelton, but he appeared to have a healthy respect for their wretchedness.

"Lady Beckman will have things well in hand in the ballroom, of that you can be assured," Mrs. Wellburton said.

"Yes," Lord Mendbridge said, "of course she will. Now girls, as my sister notes, Lady Beckman will have things in hand. Do not become afraid that I am not here to arrange things."

Penny nodded and smiled at her father. The very last thing she would fear at this moment was that her father would not stay to arrange anything.

Lord Mendbridge turned and hurried toward the card room, the fear of being left to Mr. and Mrs. Jelton nipping at his heels. Mrs. Wellburton smiled and squeezed Penny's hand before following her brother.

Penny looked at Kitty. Kitty looked back with wide eyes and began to laugh.

"Goodness," Kitty said, between giggles, "Lord Mendbridge has managed to arrange things most unsatisfactorily. I am to dine with the ox head and you are to attempt supper while Lord Grayson explains what he does not know of Cardinal Wolsey."

Penny had been mortified, but seeing her friend's good humor over the circumstance eased her feelings.

"I know you would not wish to dance with Lord Cabot," Kitty said, "but I suppose it could not have been avoided. As it is, at least it is the first and you will be done with it early."

Penny nodded. It was of course true. If she must dance with Lord Cabot, it was well that she get it over with.

Those thoughts, the ones that hovered at the top of her mind, did not so much reflect the thoughts beneath them. The thoughts she would never say aloud.

They would dance, as they had so often before. All those times when it had been exhilarating. And now, so much had changed. Balls had once been so bright, but now their luster seemed to have dulled.

⋙⋘

HENRY MADE EVERY attempt to hide his aggravation after he'd been summarily directed on how to fill out both Miss Darlington and Miss Dell's cards and then sent away. Why must he take Miss Dell into supper? Why should it be his responsibility to squire her because she was not yet out? It should have been a perfect opportunity to speak at length with Miss Darlington. Now what? Would he be expected to discuss algebra as Miss Darlington had hinted to him? Well, perhaps Mendbridge had it right, Miss Dell would certainly not be in any danger from *him*.

At least Grayson had been his replacement for the hoped-for supper with Miss Darlington. He was certain she did not care for Grayson's waterfalls of compliments. It was, at least, better than Burke. Though, he was surprised Lord Mendbridge had not held out for Burke, since he seemed so intent on managing the ladies' cards. Perhaps Burke was not to attend.

Henry paused. Why was he thinking of who had taken his place? He had hoped he would be afforded the opportunity of another conversation with Miss Darlington. Another chance to see if she might soften toward him. He was not at all comfortable with their current standing, which was no standing at all. He could not be comfortable with knowing another person held him in ill-regard.

But that was all.

As he was not to have that opportunity, what care he over who took his place? What matter if it *were* Burke?

"Bad form taking Miss Dell into supper," Grayson said next to him. "You very well know I favor the lady."

"I had not the slightest preference in it," Henry said. "Mendbridge as much as ordered me to."

"Did he?" Grayson said. "Ah well, a ruse to keep me away I'll reckon. Fathers and guardians do tremble at the sight of me."

"If they tremble," Lord Dalton said, joining them, "it is only to fear that you are in danger of ceasing to breathe on account of a diabolically tied neckcloth cutting off your windpipe."

Both Henry and Lord Grayson ignored Lord Dalton's barb, Grayson being entirely immune to insults over his careful dress and Henry finding he could not care less.

Grayson spotted Miss Sassbury across the room. He headed speedily in that direction.

"I supposed Mendbridge *forced* you to take the first with Miss Darlington?" Lord Dalton asked Henry.

"In fact, he did," Henry said. "Though I had rather have taken supper. Miss Darlington still seethes and I do not like it. I would not like it for anybody to think so little of me."

"Well," Dalton said, slapping his friend on the back. "Mendbridge is a sly old fox. Do not think for a moment that his bumbling appearance has any foundation in truth. He knows what he's about."

"What is he about?" Henry asked. He had been sure that Lord Mendbridge had not been about anything other than being his jolly and rather oblivious self.

"There has been talk that there is an announcement regarding Miss Darlington's future in the offing," Dalton said. "Considering how often you squired the lady to supper over the last two seasons, I can see how he would wish to avoid that picture going forward. Ah, there is Crimpleton. I need to ask him about his views on the bets being laid. He can be uncanny at times."

Dalton strode away, leaving Henry standing alone. He glanced behind him and saw Miss Darlington and Miss Dell talking to Burke.

Of course, Burke. That was the announcement in the offing. He'd known it since the night of that first dinner. It was a match that would please everybody. Including, as it looked just now, Miss Darlington herself.

It was all wrong, though. Burke did not suit Miss Darlington. Oh, naturally, everybody would say otherwise. Burke had a fine stable and was a respected horseman. What better match for Miss Darlington? Then, he was to be a duke so his prospects could hardly be better. And, if Henry were forced to admit it, Burke had a pleasant temperament. Burke was not likely to be rude to a lady and then be left to figure out why he'd done it and how to redeem himself.

An awful feeling crept over Henry as he stood at the edges of the ballroom floor, hardly cognizant of the swirls of people around him.

It should be him. It should be Henry Roland, Viscount Cabot and son of the Duke of Wentworth for Miss Darlington.

How could he not have seen it was so!

CHAPTER NINE

HENRY SWALLOWED HARD, his throat suddenly gone tight. He had just wondered how he had not seen that it must be him for Miss Darlington. But he *had* seen it, somewhere in his stupid mind. He'd known all along. He supposed he'd thought, well he probably ignored the idea because…well because there seemed to be no hurry. Why examine a thing when there was no need to decide? Why not just go along pleasantly? There had seemed to be time, endless amounts of time.

That idea of endless amount of time had suited him. He'd agreed with his friends that they ought not go hurtling into marriage so soon. They ought to go on as they were, very pleasantly as it happened, and then at some point they would marry. They'd all seen the sense in it.

He still remembered that first day he'd laid eyes on Miss Darlington. He'd ridden through Hyde Park and passed a lady merrily reining in a spooked horse. The scene had startled, none of it as it should be. The horse was far more enormous than one would expect for a petite lady. Rather than shrieking in a panic, she laughed as she wrestled the animal back under control. Her copper curls bounced as she masterfully worked the reins and held her seat. The horse's nostrils had flared and the beast gave one more back kick before settling, all the while the lady goodhumoredly scolding her mount for being a ninny over an errant squirrel.

Then, he had realized it was Mendbridge himself who escorted this veritable Epona and instantly surmised that the lady must be his daughter. He had seen to it that they were swiftly introduced.

It was not a day later that he had boldly put himself down for supper at the Tremane's ball. Since then, it had been a regular thing, except for those times when Burke or some other man had beat him to it.

Now Burke had beat him to it for the rest of his days. Burke had not assumed he'd got endless time. The engagement would be announced any moment. My God, it might even be announced before they left Newmarket.

Though Henry had been flummoxed to understand how Hampton, Lockwood, and Ashworth had found themselves married when they all swore they had no notion of it, now he began to see how it had happened to them. They had suddenly realized the truth of it. The only difference between him and his three friends is that they had realized in time while he had not.

If he'd never said those hateful things to Miss Darlington, he wondered if Burke would have got his chance. As it was, he'd laid the groundwork himself.

What a fool he'd been! How had he ignored the fact that nobody would suit him as Miss Darlington would? Why on earth would he think there was all the time in the world? Had he ignored the existence of other rivals altogether? Had he not bothered to wonder if Miss Darlington was in agreement with him over endless amounts of time?

The music struck up, shaking Henry from his awful realizations. He had taken the first with Miss Darlington and he must at least get through it creditably. He may have singlehandedly ruined his chances at happiness, but he must at least hold on to his dignity.

That was the main thing. He could never let on that he cared one way or the other. My God, he could not bear the humiliation of being seen as a lovesick idiot who'd been passed over. The moniker would never leave him. Worse, he was friends with Burke. He would see them both regularly over the years. How could he bear noting Burke shaking his head in pity when he thought he was not observed? How could he countenance finding invitations to Burke's house had dried up because his lady felt it was awkward?

He already skated dangerously on that pond of thin ice—his attentions to Miss Darlington over the past two seasons had been marked. And, *remarked*, no doubt.

No. Nobody was ever to know anything about it. He must show that it was nothing to him. Nothing at all.

LORD CABOT HAD come to collect her and Penny thought it was almost too cruel that she must dance with him again. It was so like any other ball of the past two seasons that it only served to remind her of what had been, in stark contrast to what was now.

She did not suppose the lord enjoyed it any more than she did, as he had been looking stone-faced so far.

As they waited for their turn, Lord Cabot said stiffly, "I suppose Burke will be disappointed that he is not to take you into supper."

"If he is," Penny said, "he cannot be more disappointed than I." While she would not directly comment on the dreariness of being escorted into supper by Lord Grayson and his high-flown compliments, she could not resist hinting that she did not look forward to it.

"I see," Lord Cabot said.

Penny supposed he *did* see. She had not made it a particular secret from him that she had never fallen under Grayson's spell, as so many foolish ladies had.

"I suppose *you* must be gratified that my father has arranged for you to take in Miss Dell," Penny said. "Though I think you shall discover that my friend, though she is learned, prefers a steady temperament with her scholarly pursuits."

"Her temperament strikes me as steady enough," Lord Cabot said. "As for her pursuits, I would not know."

Penny swallowed a sigh. He would continue dissembling. She did not know to what purpose. He knew well enough that she and Kitty were close friends. Did he imagine he was to reveal himself the highly educated man to impress Kitty and it would remain unknown to herself?

"I really do not see why," Penny said, "if someone wishes to be well-read and educated on a variety of subjects, that proclivity should be under wraps."

"I do not see why either," Lord Cabot said, his brow wrinkling.

"Then why would a person go on with it?" Penny asked. "Why would a person pretend at being one thing when in fact they were another?"

Lord Cabot did not answer and Penny plowed on, even though she knew she should not.

"Unless, of course, one delighted in pointing out the lack of information in others. I suppose it is all just a game." A *meanspirited* game, Penny thought to herself.

"If you mean to imply that I shall be discomposed by Miss Dell showing me up in some intellectual fashion, the notion is ridiculous."

"As I now understand it, Lord Cabot."

They had no further conversation after that. Rather, they went through the changes with neither meeting the other's eye. Though Penny very successfully avoided looking into his eyes, she was not as successful at ignoring the warmth of his hand through her glove. She had always noticed it. Some gentlemen had cold hands, some felt more neutral as if they were not one way or the other. Lord Cabot's hand was always very warm, as if his vitality could not be contained by a glove.

She must stop thinking of his hands or his legs or any other part of him!

HENRY LED ONE lady after the next through the dances. He supposed he was a wretched partner. He had little to say and none of it amusing.

How could he be amusing at such a moment? He knew the thing was all but settled between Miss Darlington and Burke. And yet, when he'd come right out and said that she must be disappointed that Burke would not escort her to supper, he'd somehow hoped to hear otherwise. He'd not heard otherwise, she'd claimed she was *more* disappointed than even Burke would be!

He supposed he'd harbored some idea that there might be the slightest chance that the match was being pushed by Mendbridge and not favored by his daughter.

But no. She was even more disappointed than Burke. It could not be more clear. After all, anybody might expect a lady to demur, even if she *were* more disappointed. To come right out and say so was verging on the announcement itself.

It hinted that she did not only find the match satisfactory. She thought she was in love with Burke!

It was nonsensical. Why should anybody fall in love with that swine?

Henry checked himself, as he knew very well that Burke was not a swine. He dearly wished the man *was* a swine. Or a scoundrel or a reprobate or deep in debt or secretly married or all of those things together. Then, he might expose him in some manner. The idea was beneath him and not very gentlemanly, especially since Burke was his friend, but there it was.

The inconvenient truth of it, though, was that Burke was the most sensible of them all and had never done a thing he could point to as being outrageous.

Though, he wondered at Burke not telling him directly of his preference for Miss Darlington. He might have mentioned he intended to approach Mendbridge with the idea. Certainly, Burke had noticed how often he'd taken the lady into supper or claimed the first. It would seem the honorable thing to tell a rival they were to be defeated before that rival was bowled over by hearing the news publicly. Was there some breach of protocol in it? Or decency?

He might just take that up with Burke.

Not at this very moment, though. He'd got through the dance with Miss Dell in near silence and now he must lead her into supper. He understood from Miss Darlington that Miss Dell was set on exposing his less than well-read habits. Let her, he could not care less. If the lady was intent on questioning him about algebra, she would soon be apprised of the idea that he'd received a book on the subject and not bothered with turning beyond the first page of it. Nor would he ever.

Algebra could go to the dogs!

PENNY FELT HERSELF prickly upon finding herself next to Lord Grayson at supper. She had always found his penchant for outlandish compliments tiresome. *Now*, however, she found there was a particular sting to their absence. The lord had not mentioned a thing about her person and instead had only endlessly spoken of Kitty.

As he waxed on, Penny examined her feelings. She supposed it rankled that she'd become so accustomed to attentions that seemed to have suddenly flown off from every direction. Lord Cabot did not admire her as she had once thought and not even Lord Grayson could be bothered to compare her hair to the fires of Venus as he had so often done.

Had she lingered too long through the seasons? Were two seasons enough to blunt the charms of Miss Darlington?

Heat warmed Penny's cheeks as she wondered if she was on her way to becoming a spinster. New, younger girls would come on the scene. Miss Darlington was no longer a novelty. Perhaps her looks were fading and she had not even noticed! Had not her aunt cautioned her about the hours she spent in the sun while on horseback? Perhaps she was becoming just the eccentric lady that drove a High Flyer.

It was a ghastly idea.

"I say, though," Lord Grayson said, "why *does* Miss Dell read so much? Does her father force her to it?"

Penny made herself attend to Lord Grayson. Though, what he was on about now she did not know.

"Miss Dell reads because it gives her pleasure," she answered.

"Are you certain?" Lord Grayson asked.

"Yes, quite," Penny said.

"I don't see the pleasure in it, myself," Lord Grayson said. "I think, why bother storing up all sorts of useless facts that have no bearing on one's life?"

"I suppose people are different," Penny said noncommittedly.

"I think she'll give it up when she's out," Lord Grayson said. "There will be so many entertainments that there will be no time for Cardinal Wolsey and his ilk."

"I think you do not know my friend very well," Penny said.

"Oh, people change," Lord Grayson said, staring down the table at Kitty.

"They certainly do," Penny said bitterly. "One may think one knows a person, and then discover that they never did. Then that person they thought they knew might try to flout some hidden knowledge in order to impress some other person."

Lord Grayson laughed. "You overestimate me, Miss Darlington. If I had some hidden knowledge, I would present it in a flash to Miss Dell. Alas, I have none of it. I could not make it past the first page of that dreadful book on the cardinal."

Penny was confounded by Lord Grayson. Why on earth would he think she spoke about *him*?

"It is the scholarly Lord Cabot who walks around hiding all his knowledge," Penny said bitterly.

Lord Grayson laughed. "Cabot, a scholar? The notion is ridiculous."

"You needn't bother, Lord Grayson," Penny said. "I know all about it. Lord Cabot intends to put his accomplishments on display for Miss Dell's edification."

"Does he?" Lord Grayson said, a tinge of outrage in his tone. "I am surprised his thoughts would run in such a direction. One would think the only thing on Cabot's mind just now would be escaping the moneylender's noose."

"Moneylender?" Penny asked in some surprise.

"Yes, Miss Darlington," Grayson said peevishly. "I have it on good authority that our Lothario has gotten himself in deep and his filly is his only way out. I wonder how Miss Dell would view *that* particular piece of knowledge?"

Penny did not answer, though she was shocked by the idea. A gentleman turning to a moneylender was generally the beginning of his end. And to borrow for a horserace? What would he do if he lost?

Well, he would not have to flee as so many young gentlemen before him had done. Certainly, his family would not allow it.

But if his family were willing to come to his rescue, why had he gone to a moneylender to begin? After all, what did anybody really know of the financial position of the duke? Had property been mortgaged? It might be so and the whole thing kept quiet. Many a vast holding had been revealed to be wobbling on shaky ground before now. As she knew from Lily, Lord Ashworth had brought his father's estates back from the brink of ruin. Nobody had the least suspected that had been his raison d'être for gambling.

Penny narrowed her eyes. Might there not be a monetary cause for Lord Cabot's sudden interest in Kitty? Her dowry was generous, exceedingly so. Far more than Penny's own. In truth, Penny had sometimes feared for her friend's coming out on account of it and only mollified herself when she considered Kitty's good sense.

Penny sighed. It seemed the layers were being peeled back on Lord Cabot's character. He was never who he had represented himself to be. He was devious, bad tempered, foolish, and self-interested. He might very well find himself on a packet boat to the continent one of these days and she would not be sorry about it!

HENRY DID HIS best to suffer though the supper with Miss Dell. She had not the slightest interest in horses, as he had discovered. He'd ventured the subject thinking any of Miss Darlington's friends must have at least a passing interest and it would be a deal more pleasant than algebra.

Miss Dell thought horses were convenient. *Convenient*, she'd said.

A poker to stir a fire was *convenient*. A side table to set one's drink on was *convenient*. Having enough money in one's pocket to do as one wished was *convenient*. How on earth could the noble creature that was horse be reduced to a mere convenience?

Despite his outrage over her ill-informed opinions, Henry decided to launch the topic that had been eating away at him all night.

"I suppose Miss Darlington is devastated that she was not taken into supper by Lord Burke," he said out of nowhere.

Miss Dell looked at him quizzically. "Devastated may be too strong a term, Lord Cabot. Though you would be right in thinking the lady does not love an endless stream of meaningless praises and Lord Burke would never be guilty of it. He is a gentleman who says what he means."

"I imagine he's said quite a lot recently," Henry said, though even to his own ears he sounded petulant.

"If he has, I am sure it was all full of good sense," Miss Dell said. "Though I am not certain I can say the same for your friend." Miss Dell paused for a moment, then said, "Why *does* Lord Grayson go on in such a manner?"

Though Henry understood perfectly the meaning of Miss Dell's query, he had no interest in a lengthy discussion about Grayson's flirtations. He said, "Grayson goes on as he chooses. I only wonder that some people do not think carefully about their future, and what would be right, only because of a misunderstanding."

"Do you say I have misunderstood Lord Grayson's temperament?" Miss Dell asked in some surprise.

"We all understand *him* well enough," Henry said. "I would only hope that *everybody* had such understanding about *other* people and did not make choices they would later regret. One ought to think of who one is actually suited to. That is all I say."

It was well that was all that he *did* say. Miss Dell's attention, thankfully, was taken by Mr. Grettinger on her other side before she could press him to elaborate on his cryptic speech. God knew what he might have said next.

All in all, it had been a most unsatisfactory evening.

THE NEXT DAY passed by with the house going on quietly, though tension hung in the air throughout Newmarket. The races would begin the following day and the town was anything *but* quiet. Stalls were being erected to sell everything from refreshment, to a reading of fortunes, to the inevitable thimblerigging games. Carriages filed in, and every scallywag from London who thought they might chance upon an opportunity had made their way there on every possible sort of conveyance.

Lord Mendbridge's men were hard at work building their private stand adjacent to the common seats. For himself, the lord would not have minded to sit in the general stands with whoever happened to turn up, but he would not place his sister or his daughter in such circumstances. One not so careful might find themselves sitting next to a pickpocket intent on relieving one of one's purse or a farmer in his cups who might forget himself and pinch a knee.

Penny had been to the stables and had found the place as calm as she had expected. Nobody wished to spook the horses or alarm them in any way. This was, as usual, only partially successful. The distant sounds of building were not entirely muffled and even if they had been, horses knew well enough when something was in the air. They felt it on the people who came to care for them, they felt it on their owners. It was as if some sort of vapor emanated from those who worked so hard to pretend nothing particular was in the works. Horses knew, they always knew.

Penny and Doom had walked the line of stalls, listening to gentle stamping and soft nickers as they passed by, and checked on Zephyrus and Bella. Both horses were in good order, though she could see in each an alertness that signaled something coming. Bella seemed the less eager to discover what that might be, as she had backed herself in her stall. Penny noted her upright ears and her eyes a smidge too wide and knew she was right to not have entered the filly in the thousand guinea stakes. Zephyrus, to her delight and approval, seemed all eagerness and gently kicked his stall to be let out.

Penny ordered that they both be turned out at a nearby field as that was likely to settle them. She knew that Zephyrus could not put his attention on both the atmosphere of change and the eating of grass that he liked so well. Bella was used to having Zephyrus nearby while she grazed and would take comfort in it.

On race day, they would be let out at dawn for a short period, and then taken back into their stalls to rest for four hours. This,

Penny judged, would keep Zephyrus in spirits while allowing his stomach to settle before the race. A horse's spirit, she well knew, was half the battle. Further, allowing Zephyrus and Bella to go out when the other horses remained confined would have the benefit of irritating their stall mates. Though she knew of no horse language, she could well enough guess their thoughts on seeing other horses turned out. A vague discontent would settle over them and who could they blame but their caretakers? Let the other owners, who thought they knew so much, stick to their routines. She was certain she had the better of them.

Of course, she knew Lord Cabot was in agreement with her, as they'd had many discourses over the subject. She supposed he could just as well choose another field for his filly.

Now, Doom came jogging back from having turned out her horses. "Zephyrus is in fine form," he said, "he done his usual race around the fence to show who's in charge and then bucked a few times for good measure. Bella did as *she* always does, she watched him admiringly and then settled to graze."

Penny was satisfied that all was as it should be. "Let us go then, the boys will bring them in later. I wish you to rest today and go to bed early. The morrow will take all your strength and concentration."

"I'm ready, miss," Doom said with all confidence. "This place is in me bones."

Penny smiled and they proceeded to walk the line of stalls back out to the carriage. She noted a slight boy hanging about Lord Cabot's stall. His rider, no doubt.

"What ho?" Doom suddenly called to the boy.

The boy glanced over his shoulder at their approach. His eyes grew wide and he sprinted out of the stable. The dust he kicked up remained the only evidence that he'd ever been there.

Penny looked at Doom quizzically. Her groom was looking just as quizzically at the spot where the young boy had so recently stood.

"What is it, Doom? Are you acquainted with Lord Cabot's

rider? But why should he have raced off like that? He looked near terrified to see you."

A sudden thought came to Penny and she sighed. "You have not got into some scrape with the fellow? This is neither the time nor place for boyish scuffles."

"I ain't fought nobody in a month and *that* ain't the lord's rider," Doom said. "That there is the assistant to the grocer Mrs. Lowell has taken on. She dumped Slincher and went with Cumberbald on account of a pineapple and Turkish dates."

Much of what Doom ever said to her was mystifying, but Penny thought this particular bit of news was more obscure than usual.

"His name is Freddy," Doom went on, "and he hangs about the kitchen ever so much. Mrs. Lowell has taken a liking to him, but for myself I ain't so sure. The two of them are forever gossipin' about house business while he eats her cakes. As a general thing, it used to be *me* that was talkin' and eatin' the cakes."

Penny suppressed a smile. It seemed Doom had been replaced as eater of cakes and exchanger of news and was not particularly amused by it.

"I got my suspicions, is all," Doom went on. "Nothin' solid-like, just a feelin.' Where did this Cumberbald come from out of nowhere? How does he send that fellow with a pineapple? Mrs. Lowell says it's a present fit for a king."

"Ah well," Penny said, "I suppose Mr. Cumberbald is ambitious and as for that rascal, he ought to be out working and has slipped in to get a look at the horses. No harm done, he is only a boy, after all."

Doom did not seem convinced, but then Penny reasoned he would not be. The usurper of Mrs. Lowell's affections was not likely to be looked upon kindly.

CHAPTER TEN

Mr. Farthingale was well-pleased with the developments of the last twenty-four hours. The betting had ranged wildly on the three-year-old filly race. One moment, Cabot was expected to die of his injuries, and heavy betting on *that* particular development had leaned toward Tuesday. But then, as if the angels in heaven smiled down upon him, Cabot had left his bed and danced the night away at a ball. If there was anything that could convince of a death not being imminent, it was to find the patient dancing at a ball. All ideas of Cabot's early demise had been cast aside. Farthingale had himself lurked in the bushes outside of Lord Beckman's house to confirm that the rumors were true—that Lord Cabot was indeed on his feet again and would attend the races.

He'd been more than satisfied over what he'd observed. Cabot had leapt down from his horse as if there had never been a thing wrong with him. Then, Mr. Farthingale had spent a deal of time crouched outside a window of the ballroom and was exceedingly pleased to see his quarry dancing with nary a limp.

The following day, as the news spread like a fire across Newmarket, he'd risen early to seek out Mr. Plastermen. That gentleman had a few advantages when it came to the bet-taking trade. He had been in the business for years—he was no fly by night. Further, his London address was well-known, so there was little danger of the fellow attempting a dodge to avoid paying up. And most appealing, Mr. Plastermen ran a sophisticated operation—one could bet to win or lose, or which order the horses would come in, or by how many feet one horse would beat another, though that one was notorious for sparking arguments. One could even bet against another gentleman's bet. If one knew Lord so and so had laid a hundred pounds on a particular horse that was unlikely to win, one might wager against the outcome. Every so often, an outlandish bet would surface—how many black horses would place, or if a horse with a white sock would win. How Mr. Plasterman kept it all straight, Farthingale was not certain other than knowing he was a great student of odds and chance. For himself, Farthingale did not much care how Plasterman did it, as he liked to ensure the odds ran in his favor through his own actions, and not from some dusty theory.

Mr. Plastermen had been happy to accept a large bet against Cabot's Bucephalus. Farthingale proclaimed he knew well enough that Bucephalus was the superior horse, but he was certain all was to be up for Cabot by Tuesday. He'd even heard, though he certainly had not, that relatives from all over England made their way to the deathbed. The early demise of the lord would leave horse and rider dejected and at sixes and sevens— they could not hope to win. If, Mr. Farthingale said with a convincing pound of fist in hand, they even found the strength to turn up at all! He was certain he'd convinced the man that the news of Cabot's regained health had not yet reached his ears. It had, though. It most delightfully had. The bets would come in swift for Bucephalus, with only himself knowing that Bucephalus would not race from an entirely different cause.

Just now, his bets having been secured and he having returned to his room at the Bull and Bell, he opened his door softly. He peered up and down the corridor to assure himself that the tavern's halls were empty of ears that might listen. He shut it again and turned to Freddy.

"I will wake you near dawn. You will want to get there early enough to gain access to the horse, but not so early that some night-watch or other would challenge what you do there. Dose the cup, deliver the berries, and be off. Having accomplished that little errand, our fortune is made."

Freddy eyed the brown sack in front of him. He opened it, peered in, and then tied it closed. "She ain't gonna keel over though, is she?" Freddy asked. "I don't like killin' animals. I might eat a chicken with gusto, but I ain't never gonna wring its poor little neck."

Mr. Farthingale examined his protégé, ever surprised by the boy's delicacy of feeling. He was particularly bemused by the idea that Freddy was far more concerned with the horse than he apparently was with the health of its rider. He said, "She will not keel over, as you so delightfully phrase it. She will merely be out of sorts and in no condition to run a race. Nor will her rider be in any shape to turn up. They will take the day off together."

What he said was probably true, he did not expect the horse's dose to be fatal. Nor did he wish it to be. He wished the dose to produce only an unsteadiness of gait. Just enough so that all would see the horse was indisposed without being able to pinpoint the exact nature of the complaint. A dead horse would invite too many unwelcome inquiries. He had guarded himself well enough by placing his bet against Cabot so early in the day, it would be entirely believable that his bet had been laid because he had been in ignorance of the lord's recovery. *Not*, that he had known there was anything wrong with the horse. Still, he would prefer nobody look at him and his bets too closely.

On the other hand, he was not particularly experienced with poisons. He had a vague idea that such substances could not be entirely relied upon to do exactly as one hoped. He must be ready for any circumstance that might arise.

As always, he had considered his options and chosen two different strategies. If the poison were not enough to affect the horse, then he must hope its rider was incapacitated. Finding another suitable rider on the morning of a race was highly unlikely.

For now, things went along swimmingly. The idea that Cabot was recovered and the gentleman's horse had all along been the superior creature was spoken of everywhere. The bets flowed heavily in favor of Bucephalus. With any luck, he would leave Newmarket with a tidy sum and Lord Cabot would still be in debt to him for three hundred guineas. That particular amount might not be readily paid, but it would be paid eventually.

Business was, as always, moving along at a satisfying clip.

DINNER THAT EVENING at Mendbridge Cottage would be a quiet affair. At least, a quiet dinner would be attempted, but Penny well knew that Petit would turn up at the door to the dining room more than once before the meal was through. As a usual thing, there would be multiple matters that would come up at the last minute from the stables. This year, her father had four horses in the races and so she might multiply the interruptions. Other gentlemen might abhor their stablemaster interrupting their dinner, but Lord Mendbridge would abhor it if Petit *didn't*.

Mr. Thornbridge was to come and dine, an old friend of Mrs. Wellburton from her married days. He was a widower and Penny often thought he was a bit soft on her aunt, though he had made no move over the years to express his admiration in any firm fashion. What Mr. Thornbridge *had* displayed, over their many meetings, was a singular lack of information when it came to horses. For that reason, he would be seated next to Mrs. Wellburton, that being as far as he could be placed away from her father. Lord Mendbridge was tolerant of the gentleman, as he was so favored by the lord's sister, but nobody would think to burden him with the man's company over an entire meal. That would leave Kitty to Mrs. Wellburton's other side, as she also had little interest in horses. Lord Mendbridge was exceedingly fond of

Kitty, but this night would not be the moment to test that fondness. The lord generally had horses on his mind and the night before a race would entirely crowd out any other possible subject.

That would leave Penny to her father's left and Lord Cabot to his right. She had little hope of being much engaged by Mr. Thornbridge on her other side, as *he* would be too much engaged with her aunt.

At least it was not to be a long and drawn out affair. Lord Mendbridge was of the opinion that the night before the races ought to go on soberly and end early.

Penny and Kitty had gone down at the last possible moment, so as not to be kept lingering in the drawing room with Lord Cabot. Neither wished to extend any particular conversation with that gentleman. Late last evening, Kitty had confided to Penny her difficult exchanges with the lord over supper. The man spoke in riddles, *petulant*-sounding riddles. What he had not done, to Penny's surprise, was unveil himself as a scholar. Rather, Kitty said, he appeared every bit the ox head she'd initially taken him for.

Penny had not known what to make of it, other than to assume that the lord had some other grand plan in mind. Perhaps he thought to continue to make himself look dull for a time, so that the sudden revealing of vast quantities of knowledge would be all the more stunning. She supposed she should not bother to hazard a guess, as the lord was a confounded sort of person who might be counted on to enact any sort of bizarre scheme. Had he not toyed with *her* for months before revealing his true self?

Penny had told Kitty of Lord Cabot's having gone to a moneylender so that he might enter his horse in the race. Kitty said it was only further confirmation of Lord Cabot being an ox head, as there could be nothing more idiotic. When Penny had hinted that Lord Cabot might have an eye on her dowry, Kitty had laughed and said, "He'd have to pry it from my hands while pointing a pistol at my head."

Penny had found herself cheered by that notion. If Lord Cabot was so foolish as to bury himself in debt, he could well pull himself out of it by his own devices. He would *not* be rescued by Kitty Dell.

Now, as they entered the drawing room, Penny saw that Mr. Thornbridge had cornered Lord Cabot in a conversation. She was all but certain her father, who now stood at the window, had been in the vicinity and quickly taken himself off. Mrs. Wellburton sat on a sofa, listening to her friend's one-sided discussion and nodding in approbation over his considered opinions regarding the Luddites and their condemnation of lace-making machines.

"Ah, there they are!" Lord Mendbridge said upon seeing Penny and Kitty enter the drawing room. He said it with perhaps more enthusiasm than might be expected and Mrs. Wellburton understood her brother perfectly.

She rose and said, "Let us go through."

PENNY FOUND THE dining table was one of two worlds. On her aunt's end, it was filled with news of Mrs. Wellburton's old neighborhood and endless merriment—apparently a local dowager was up to her old tricks and everybody was terrified that the traditional Maypole was not to come off, as the elderly lady did not find it seemly.

On Penny's end of the table, it was all speculation on the morrow's events, with the rather regular appearance of Petit come to whisper some matter into her father's ear. They had come to dessert before Penny was at all confident that they had seen the last of the stablemaster for one evening.

Just now, her father spooned his trifle and said, "I am always skeptical of the three-year-old filly race. A young filly hardly understands herself and one never knows what she'll decide to do next. I would not lay a large wager over it."

"I must protest the idea, Mendbridge," Lord Cabot said. "My own filly's mind is singular. She likes to gallop as fast as she can in whatever direction she's pointed in."

"So she's led you to believe," Lord Mendbridge said, "though she might change her mind at an inconvenient moment."

"I doubt that she will," Lord Cabot said. He looked across the table at Penny, as if he were on the verge of challenging her in some manner. "Though," he said, "it is not *always* a bad thing for a young female to change a mind on some matter."

Penny bristled, as she always did over the idea that the females of this world, be they person or horse, were supposed to be flighty creatures who reacted without reason and could not settle on an opinion. She particularly bristled that the notion came from Lord Cabot. "I object to the idea that it is only a filly that might change course," Penny said. "I am certain a colt is equally likely. In fact, colts, in particular, may zig and zag in a most irrational manner."

"Yes," Lord Cabot said, "I will concede that point. A colt might be going happily along one way when it suddenly realizes it ought to go another. Of course, the colt can only hope that others see the sense in that change of course. Or realize that the colt meant to go that way all along. And was only delayed."

"I do not see that a colt thinks so very deeply over its inconsistencies, my lord," Penny said.

"Oh, I don't know," Lord Cabot said, "colts might think deeper than you would imagine."

"And a filly would not?" Penny said.

Lord Mendbrige had been looking back and forth at his dinner partners. Finally he called down the table to his sister. "My dear, I think we all grow tired."

DOOM WAS UP before the sun. He would get to the stables at four, well in time to let Zephyrus and Bella graze for an hour in the predawn light and be put back into their stalls to rest a suitable time before the races.

He'd trotted down the dark lanes with confidence, he now

having been down them so often that he knew every dip and rut. The stables remained dark and Doom smirked to himself that the grooms were a bunch of layabouts.

As he made his way down the line of stalls, sleepy horses peered out at him. Zephyrus softly kicked his stall door before Doom was even in view, the horse having become accustomed to the sound of his footsteps.

He led the horses out to the east field, Bella dutifully following behind her leader wherever he might go. He closed the gate behind them, took himself back into the stables, and found a haybale to lie down on. He would relax for an hour, bring the horses in, and then have the breakfast that Mrs. Payne had thoughtfully packed for him. She'd said she'd made him his favorite—a mound of bacon stuffed between two pieces of toast.

Only a year ago, on a morning like this, he'd have found himself standing in the chill mist of a London street, holding a horse and fighting to stay awake. He'd have been waiting for hours for some drunken sot of a lord to decide he'd had enough of fancy wine and throwing away his money at a hazard table. Bacon between buttered toast would have been, back in those hungry days, the stuff of dreams and imagination.

Life had changed so much that he sometimes could not believe his luck.

Through his lazy mental wanderings, he heard someone make a noise at the other end of the stable. He rolled to his side and recognized the man who would ride Lord Cabot's horse. Doom had seen him from time to time, he was a slight and grizzled individual named Rupert. He was not surprised to see him now, nor to see him lead out Lord Cabot's horse. Miss Darlington had said that the lord would likely have the same idea of turning out his horse early. Doom had sometimes wondered if Miss Darlington did not give away too much of her strategies to Lord Cabot, though he supposed all that nonsense had come to an end. As far as he understood it, the only two inmates of the house who did not despise the lord were his valet and Lord

Mendbridge himself.

Doom rolled over and shut his eyes.

A HAZY ORANGE light peeked in through the slats of the stable walls and Doom sat up, judging the time. It must now be going on half past five and time to bring the horses back in. After that, he would have his breakfast.

He hopped down from the haybale and made his way outside.

The air was crisp with the morning chill that would burn off by race time. Doom turned the corner and the field came into view. He stopped short and squinted his eyes, rubbing them for good measure.

As far as he could make out, that blasted grocer's assistant stood by Zephyrus and Bella at the far fence. What in blazes was that fella doing there, and at this time of day?

"Hey!" Doom called. "What do you do there?"

The boy's head snapped up at the sound. He looked in Doom's direction and then sped off into the trees with a sack in his hand.

Something was not right.

In a flash, all of the niggling ideas about Freddy came to the forefront of Doom's mind. He'd written them off as only his aggravation at finding the boy so often fawned over by Mrs. Lowell. But now, they came rushing forward to present themselves. How was it that this country grocer, Mr. Cumberbald, had suddenly sent a pineapple when he now understood they were near impossible to get? How was it that the man's prices were so low as to seem improbable, or so Mrs. Lowell had said. She'd been convinced that Cumberbald only wished to secure his place as Lord Mendbridge's supplier. Doom had thought that, supplier or not, Freddy came to the house with endless small packages instead of one larger one. Those frequent visits had not seemed necessary.

Then, Freddy had been spotted in the stables only yesterday

morning. Why had he been there?

An unknown boy had weaseled his way into the house and now began turning up nearby their horses.

Doom could not work out the whole of the scheme, but he *could* be certain the boy was up to no good. As it was race day and the boy lingered unaccountably near Zephyrus, that no good must have to do with the betting.

He set off in a run after him.

FREDDY HAD BEEN used to following Mr. Farthingale's directions without fail. If the gentleman said do it this way, then it was done exactly that way. Up until this morning, his master's directions had always been meticulous. He'd thought, upon laying his head down the night before, they were meticulous once more.

He was to go to the stable just before dawn. He was to take the small vial of laudanum Mr. Farthingale had provided and go to the cabinet that held Lord Cabot's things. Inside he would find, among the brushes and gear, a chipped and stained teacup. He was to empty the vial into the cup and swirl it around so it was not obvious. When Lord Cabot's rider took the cup to the grooms' quarters for tea, as he did every time he came, he would dose himself. It might not have worked on a fella who took better care of his cup or less sugar in his tea, he might have noticed the stain of the liquid or tasted its bitterness. Farthingale assured him he had spied on the groom's habits thoroughly—the inside of the cup was already stained brown and the man used as much milk and sugar as he could find. He had described the whole set-up as "an affront to tea."

Once that was done, he would seek out the filly in Lord Cabot's stall. That part was easy enough, he'd already been there. The stall was one of the first in the line and conveniently labeled as being for Lord Cabot. Feed the horse the contents of the sack and be off. If the horse wouldn't go for it, mix it with some oats.

Both the horse and the rider would be incapacitated. Farthingale liked his plans to have layers, as if one didn't go as planned a person could hope the other one would. The horse, though. That was the most important part of it. A rider *might* be replaced, though unlikely. The horse could not be replaced.

He'd reached the stables just as the sun rose and the first part of the plan went off without a hitch. The stables had a series of closet-like tack rooms where the boarders could keep their gear and colors. Within the room was a cabinet that locked to keep safe the things deemed of value. Why Rupert would keep his teacup locked up, he didn't know but it had not slowed him down a minute—he'd been letting himself into locked doors since he was able to walk. He'd poured the laudanum into the cup and swished the thick brown liquid around so the sides were coated. Considering the state of the cup and the years of stain embedded in its porcelain, he very much doubted this new addition would be noticed. Then, he'd locked it up again and made his way to the horse's stall.

It was empty. The horse was gone. *That* was when the plan began to unravel.

He'd run outside, having no notion of where the horse could be. Had the lord moved the animal to Mendbridge Cottage?

He'd quickly jumped behind a post in spotting Rupert, Lord Cabot's rider. The fellow was walking into the stable, though Freddy had not had any notion he'd been on the grounds. It seemed he'd got to the fella's teacup just in time. But what had the man done with the horse?

Freddy stole along the outside of the stable and made his way to the rear. He turned the corner and two fields with horses grazing came into view, one to the right and one to the left. Two fillies who looked exactly alike grazed in two different fields. Farthingale had not said anything of the possibility that the horse might be out of its stall! Which one was Lord Cabot's horse? How was he supposed to tell the difference between the two?

Should he wait until they were brought back in? Then, he would know who was who. But it would be too late! There would be too many people about. As it was, he'd been lucky to not have been caught dosing Rupert's teacup.

He must do something, he could not return having done nothing. There was too much money at stake. But what was he to do?

As he did not have much to go on, he used his deductive skills to reason out what he *did* know. Lord Cabot was a lord, with prospects rich enough to borrow heavily. The gentleman would be a duke someday. It stood to reason that a man of that stature would have more than one horse at the races. So, it must be the filly who was out grazing with the stallion.

It seemed likely enough. He must just pray he'd guessed right.

He wondered, as he made his way over the bumpy tufts of grass toward the fence, if he could actually get the horse to eat anything. It was one thing to have a horse in a stall, and another to attempt to lure one to a fence. And, he hadn't been thinking clearly enough to bring oats in a bucket.

Still, the time was getting late. He must try what he could.

Fortunately, these two horses did not seem to be the wary type. They had looked at him curiously. He distinctly saw the stallion stare at the bag in his hand. That horse began to walk over to him, probably imagining he'd brought apples. The filly dutifully followed him.

It was not the ideal situation. He'd probably have to feed some of the berries to the stallion too, as he was unlikely to allow one of his herd to eat ahead of him.

When the horses reached the fence, he'd opened the bag and taken out a handful of the berries. Mr. Farthingale had dusted them with sugar to lure the horse in.

The stallion pushed the filly out of the way and bent his head to smell his hand. He shook his mane, turned, and walked away. The filly approached, seeming in a hurry lest she get pushed aside again, and took some of the berries from his hand.

What luck! The stallion was not interested and the filly was. Certainly, the morning was finally turning his way. He must only get her to take a few more handfuls and he would be off.

As he reached into his sack a second time, he heard a voice break the quiet of the morning. His head snapped up.

It was Doom, one of Mendbridge's grooms. And the fellow was running toward him.

He could not be caught.

CHAPTER ELEVEN

HENRY HAD BEEN up with the sun. He'd gone along, this past week, in all confidence about the race. Other things had distracted him, particularly Miss Darlington, but he'd not worried over his prospects at the races.

Now, though, the day had arrived. Somehow, it being so close to coming off had filled him with trepidation. What if something should happen? What if the unthinkable should occur and he lost? He was in debt to Mr. Farthingale for three hundred guineas and in a fit of confidence the day before, he'd laid some heavy private bets. Should he lose, he would be out near two thousand pounds. Two thousand pounds that he did not in fact have.

Good God, would he be like Mackery, sinking slowly deeper into debt until there was nowhere to turn?

No, of course that would not happen. His father would hardly permit his eldest son to fly to the continent with creditors on his heels. Dukes' Pact or not, his father would come through if absolutely necessary. One would hope.

On the other hand, the old man could get exceedingly testy when his gout flared up. Nobody would soon forget the day on the estate when he'd fired all the servants because somebody had watered down his port. It had been fortunate that Henry's mother had been the one to water it down and had rehired the servants before an hour had gone by.

My God, if his father was particularly irritable, he might attempt to use a large debt as leverage—*marry, and your debts will be paid. Otherwise, you can return from Spain or Belgium or wherever you've taken yourself off to when I am dead and you inherit.* Henry's mother would not be likely to interfere on that sort of directive, she was in wholehearted agreement with the Dukes' Pact. As for his grandmother…she'd probably buy him his ticket abroad.

He'd have to go. He could not linger in England with gentlemen's bets gone unpaid. He had no hope of paying any of those debts with a dowry. If he had thought he was against marriage before, now he knew it to be impossible. He would never marry. The only woman in the world for him was Miss Darlington, and she would marry Burke.

"That's it, then," he said softly. "If it all goes wrong, perhaps Mackery's contessa will find room for one more ne'er-do-well in her villa."

"I'm sorry, my lord?"

Henry realized Jarvis would think he'd lost his mind. He must not allow his thoughts to drift to Miss Darlington! There was too much at stake, he must be focused on the business at hand. Though, if he were to examine it closely, there was not much business for him to actually accomplish other than turning up and watching his fate unfold with the race.

"Should you like to be off to the stables at once, my lord?" Jarvis asked, polishing a smudged boot buckle with the cloth he always seemed to have on his person.

"I should like to, but we both know Rupert would be incensed," he said. His groom was skilled and had no need of his interference. In truth, he'd always been rather bold in sharing his opinions, and his opinion on a race day was: "Don't bother me or the horse. Nobody in fine clothes need be in the stables."

"Ah, yes, Rupert," Jarvis said, as if he'd just bit a lemon.

"You see how it is, then," Henry said.

"As clear as glass."

Once, Henry had ignored Rupert's precept of staying out of the way while they were at Epsom Downs. He'd been paid for his trouble with a slew of insults, most of which he did not care to recall as they referred to his manhood and his person.

Another groom would have been dismissed on the spot for such effrontery, but what could one do with Rupert? He'd known Henry since he was a boy and had knocked him on the head more than once in those early years. Further, he was too valuable to dismiss. As it was, the fellow's salary was always being raised because some lord sought to poach him with a more attractive offer. If one thought of buying horseflesh, did not one always call upon Rupert to gain his opinion?

Henry had bought Bucephalus on the groom's recommendation. Rupert had eyed the horse and watched her move, he'd examined her teeth, and felt along her ribs, and laid his ear against her chest. Then, he'd done what only Rupert could do, he'd had a long talk with the horse. He'd pronounced the current owner a great booby of a man and the horse herself a jewel.

No, as much as he'd like to gallop down to the stables and supervise all the preparations, he would keep himself well away from Rupert's wrath.

"I suppose Miss Darlington will go down early," Henry said, "as she does not have her own Rupert to keep her away."

"The lady's rider is too young to have yet reached the storied heights of incivility Rupert currently occupies," Jarvis said drily, "though he seems to aspire to it. The young ruffian's name is Doom."

"Doom?"

"Apparently his mother and father looked upon the infant with something less than sanguine feelings and named him thus. He has the effrontery to glare at me whenever we chance upon one another."

"I suppose you cannot blame him for glaring, I suspect he only follows others' leads. Do they all continue cool below stairs?"

"Oh yes," Jarvis said, his hand visibly tightening on Henry's boot. "One would think I am the devil himself. I have been served so many ends of meat that I believe they may be buying them specially for me."

"Confounded people," Henry muttered, "I suppose they will all love Burke. Burke will be celebrated, as will his valet."

"Lord Burke?" Jarvis asked quizzically.

Henry bit his lip. He must stop thinking about Miss Darlington, and Burke and, well, the whole mess. It was race day. He must turn his full attention to that.

Though, he noticed his thoughts were not to be so easily directed. They would keep drifting back. As he was naturally a rather hopeful individual, they kept drifting further in the direction of ideas that might solve the whole problem.

What if Miss Darlington had not firmly made up her mind? Or what if she had, but her mind could be changed? After all, nothing had been announced yet.

Had not many a lady thrown over a fiancé before the banns? Or, if not many, then some? Or if not some, then at least one?

It could not be unheard of! He should take his chance, for if he did not, it would always weigh upon him. A man should not live his life wondering what might have happened if he'd tried something.

No, a man could not live with such a notion.

"I will do it," he said softly. "I will do it tonight at the club's ball."

"Celebrate your victory, my lord?" Jarvis asked.

"Yes, let us hope to be victorious." Henry answered. "Even if it results in another gentleman's loss."

"Does it not always, my lord?" Jarvis asked, beginning to look at him strangely. "Only one horse can cross the finish first."

"Then let it be me," Henry said.

DOOM REACHED THE edge of the woods. Far ahead, he saw a brief glimpse of Freddy. The boy was following the only path visible, he should not be hard to catch. Doom set off as fast as his legs could carry him.

Had he been any other groom, he might not have had a very good chance of catching up to the scoundrel. After all, a person guilty of a crime and desperate for escape usually had the advantage—fear would propel him faster than his pursuer. Fear made one quick and nimble. Doom had firsthand experience of it, having spent a deal of time running for his life through the streets of London.

Every time he stole something for his supper, he led his pursuers on a merry chase. At times, he might be forced to elude a dozen men, as there was nothing people liked more than to chase down a thief. He'd become expert at dodging and weaving, jumping over fences, running through back gardens, pulling himself up drainpipes, and making wild jumps between roofs. Now, he had only to jump over tree roots and stones and duck under branches.

Freddy glanced over his shoulder and Doom saw him throw the sack into the brush and head for a farmer's fence at the far side of the woods. He pumped his legs ever faster.

Freddy was nearly over the fence when Doom caught up to him. They struggled, Freddy trying to go forward and Doom just as hard pulling him back.

"Get off me if you know what's good for ya!" Freddy yelled.

"I ain't never, you sinner," Doom yelled back.

"I ain't done nothin.'"

"You have, I know it."

As they wrestled atop the rough wood fencing, Freddy forced Doom's forearm across the top rail. Doom fought against it, but the boy was strong and as determined as a badger. Freddy maneuvered himself above Doom and put his foot atop Doom's outstretched arm. He threw his weight upon it.

A sickening crack reverberated in Doom's ears and a searing

pain shot through his arm, a few inches above the wrist.

Freddy wrestled out of the grasp of Doom's good arm and leapt down from the fence. He ran across the farmer's field as Doom collapsed to the ground. His arm was broken. He knew it well enough from the feeling of it, though looking at it would have told him too. His forearm hung at an odd angle, as if it had grown another joint.

The devil had broken his arm! He'd never fared so badly in a combat.

He must get back. He must get back to the stable and to Miss Darlington. She would know what to do for him, and for Bella too. He'd had every intention of beating the truth out of Freddy, but the scoundrel had got away.

The sack. It was in the woods. If he could somehow find it and make his way back to the stables quickly, Miss Darlington would know what to do.

Doom took a deep breath and stood, holding his arm. Every step would be awful, but he must find the sack and get himself back. If he collapsed in the woods he'd be on his way to the gangrene before anybody was to find him.

Despite his name, Doom had never been in the habit of thinking the worst might happen. Though, he could not stop his thoughts from settling on the idea that his arm might not be saved. It was not an unusual thing. How many fellas had he seen on a London street with something missing on them? One never knew if it were the war or an accident, but they could not work. Nobody hired a man without all four working appendages. Nobody raced a horse without two working arms. If he viewed the doctor coming at him with a saw, would he not *rather* die in the woods?

He pushed those thoughts away. Whatever was to happen to him, he could not let down Miss Darlington. He could not let down the house. They had taken him in and made his life comfortable, short though it might turn out to be. Zephyrus was a fine horse and Bella was the apple of Miss Darlington's eye—if they could be saved from whatever trickery was in the works, he would do it. He would not let Miss Darlington down.

He put one foot in front of the other, doing his best to ignore the shooting pain that came with every step. He must just keep his mind on two things—find the bag and get back to the stable.

PENNY HAD DRIVEN herself to the stables. There had been some clucking from Mrs. Payne over it, that lady certain that nobody in the house knew she meant to set off alone. Mrs. Payne had been right, as it happened. Her aunt would not like the idea at all. However, Doom would have gone over two hours before and he was the only groom she ever took as a tiger.

She had not run into any trouble on the road, nor had she expected to despite Mrs. Payne's head shaking and tsking as she departed. She well knew there would be two kinds of gentlemen in Newmarket at the moment—those sober-minded individuals who took race day seriously and were no danger to anybody, and those rogues who might be a danger, but who had stayed with their gin in a tavern far into the night and were still abed with heavy heads.

As she pulled the phaeton into the yard, she could not quite believe her eyes. She stood up to get a better view in case she'd been mistaken.

There was no mistake. Zephyrus and Bella were still out in the field! It was far too late for them to be out.

She leapt down from the vehicle, trusting that her horses would not wander off. No groom was in sight to unhitch them and she would not stay to wait for them. She picked up her skirts and ran down to the field.

Her horses came to the gate willingly. She had brought no lead, but she knew they would follow her back to the stable with high hopes that they were to be fed some oats when they returned to their stalls.

Zephyrus seemed in fine form, but how much grass had he eaten? The time grew late, was it even safe to enter him? She had a sinking feeling that it was not safe.

She could kill Doom for his inattention! The boy had no doubt fallen asleep in a hayloft and now he may have cost her the race!

She glanced behind her and noticed Bella lagged behind. "Come on, girl," Penny said, careful to keep her voice pleasant. She did not wish for either of the horses to suspect her mood just now.

Bella did as she was asked, but Penny stopped and looked at her critically. The filly seemed not herself. She was tentative in her steps. Penny could not imagine what had discomposed the creature.

"Come now, Bella, we are almost back. You will be safe and sound in your own stall soon enough."

Bella walked forward and Penny kept talking to her.

"I imagine you feel something is in the air today and you fear you may be asked to be a part of it," Penny said soothingly, as they reached the stable's back doors. "You are not to worry over any such thing. I decided long ago that you are not yet ready, so you will just have to satisfy yourself by staying here and then hearing all about it later."

She opened Zephyrus' stall and the horse went dutifully in. She closed his gate and turned to Bella.

The filly was close behind her and pushed her head against Penny's arm. "There girl, all is well."

Bella raised her head and Penny took a step back. She peered into Bella's eyes. Her pupils were as saucers.

She shouted, "Grooms! I need grooms!"

One of the boys poked his head around a corner. "Miss Darlington?" he asked, no doubt surprised. Penny was not in the habit of asking for their help on any matter. Seeing the look on her face, the groom threw away the hay stalk he'd been chewing and ran down the line of stalls to her.

"Look at her eyes," Penny commanded.

The boy looked, then quietly whistled.

"There is deadly nightshade in your fields!" Penny said. "Clearly, that is what it is, there is nothing else that could account for her pupils so large. As well, her gait was unsteady."

"It canna be," the groom said, "we walk them fields every week."

"Then you have missed it," Penny said. "Find the other grooms. I will need a charcoal slurry. Quickly!"

The groom ran off and Penny spoke softly to Bella, walking her into her stall. She closed the door and ran to her tack room. She took Zephyrus' bit, which would be far too large and cause Bella to open and close her mouth to get away from it. Then, she unlocked her cabinet and took out one of the specially made plungers that had been oft used to dose horses in her father's stables. Its barrel was thick tapered glass, with a sturdy leather cap and a plunger of polished wood.

Bella would not like it, but charcoal must reach the stomach to stop any further ill effects of the nightshade.

Penny paused and looked into Zephyrus' stall. That horse's pupils were normal and he was alert. Penny very much doubted he'd eaten any of the berries. Deadly nightshade was a young horse's mistake. He would be too clever for it. Still, the enormity of what had happened settled upon her. There could be no debate, she did not dare race him with only two hours to spare. There was too great a risk for colic and she had no notion of what had occurred in that field before she arrived. She would never do anything that might harm one of her horses.

As she resigned herself to sitting out the races this year, Penny could not help that her blood boiled over the cause of it. There should never have been nightshade allowed to grow in those fields! And where was Doom? Had Zephyrus been brought in on time as he should have been, Zephyrus would be racing yet. How could he have been so reckless and imprudent!

Doom had convinced her that he was ready for such responsibility. She should have known he was too young.

DOOM HAD STAGGERED back down the forest path to the spot where he'd been sure he'd seen Freddy throw the sack. The ground was riddled with tree roots, diabolically disguised under ferns and fallen leaves. He ranged round the area, tripping his way through. He fell once, but had the presence of mind to turn himself to avoid falling on the arm that was already broken. He ignored the fact that the fingertips of that arm had grown numb and how that was surely a very bad sign.

Finally, he spotted the sack at the base of a tree. He picked it up and peered in. A pile of berries coated in white sat at the bottom, along with a vial of brownish liquid. He could guess the berries to be nightshade, but as for the vial, he had no idea. Miss Darlington would know, though. She knew just about everything.

He must just get back to her.

Doom looked up to the sky and his heart sank. He should have had the horses in well before now.

Were they even still alive? Had Freddy been able to get to them both? He thought not; he thought it had just been Bella. Poor, sweet Bella.

As he trudged through the forest, one foot painfully in front of the other, he could not help but speculate on why Freddy had done such a thing. He knew very well that all sorts of underhanded schemes went on around a horse race, but poison? Would somebody really dare it nowadays?

Meddling with horses had fallen very out of vogue after Mr. Rampart's hanging the year before. The fellow had been deep in debt and concocted a rash plan to put himself right again. He'd stolen a fine horse from somewhere up north and cleverly dyed the beast to appear nothing like itself. Then, he attempted to injure the horse who was favored to win. He'd planned to cut the horse's tendon and then pound a nail through a board in the stall and leave it sticking out as if the nail had caused the damage. He'd been caught at all of it.

Somehow, when he'd crept into the stables in the middle of the night to injure the favorite, he knocked over his own lamp. A fire broke out. The grooms in the apartments above were alerted fast enough and got the horses out while throwing buckets of water willy-nilly. Mr. Rampart had been caught running from the scene badly burned and his horse had conveniently begun to shed its dye from the buckets of water that hit him. He'd known the game was up and confessed to all.

Rampart might have supposed he could confess without trading his life. After all, not that many horse thieves were executed anymore. He should have realized that adding in an attempt to fix a race, injure another horse, lay the blame on Lord Hasselby's stable, and then burning down the stable was rather more than any judge might find sympathy for.

Nobody involved with horseracing would forget the man's screams as he was hauled up to the gallows. And, had they been lucky enough to avoid witnessing the spectacle, the newspaper had provided a lurid description. Criminals, as Doom well knew, liked to keep risks low and rewards high. Mr. Rampart had taken too big a risk and paid too big a price.

It seemed impossible that Freddy would attempt such a thing. And if he did, who did he work for? Who was this mysterious Mr. Cumberbald anyway?

Doom reached the edge of the tree line, the stables just ahead. He limped gratefully toward it.

CHAPTER TWELVE

I T HAD BEEN one of the most unpleasant half hours that Penny had ever spent in her life. The charcoal slurry had been brought and loaded again and again into the syringe.

Bella, despite her hazy state, had been irate about it. Each time the plunger had been refilled and Penny gripped her cheek to shoot it to the back of her tongue, Bella had yanked her head in a fury.

She was certain Bella's thoughts ran along the lines of: "I would trample you if I had the means."

Penny had worked as quickly and efficiently as she was able so that Bella need not suffer overlong. Finally, the last dose of it was in. Now, all they could do was wait. Penny was hopeful. After all, Bella had been able to walk back to the stables on her own. There was every chance that she'd eaten some of the berries and then quickly lost interest in them.

She laid her cheek against Bella's and whispered, "I am so sorry, but it was for your own good."

As she said it, she remembered all those times as a child that she'd been told something was for her own good. She'd not ever seen the sense in it, and often thought she was being lied to. She suspected Bella felt just the same.

"Miss. Miss!" one of the grooms said, tugging on her sleeve. She let go of Bella and turned. He was pointing to the stable doors. Doom staggered toward her.

She saw in an instant that he'd been injured.

"Doom! What has happened? Where have you been?"

He held his hand out, clutching a brown sack, as he made his way unsteadily toward her. "Freddy, the grocer's boy. He fed this to the horses, Bella at least. Nightshade, I think. And there's something else in there, but I don't know what it is."

As Penny took in his words, she just as quickly noted his opposite arm hanging at an odd angle.

"Your arm!" she cried.

"It's done broke," Doom said. "I chased that hooligan and he broke it over a fence rail."

Penny stood there in momentary shock. The grocer's boy had poisoned her horse and broke her rider's arm? Why?

Her commonsense took over just as fast. There was no time for *why*. She had done what she could for Bella, now she must do what she could for Doom.

She turned to the grooms, who were white-faced. To the oldest, whom she knew as Johnny, she said, "You must take Doom to Mendbridge Cottage in my phaeton. It stands just outside. Fold up a horse blanket to prop up the injured arm, it must not be jostled about. Send someone for Doctor Prentiss. Take Doom to the front doors and tell the butler, Mr. Montrose, that I have directed he be put in a bedchamber in the house. He will do as you say."

Penny took the sack from Doom's good hand. "You have been very brave, Doom, and I am ashamed of what I have thought in discovering you missing."

Doom smiled weakly. "You thought I be shirking. Not a chance."

"I should have known better."

"I can't ride Zephyrus, though," Doom said regretfully. "I was all set to put on the colors and take him to victory."

"Never mind the race," Penny said. "There will be other races. Now, you will go carefully to the phaeton and Johnny will take you back. I will see to the horses."

"I done interrupted that jackanapes afore he got far with it," Doom said proudly.

"I believe you have," Penny said. "Bella is not happy just now, but I have every confidence in her recovery and it will be due to your good efforts. Do go with Johnny, the doctor will be there as soon as he is found. Mrs. Wiggins and Mr. Montrose will take care of you until he arrives."

Johnny led Doom out of the stables. Penny opened the sack. As she did so, both Zephyrus and Bella backed in their stalls, as if they knew its contents were the author of the morning's disaster.

The berries were indeed nightshade and appeared to have been dusted with sugar. She grasped the vial and pulled it out. It was a quarter filled with a brownish liquid. She wrestled the cap off and smelled it. It had an unpleasant odor. Penny put a drop on her finger and tasted it. It was bitter. She recognized it instantly. It was laudanum.

Laudanum? Had that boy planned to dose her horses with nightshade *and* laudanum? She did not see how he thought he might accomplish it, no horse would willingly take it. Perhaps he meant to smear it on the horse's gums? It would have been a dangerous gambit and one that might have resulted in the loss of a few fingers.

She peered at Zephyrus. His pupils were quite regular. Unlike the nightshade, if the horse had taken laudanum his pupils would have constricted.

Perhaps the boy had the laudanum with him as his own habit? Many a person had been treated with the medicine for some complaint or other and then found themselves loath to part with it. Though, for a grocer's boy, one might have thought ale or gin the more likely vices.

No matter. It did not seem as if the laudanum had been used on the horses. The trip to Newmarket was to be a disappointment, but as she'd told Doom, there would be other races. Bella had not grown worse and seemed a bit more alert than she had been. That was a very good sign. Illnesses rarely remained the same, they grew worse or better, and Bella was going in the better direction. As for Doom, Doctor Prentiss had proven himself skilled in treating Lord Cabot and so Penny had every confidence in her tiger coming through no worse for the wear, too. He would be out of sorts for some weeks, but he was young. He was strong enough to fight off an infection and his bones would knit quickly. The servants would spoil him silly while he recovered.

She had told Doom she was ashamed of her thoughts in finding the horses out and him nowhere in sight. She was, and she also felt exceedingly stupid. The boy had never given her a reason to doubt him.

She would not leave with a victory in her reticule as she had planned, but she hoped to leave with both her tiger and her horses alive. For that, she must be grateful.

As she stroked Bella's cheek she thought the filly was becoming more sanguine then she had been. She nuzzled Penny's hand. "There you are, pretty girl," Penny said. It was one of the things she loved about horses—if they were loyal, they would not hold a grudge long. Trust was the key. Let one who was not trusted do something inexplicable and a horse would never forget it. But if one was trusted, as she was by Bella, the rancor over a charcoal slurry was not likely to last.

One of the younger grooms who had gone out to assist Johnny in getting Doom into the phaeton came hurrying toward her.

"There is not a problem?" Penny asked. "Do not tell me my horses have wandered off with the phaeton."

"No, miss," the boy said, "Johnny and Doom done got off quick enough. It's only that Johnny, he's our leader, you see. And now he's gone."

"Yes, I know it. I did send him. Surely you understand your duties and do not need him peering over your shoulder?"

"It ain't duties what's the difficulty," the boy said, kicking at some hay. "It's that when a thing is unexpected, you see, then we tell Johnny and he says what to do."

Penny took pity on the young boy. It must have been quite the morning for him. "You're not to worry over it," she said, "I have things well in hand."

Though she thought the boy would be comforted by her words, he did not seem so in the least.

"But you see, miss, we lads has got a room." He helpfully pointed at the rafters to indicate where the room was.

Penny waited for him to go on.

"It's a room for our convenience," the boy said. "There ain't no cookin' mind, as we don't want the stables afire, but we do bring jugs of tea. And, we keep up there all the things a body needs for tea—sugar, fresh milk from the farm, rolls from the kitchens…"

Penny could not imagine why the boy thought she ought to know any of it.

"We lounge there when we aren't workin' and it's ever so nice."

"I'm delighted for you," Penny said, wishing the boy to come to the end of his descriptions.

"We got some comfortable chairs and whatnot," the boy went doggedly on, "and we don't mind other fellas stoppin' in. Doom knows all about it."

Penny was becoming exasperated as she began to understand the boy's ramblings. "If you wish to point out that you have sometimes supplied Doom with tea," she said, "and you hope some renumeration might be had, I will see to it before I leave town. Is that sufficient for you?"

The boy looked completely confused. "No, miss, we don't need to be paid for the courtesy, we is always happy to share what we got. It's just now, though, Lord Cabot's rider, his name is Rupert. Well, he's in a bit of a pickle. Johnny would know what to do but the rest of us don't."

"What do you mean, in a pickle?" Penny asked, nearly amazed that there might have actually been a point to this meandering conversation.

"P'raps the better thing is to say that he *is* pickled," the boy said, appearing just as relieved as Penny that he'd finally got to a point.

"Good Lord," Penny said, laughing. "Do you mean to say that Lord Cabot's rider is drunk?"

"That's about the size of it," the boy whispered. "Though, it's an odd thing. He came in as he always is, kinda gruff if you don't mind me sayin.' Then he has his tea and he becomes all friendly-like. He's jokin' and laughin' and I thought well that's a nice change. Then he starts sayin' things that don't make sense, like there's horses in Africa what are black and white stripes and nobody can ride the beasts. He's gonna go there and show 'em all how it's done. Then he falls asleep. We tried to wake him but he won't get up."

The boy's story was extraordinary, but then she supposed the whole morning had been so. Penny turned and looked at Bella. Pleased that the filly was seeming more and more herself, she thought she might step away for a moment to investigate the groom's rather wild claims.

"Stay here and keep an eye on Bella," she said. "I will go and see for myself what is the matter with Lord Cabot's groom."

The boy nodded, appearing relieved that this problem, whatever it was, had been taken off his shoulders.

Penny knew the way perfectly well. It had not been a secret to her that the grooms had a room overhead. Grooms frequently did and she had heard their footsteps and laughing above her often enough over the past week. She strode to the front end of the stables and the winding staircase tucked behind a corner that led up to the floor above.

Upon reaching the top, she found the rest of the boys standing in a semicircle in front of a faded and patched sofa. They parted as she approached.

Lord Cabot's grizzled groom sat with his head lolling back and a small dribble running down his chin.

"For heaven's sake," she said, looking at him. "What is his name again?" she asked the grooms.

One of them stepped boldly forward and said, "His name be Rupert. We suppose he's a minute away from bein' sacked."

Penny looked askance at the boy. "It will not be within your purview to do it though, will it?"

The boy looked abashed, and though Penny had provided him a set down, she thought he was entirely right. This particular groom would not be employed long. Lord Cabot would likely be enraged, as he was unlikely to find another rider so soon to race time. Especially not for the filly race. It was to go off first and the rider need not only be skilled, but exceedingly lightweight. Any man fitting that description was already engaged.

Another idea followed just as quickly. Lord Cabot had pinned all his hopes on the race. He'd gone to a moneylender over it. And now his feckless groom had caused him a world of trouble.

She leaned over and shook his arm.

Rupert lazily opened his eyes and smiled at her. "You're pretty thing. Ain't she a pretty thing, boys?"

The boys tittered behind her, as boys were wont to do over any kind of vulgarity. Penny slapped Rupert's cheek and said, "None of your insolence, if you know what's good for you."

This seemed to strike Rupert as being worthy of consideration as he wrinkled his fuzzy brows in concentration. Then just as suddenly, he smiled again. "It ain't no matter, anyhows," he said. "I'm off to Africa to ride the zebras. Just see if I don't."

Penny had been leaning close to the man, but had not smelled that familiar reek of alcohol that would be expected to emanate from an inebriated individual.

He looked into her eyes and muttered, "Zebras. Just see if I don't."

As he'd looked her in the eye, Penny had looked *him* in the eye. Though the room was dim as the windows were few and small, his pupils were pinpricks. She began to suspect that it had not been her horses that were to be dosed with laudanum. It had been Lord Cabot's groom.

But how? Why? What purpose would it serve to disable *her* horses and the *lord's* groom?

Penny stood stock still. Bella had not been the real target. The grocer's boy, who Penny was now certain did not work for a grocer at all, had come to poison Lord Cabot's horse. The filly was a near copy of Bella, but for the few white hairs on her withers. What he'd found when he arrived was two identical horses out grazing. He'd probably counted on finding the horse in its stall and had found himself in a quandary. How had he decided to go for Bella? Perhaps he'd tried it with both horses and Bucephalus wouldn't take it?

She could not be sure what had happened, but she had passed Bucephalus back in her stall and she looked no worse for wear. *That* horse had not fallen for the ruse. It had only been dear Bella, and her impossible sweet tooth, that had not been able to resist the sugar that laced the poison.

Now here was Lord Cabot's rider, incapacitated. It *must* have been purposefully done.

"Rupert," she said, shaking him. "Did you take anything today? Did anybody hand you something?"

The groom stared at her quizzically and said, "Have you seen the zebras? I saw a drawing of one once. I pray they be real. Lord, I do pray it."

She would not get a lick of sense from the man. Penny glanced at the teacup that sat on a roughhewn table by Rupert's side. She picked it up and examined the inside of it, running her index finger along the sides and bottom. Along with a ridiculous amount of wet clumped sugar, she noted something sticky. Something brown. She tasted it and knew at once what had happened. Somehow, the scoundrel had got the laudanum into Rupert's tea.

The poor man. As one of the grooms had mentioned, he likely would be dismissed, though it seemed no fault of his own. And Lord Cabot, what of him?

She should not care a whit what was to happen to Lord Cabot. In fact, if the lord had chosen to enter the dark realms and seedy alleyways of moneylending, he might face whatever consequences for it. If his family could not rescue him, then he could just go off to some distant shore until some solution were found. Or perhaps he'd be like Mr. Brummel, who she'd heard was slowly falling to ruin in Calais.

It would serve him right.

And yet, as much as she was loath to admit it, she might miss the crinkle of his eyes and the timbre of his voice.

No, she would not, she was being a ninny. She would only miss what she thought he had been, not who he was.

Though her logical mind was firm on that idea, her heart was a more wayward creature. Her heart *would* paint a world without the gentleman as rather grey and lifeless.

"Oh, bother!" she cried.

The grooms fell back at this outburst. Rupert smiled and said, "You've seen the zebras, I expect."

Penny ignored Rupert, entirely taken up by her own thoughts. *If* she were going to do something about this situation, *if* she were to make any attempt to assist Lord Cabot, she must act quickly and decisively.

She took a deep breath and turned to the grooms. "He is not drunk," she said, with every effort to infuse her words with authority. "I happen to know that our housekeeper was treating him with saffron for a stomach complaint. It is that substance that is in his tea and has produced this unfortunate result. It is not uncommon, I am afraid."

Penny hoped the lie would be believable. Saffron was exceedingly expensive and so it was unlikely that any of them would have any experience with it.

"Fortunately," she continued, "the effect will not last long. He will be recovered in good time for the filly race."

"But miss," one of the bolder grooms said, "the fillies must be got on their way in the next half hour! I can hear a few of them getting ready below us as we speak!"

"I see you doubt my understanding of saffron," Penny said sternly. "Did you not all view how quickly the effects came on? Have you ever seen ale or gin or any other drink come on with such speed?"

The boys all shook their heads.

"And does it not follow that a thing that can come on that fast must also depart as quickly?"

As it appeared, the grooms did see a certain logic in that idea. And, as they none of them had much knowledge of medicines of any sort and none whatsoever of saffron, the idea began to take hold.

"That's a rum thing, that saffron," one said.

"I wouldn't like it for myself," another said, "no matter how bad my stomach ached."

"That is quite enough debating about it," Penny said. "Carry him down to Lord Cabot's tack room, I will see to the rest. I presume you have other things to do?"

The boys nodded, and in truth they might not have had other things to do that could not wait, but they were all eager to get out onto the turf and secure a spot to watch the race.

"Get on with you, then," Penny chided. "We have not got all morning."

⫸⫷

THE BOYS HAD got Rupert down the stairs, though not without a few bumps on the groom's head as they turned corners. They'd taken him into Lord Cabot's tack room and placed him on a bench, leaning his head and shoulders against the wall. The groom snored peacefully.

The boys had stood back and looked at the slumped groom dubiously, but Penny said, "You ought to go if you're planning on getting close enough to watch the race. I will watch over Rupert until the effects of the saffron wear off. As they will, very suddenly."

Penny did not know if they had been wholly taken in by the tale, but no boy their age would risk missing the race. As if fish swimming in a lake, they turned as one and darted out the door.

Penny closed it behind her and stared at Rupert. Was she mad to even contemplate what she was just now thinking of?

Yes, she supposed she was. It did not make a lick of sense to put herself in so much peril. What if she were caught? She did not much care for any talk about herself, but how would it reflect on her father? Or her aunt? Not very well, she was sure. Especially not her aunt, who had raised her and would have been credited with the task of imbuing her with a feminine sense of decency.

And what did she risk it for anyway? To save a man who had treated her so cruelly?

Yes, she supposed that was exactly what she contemplated. She did not love him now. Not since she had seen what he could be. But she could no longer deny to herself that she had loved him once. She still loved that man she'd known. She loved what she'd thought him, and of what their future might be. She supposed she'd never stop loving *that* man, though it had only been an illusion.

Penny glanced around the tack room. Neatly hung on the wall were the groom's riding clothes, the lord's colors a black and green stripe. When she had stared down at Rupert in the groom's quarters and considered what ought to be done, she had not failed to notice that she and he were very close to the same size.

CHAPTER THIRTEEN

FREDDY SEARCHED THE crowd for Mr. Farthingale. He'd been supposed to meet him at the tavern, but he'd been delayed by the events of the morning and found his master already gone. Farthingale wouldn't like to hear the tale of what had not gone perfectly right at the stables, but he best get it over with.

He spotted the gentleman, easily found by his tall stature and the faded hat with frayed ribbon that he wore to appear not over-prosperous. Freddy ducked and weaved through the throngs of people making their way to the Rowley Mile.

He tugged on Mr. Farthingale's coat sleeve.

Mr. Farthingale instinctively covered his hand over his inside coat pocket, a habit of living in London surrounded by pickpockets that would not go amiss in Newmarket.

Seeing it was Freddy, he instantly took note of the state of his protégé's clothes and the look on his face. He pulled Freddy from the crowd that coursed down the lane and hustled him into a wooded glen.

"Too long to tell ya the whole of it," Freddy said, before Farthingale could start asking questions that might lead to unfortunate answers. "The gist is I got some of the berries into the horse and all the laudanum into the rider's teacup. Miss Darlington's groom done interfered with me, though I reckon I broke the fella's arm for his trouble."

As he said all this, Freddy failed to mention that Cabot's stall had been empty, that there had been two identical horses out in the fields, and that he'd had to roll the dice on which one to approach. He was not an idiot, and it had occurred to him that if Miss Darlington's groom had gone after him, it had been Miss Darlington's horse that he'd dosed, and not Lord Cabot's. He would have to trust in the idea that he'd dosed the rider enough to make that unfortunate circumstance moot.

Farthingale grasped Freddy by the shirt collar. "*Some* berries better be enough. Should it not be, you will find yourself on the streets again. Or worse."

Freddy wriggled from his grasp. "I done poured three quarters of the laudanum into that teacup, it ain't possible the man gets on that horse if he even drank half of it."

Farthingale stared down at him, not looking appeased by this prediction.

"And who they gonna get to ride the filly, even if she ain't the worse for it?" Freddy said. "There ain't time, and there ain't riders hanging about with nothing to do."

"What if Lord Cabot decides to ride himself?" Farthingale asked.

"Him!" Freddy said, forcing himself to laugh. "That great beast of a man can't get on that filly's back. She'd collapse at the half mile. That groom of his don't weigh much more than me—*that's* what the horse is used to."

Farthingale slowly nodded. "You had best be right. If I lose, we are ruined."

Freddy used all his self-control to avoid swallowing hard, though that was precisely what he would have liked to have done. Ruined? He'd no idea his master had got them in so deep. He did, however, have an idea that the outcome of the race was in no way certain.

HENRY WAS FEELING more cheerful than he had been in some time. He'd thrown off the uneasiness of the morning as being nonsense. Of course he would succeed. Before the day was through, he would win the thousand guinea stakes, have the cloud of debt lifted off his head, and if the fates would be kind, he'd win the hand of Miss Darlington too.

The stand Lord Mendbridge had built was ideally situated. He would see the start of the race in the distance, and the end of it clearly. The race itself was well in hand, all he need do is observe Rupert and Bucephalus both doing what they knew how to do so well.

The situation with Miss Darlington was not so well arranged, but that did not mean he would not find success. He must only make his case! Surely, she would see that he was far more suited to her than Burke. Burke was pleasant, of course. But pleasant was not enough!

Surely, she would see it. She would not spoil her own happiness over some errant words he'd said that ought not to have been said.

Would she?

He did not think so, anyway. After all, when she was apprised of the idea that he loved her, she must soften.

Where was she, anyway? Surely, she would not miss the race.

Perhaps Burke had waylaid her. Damn Burke.

Lord Mendbridge elbowed him. "Eh, Cabot? What do you think of? Worrying that I'm right about fillies and your own might change her mind about wanting to race?"

Henry smiled, but did not answer. They had made their way to the lord's stand and had an excellent view of the Rowley Mile, as well as the jostling crowd who were not so lucky as to have a private stand. Though the raised seats might have kept the masses at bay, the stench of them was not so easily avoided. It was as if every farmer in the neighborhood had a deep-seated resentment against baths.

"I suppose the ladies all come together?" Henry said.

"They come in the carriage," Lord Mendbridge said. "Montrose and a battalion of my footmen and grooms will clear the way here for my sister and Miss Dell."

"But Miss Darlington?" Henry asked.

"Penny?" Lord Mendbridge said, laughing. "Don't be a blockhead, Cabot. She's got a horse in the race this afternoon. She'll stay at the stables with her eye on everything until the last moment. Petit takes care of my own but Penny likes to see to things herself. She's got her own particular methods, you know."

Henry did know. Mendbridge was right, he *was* a blockhead. How had he not thought of it? He might have gone to the stables himself and spoken to her. Keeping well out of the way of Rupert of course.

Well, at least she was not wandering round somewhere with Burke.

"Ho!" Mendbridge said, pointing. "There's Burke escorting my sister and Miss Dell."

Damn Burke.

PENNY HAD NOT had any trouble donning the groom's clothes. The pants were odd, as she'd never worn such, but she'd always wondered about them as seeming more convenient. She must only get over the idea that she was not naked, though she felt so. The hat had been more of a challenge. It had taken her quite some time to secure all of her hair inside it. It had been fortunate that Rupert's head was a deal larger than her own or she would never have managed it.

For her plan to succeed, everything must be timed perfectly. She must be the last horse out and running late. She wished the other horses and riders to become irritable in waiting so that the start would not be delayed when she arrived. The less standing around the better. She must also remember to keep her head down and appear natural riding astride. She had ridden that way before, though not that often and not in a very long time. Years ago, she had sometimes dared it on her father's estate, well away from prying eyes. It was not unpleasant, but she could never be comfortable that her riding habit did a spectacularly bad job of covering one of her legs.

She would win the race, at least that was the plan. She would do her best, in any case. She'd never ridden Bucephalus and so could not know the horse's habits. At least she was intimately familiar with the Rowley Mile. She would pace the horse before the dip, not looking for an excessive lead—many a rider had made that mistake only to lose it at the rise. At the dip, she would give the horse its head, gaining momentum downhill and using the saved stamina to take the lead on the uphill. The course was all about pacing and timing.

Once the race was finished, she would not stay to accept any congratulations, but would make her way back to the stables in all haste. Some story could be made up for that, though she did not know what. There, she would change to her own clothes and do her best to get Rupert into the colors. She did not think he would be recovered in that space of time, and that was well. She would claim he'd taken a knock on the head. That was technically true, he'd had a few knocks on the head going down the stairs. As for Rupert himself, he would not remember running the race, but then, he'd had a knock on the head. After all, what could he say about it? That he was certain he'd slept in the tack room, dreaming of zebras, while everybody else had seen him on the track?

Penny opened the tack room door and peered out. The last of the fillies in the race were leaving. Time to saddle up Bucephalus.

"YOU'LL SIT WITH us, Burke?" Lord Mendbridge said, giving a

hand up to Miss Dell. Mrs. Wellburton had already sat herself on the seats above and patted the one next to her for Kitty.

Burke nodded happily. Henry suppressed a grimace. Was there nothing too good for Burke? Why should he not be wandering down amongst the crowd of unwashed farmers?

Henry paused. Mendbridge was exceedingly fond of Burke. He wondered how the old fellow would react when Miss Darlington threw over her idea of marrying Burke and told her father she'd decided for Cabot instead. That was, if she *would* throw over the idea of Burke.

Burke sat himself in the open seat on the other side of Henry. "How do you get on, Cabot?" he asked.

"Quite well," Henry said stiffly. "You?"

"Well enough," Burke said. In a quieter voice he said, "I suppose Dalton and Grayson are wandering around somewhere, though I suspect Grayson will somehow maneuver himself next to Miss Dell."

"I don't find favor with those who secretly maneuver," Henry said.

"I don't see that Grayson makes any secret of it," Burke said, looking at him quizzically.

"All I say is, one should not rest upon one's laurels precipitously. A man should not imagine he has won a lady's heart too soon. Much can change."

Henry knew he should stop speaking immediately. He should have stopped speaking three sentences ago.

Burke's demeanor changed and said heatedly, "I do not know what you think you know about my own situation, but it is…complicated."

This cheered Henry no end. If both of the couple were in favor of an engagement, there would be nothing complicated about it.

"I cannot possibly know the complications of your situation," Henry said. "I only seek to make my own situation a deal *less* complicated. Let the best man prevail, as they say."

"Prevail in what?" Burke asked.

Before Henry could answer him, though he was certain Burke knew full well what he spoke of, an unmistakable voice reached his ears.

"Lord Mendbridge," Grayson said. "How pleasant to encounter you."

"Yes, yes," Lord Mendbridge said in all good humor, "you may join us, you too Dalton. There is plenty of room yet."

As the two men climbed the stands, Mendbridge said, "Hurry now and settle yourselves. The fillies are taking the turf."

Henry's thoughts were taken off Burke and put firmly on the track. Beyond the rails and the sea of men crowding against it, nine horses filed out and spread themselves along the starting point. He stood up, squinting at the distant start. Where was the tenth? Where were his colors?

Rupert was late to the turf? Why? Rupert was never late in coming. He liked to pick his spot, somewhere in the middle of the crowd. He had a theory that a horse went its fastest when it had at least one horse to either side. He would never be late!

My God, had some disaster struck? Was the horse lame?

Mendbridge shook his head. "It seems your filly may have changed her mind," he said softly.

"It cannot be," Henry said.

The horses had reached the starting point, some standing still, some needing to be walked in tight circles to keep them in the right spot.

Mr. Jardins waved the flag for the one-minute warning. Henry stood stock still. The race would start without Bucephalus. Not in a thousand years had it been a circumstance he could have imagined.

As the seconds ticked down and Mr. Jardins loaded his pistol for the start, Henry sank down into his seat. He was ruined.

Mendbridge suddenly grabbed his arm and shook it. "There she is!" he cried.

Henry leapt up. Relief washed over him like a sudden rainstorm. In the distance, there was Rupert, there were his colors.

Bucephalus trotted to the start with only seconds to go.

Mr. Jardins raised his pistol and fired.

They were off.

PENNY HAD TIMED it without a second to spare. Mr. Jardins had looked in her direction with a rather scathing eye, but quickly turned back to the loading of his pistol. The other riders were far too intent on their own horses. She'd worked Bucephalus into the middle of the field, trusting in the other horses' natural inclination to move away from a horse coming amongst them.

She kept her head down until the pistol fired.

Though she did not know Bucephalus, Penny was beginning to quickly become acquainted with her temperament. The horse had been a handful to keep to a walk as they approached the start, the girl's eagerness all too evident. Now that the pistol had been fired, she shot off like a ball from a cannon.

This horse was born to race.

Penny kept her focus on control amidst the thundering hoof-beats on either side of her and the shouts of the crowd ringing in her ears. As they passed the bushes, Lord Canley's Triple Jinx was to her right and running just as her line always did. Jinx and Double Jinx had been known for galloping hell for leather. Triple Jinx had the lead of her, but Penny did not think she'd keep it on the rise. The filly might be fast, but it was doubtful she was a stayer. At least, her line was not known for it.

Lord Philpot's horse, Lady Macedonia, was in front on the outside. This did not concern Penny much—the lord's horses nearly always started well and then fell back. It was almost as if there was some agreement in that line that the start was all that mattered and they might finish how they liked. Lord Philpot was always certain that his next comer was the one who'd work all the way to the finish. Penny hoped he was just as wrong this time as he'd always been in the past.

The rest of the pack had fallen a half-body back. If she could triumph over Triple Jinx and Lady Macedonia she would have it.

Penny could feel Bucephalus straining against her, frustrated that she'd not been given her head. As they approached the dip, Triple Jinx now a full head in front, she let the horse loose.

Bucephalus took full advantage of it.

Horse and rider flew down the dip, gaining on Triple Jinx. Penny felt like she was nearly flying and leaned over the horse's neck to hold her seat. As she had expected, Bucephalus hardly slowed on the rise, so joyful was she to be galloping as fast as she liked.

They gained on Triple Jinx hoofbeat by hoofbeat. The finish was just ahead.

"Go girl, go!" she said in Bucephalus' ear.

Penny could feel the energy and excitement of the horse, Bucephalus gave a final push and overtook Triple Jinx a few yards from the finish.

My God, she'd done it.

HENRY REALIZED HE'D been clutching Lord Mendbridge's sleeve. It had been close, but he was certain Bucephalus and Rupert had edged out Triple Jinx in the final moments. He let go of Mendbridge and waited for the judge to raise the colors of the horse that had come in first.

Impatiently, Henry strained his neck to watch Mr. Talbert sort through the various flags on the turf. Finally, he hauled up the black and green stripe.

As the crowd cheered, Henry sank down in his seat. He had done it. He'd won the race. The pressure of standing upon a cliff and staring down into a morass of debt flew from him. Along with that relief, he silently swore he'd never bet what he did not have ever again in his life. It was one thing to find oneself in high spirits at the end of it, but he would not soon forget the tortuous minutes when things had not looked so certain.

"Deuced strange," Mendbridge said.

"Strange?" Henry asked, a whiff of panic drifting over him. There could not be anything to go wrong now. Please God do not let the results be called into question.

"Your rider does not stop to receive his congratulations," Lord Mendbridge said.

Henry peered down to the turf. Lord Mendbridge was right. Rupert was making his way back toward the stable at a trot. What was the confounded man doing?

"It seems your groom is a less than gracious individual," Lord Mendbridge said, amidst the various people throwing congratulations toward Henry. "One might have thought he'd at least shake hands with Triple Jinx's rider as a battle well fought. Bad form."

"Rupert *is* a less than gracious individual," Henry said. "Though even for him this is a bit far. I think I will go and have a word with him. It will not be too late to congratulate Lord Canley's rider when they reach the stable and I will see that he does so."

Henry jumped down from the stand and pushed his way through the crowd, determined not to be waylaid by those who wished to relive the race with him. He had no idea how he was meant to scold Rupert over anything, but hoped he could coax the man into acting civil. As he now had ample funds to his name, he assumed he'd end up paying for the courtesy.

Did he really care, though? Might he not happily pay Rupert to hand out a thousand polite phrases? They had won!

PENNY HURRIED BUCEPHALUS into the stables, well ahead of the other riders.

She had done what she set out to do, and now she must cover her actions in some believable way.

She leapt off Bucephalus and threw the reins over a post. The horse could be seen to after she was finished with Lord Cabot's groom.

The stables were eerily quiet. She flung open the door to Lord Cabot's tack room and found Rupert asleep just where she'd left him. She hurried out of the groom's clothes and donned her own. Now came the more difficult part.

She'd never pulled off a man's pants in her life and it was about the last thing she liked to be doing at this moment, but there was no other option.

Rupert groaned and opened his eyes. He blinked several times as if to assure himself of what he was looking at.

"Miss?" he said groggily.

Penny made a split-second decision. What else could she do in the current circumstances? Rupert was awake so all thought of dressing him and telling him he'd forgotten the race on account of a bump on his head was over.

"Good," she said, "you're awake. Get dressed quickly, there is not a moment to spare."

Rupert staggered to his feet. "Blast!" he cried. "How could I have fallen asleep? Am I late for the race?"

"Later than you know," Penny said urgently. "Get dressed! Now!"

Rupert became more alert by the second. He grabbed his clothes from the peg, then halted.

"Oh, don't worry!" she said, sensing his reluctance. "I shall turn around."

Penny turned and spoke quickly as she did so. "The race has been run and you are the victor. You returned here quickly as you did not feel well. You hit your head hard before the race and began to feel dizzy at the end of it."

"What?" Rupert said.

"Pay attention!" Penny hissed. "You have won, you hit your head, you are dizzy. You must remember it. If you don't, you may explain to your master how you slept through the race."

"I never—"

"You did," Penny said, turning back around. To her enormous relief, Rupert was dressed. It was just in time, too. She could hear the other riders coming in.

"Lie on the floor if you value your job," she commanded.

Rupert hesitated, then lay down. Penny knew very well that the man's head was spinning from more than laudanum at this point, but she knew not what else to do.

She flung open the door and cried, "Quick, I need help! Lord Cabot's rider has collapsed!"

The riders were just arriving to the stable. It was not a moment before two of them had dismounted and come to her aid. As Rupert lay on the floor, looking as if he had no idea how he got there, Penny said, "He was telling me that his head ached, as he'd hit it hard before the race, and that he felt very dizzy. Then he just collapsed right in front of me."

The two men went to either side of Rupert and gently helped him up by the arms. "Do you think you can walk now? We'll help you to the bench."

"*That's* why you were so late," the other said. "I did wonder over it. One of the stable hands told us all that you were sufferin' from the effects of saffron tea."

"They said one moment you was talkin' of zebras, the next you were asleep. Now we see you woke up and got on your horse, only to fall down. I'd not take the stuff for the worst stomach in the world."

Rupert's eyebrows knit together as if he were trying to make sense of the talk swirling round him.

"Never mind the saffron tea," Penny said hurriedly. She had nearly forgot about that story and she wished everybody else would too. Why must the stable hands be telling all and sundry about it?

"I ought to be sore that you beat me on Triple Jinx," the first said, "but now that I knows you was doin' so poorly and still got on your horse, I can only admire it."

"I *am* doing poorly, I think," Rupert said, his voice tentative.

"Of course you are," Penny said. "You are no doubt concussed. It was very wrong of you to ride in such a condition, you might have fallen off and been killed. But then, I suppose your master has no care for injuries."

"A course they don't," the first rider said sullenly. "Just wait to hear what Lord Philpot will say about me not takin' the win, though I coulda told him she don't have it in her. Them of that line start strong and peter out. Always have done."

The other groom shook his head sadly. "*I* ain't sore you beat me, but Lord Canley will be. I hope your own lord sees the heroics you done today."

Penny breathed a small sigh of relief. Amidst the various complaints about their lords, it seemed nobody would question that Rupert had ridden to victory with a concussion.

Behind her, Penny heard a voice she knew all too well. "What goes on here?" Lord Cabot asked.

CHAPTER FOURTEEN

PENNY FELT HERSELF go ice cold at the sound of Lord Cabot's voice. It was one thing to bamboozle the grooms, and another to fool Lord Cabot. Still, she could not back down now. She turned, determined to control the flow of information in this unusual scene. "Your groom fell and hit his head very hard before the race. I believe he may have even experienced some moments of unconsciousness. He was able to rouse himself in time and bravely rode your horse, though he was exceedingly dizzy by the end of it. He collapsed to the ground right in front of me."

The two riders nodded sagely at this account.

"Good Lord, Rupert," Lord Cabot said. "Are you all right?"

Rupert stared at the ground and said, "I can't rightly say I'm feelin' tip-top at this moment, my lord."

"I did wonder why you turned up so late and then returned to the stables so quickly..." Lord Cabot trailed off.

"Wonder no more," Penny said. "What he needs is quiet and rest, that is the only thing to be done for such a mishap, as you know yourself, Lord Cabot. These two fine gentlemen will rub down Bucephalus, I am sure they would not mind."

The men both nodded. "Like one of our own," one of them said. "Though I won't say nothin' to Lord Philpot of the situation."

"Lord Cabot," Penny said hurriedly, lest one of the men

happen upon the subject of saffron tea, "you should have your groom transported back to Mendbridge Cottage. Mrs. Payne will look after him and the doctor can see to him. Doctor Prentiss is likely already there. For another reason."

Then Penny turned and stared hard at Rupert. "All will end well, as long as everybody does as they are told. Come now, none of us have all day."

⟫⟫⟫⟪⟪⟪

PENNY HAD CHECKED on Bella and Zephyrus before she left the stables. They were both in good order and she paid one of the stable's grooms to check on them every hour and send immediate word if either of them took a turn. She did not think it likely after so many hours, but it was well to be certain.

She'd sent another groom with a note for her father, explaining that Doom had been injured and Zephyrus would not race. She was returning to the cottage to oversee Doom's care. This sort of news might have alarmed her father, but she had phrased everything so vaguely and he would be so intent on the races, that she thought he would not be overly discomposed. As his favorite horse was running in the next, she suspected her note would eventually flutter to his feet, all but forgotten.

She'd left in her phaeton as Lord Cabot oversaw the care of his groom. Rupert had been changed back out of his colors as they waited for his own carriage.

At the house, she found Doom with his arm set. Dr. Prentiss called it a clean break that should mend well, barring any infection. Two polished lengths of wood had been placed on either side of the injured arm and secured with bandaging. The bone setting itself had been a bit of an ordeal, as Doom was inclined to fight any pulling of his arm. The doctor had finally dosed the boy with laudanum and Penny found him just as nonsensical as Rupert under the influence of it.

The only thing she found she must correct was Doom's location. She thought he'd be more comfortable in a bedchamber in the house, but he'd been complaining about it ever since he'd been put there. He wished to have Mrs. Payne care for him, and so he was carefully moved to her cottage.

Penny had asked the doctor to stay on for the arrival of Lord Cabot's groom and his alleged concussion. She'd then run down to the kitchens and put Mrs. Lowell on notice—if Freddy were to have the nerve to turn up at the back door again, she was to have the footmen seize him and tie him up. He would be turned over to the magistrate. Mrs. Lowell had been shocked over the idea, but hadn't pressed Penny for the particulars. The cook had only sighed and muttered that excellent grocers were not exactly falling from the trees and now she'd have to go crawling back to Mr. Slincher.

Having done everything she could do about this frightful day, Penny retired to her room and sank down into the chair by the window.

Nothing had gone the way it had been supposed to. Her dear Bella had been nearly poisoned, her tiger's arm broken, and…there was the other thing. The race.

Why had she done it? Why had she not just left Rupert to snore away in the tack room and Bucephalus remain in her stall? Why had she risked so much to keep Lord Cabot out of trouble?

Was she never to have done with what might have been?

Penny laughed bitterly. She was in love with a ghost, a phantom, an apparition. She was not in love with the real man, only the ephemeral being she had chosen to believe in. *That* imagined person had no more existed than a hero in a novel—pleasant to think about but not at all real.

This foolishness did not bode well for her future. How was she to marry some sensible fellow who would give her a life, and give her children, if she were forever mooning over a fantasy?

She was Marianne Dashwood, pining over a dashing and disinterested Willoughby that had never been! Marianne

Dashwood was a foolish ninny! So foolish that Penny had not even bothered to finish the book. She probably should have finished it. Penny Darlington was just as foolish as Marianne and she would have at least read about the awful price the girl paid for her idiocy.

The sounds of a carriage rolling up the drive reached her ears. Unwillingly, her feet took her to the window.

There he was. Lord Cabot, driving the carriage with Rupert sitting by his side.

She must trust that Rupert had the sense to keep his thoughts to himself. She thought he would. After all, he would have been roundly congratulated on his victory many times over. She did not think the man would argue that he'd slept through the entire thing. He might even begin to believe he did not remember a thing about the race on account of a concussion. Perhaps he would suppose that Miss Darlington ordering him to get dressed had been a fevered dream.

Lord Cabot must never know what she'd done. It would be too humiliating! For him to know to what lengths she'd gone to protect him must reveal her very stupid feelings.

She could not bear it. Whether he married Kitty or someone else, she could not bear that he grew smug over having affected her in any manner.

She must leave Mendbridge Cottage. Newmarket held no further charm for her. Tonight was the club ball and she would never get out of it. An appearance there would be far too important to her father. But tomorrow. She could leave then. She was all but certain that neither her aunt nor Kitty would be against the plan. She well knew how to convince her father, her dear father who found women such a complete mystery.

She would go home to Devon. Home to Devon's gentle countryside, and the neighborhood she understood so well. Kitty's estate was not five miles from her own and they could spend the summer as they always did—Kitty could stay with her or she would stay with Kitty. Penny would ride in the mornings, and then in the afternoons she and Kitty would walk and picnic and sit by sunny streams. She would heal herself in the peace of Devon. Bella and Doom would both be happy there. They would all heal, and then she would come back whole again for a third season. A third season that must be her final season.

She would arrive to town with a sensible eye. An eye toward marriage with a sensible individual. They would have a sensible marriage and produce sensible children. He might even have a keen interest in horses, or at least not care about how keen of an interest she took in them. She might be happy, or if not happy, then content.

She must only get through this evening.

DOOM HAD FOUGHT Doctor Prentiss like a feral cat. He felt sorry over it now, as he knew full well the fellow had only been trying to help him. On the other hand, his lack of compliance had resulted in being dosed with laudanum, a substance heretofore unknown to him. He could not say he'd like the feeling if he needed to be on his feet, he was not even certain he *could* be on his feet just now, but it had done wonders for his aching arm.

None of them in the house had understood why he'd been so stubborn on the idea that he couldn't stay there. Mrs. Wiggins had taken personal offense to the idea that Mrs. Payne was to be considered superior.

The fact was, Mrs. Payne *was* superior. Doom had only ever had vague ideas of what mothering was, but he'd discovered it from her, bit by bit. She *would* wipe his chin when he dribbled something on it. She *would* scold Petit for working him too hard when she thought he looked tired. She *would* straighten his cap or iron his shirt so he looked presentable. Of course, he always pretended to fight off such attentions, but that was only to protect his dignity.

Mrs. Lowell was kind, always giving him biscuits and cakes, and Mrs. Wiggins was pleasant enough. But nobody took an interest in him like Mrs. Payne did.

Much to his relief, Mr. Montrose and Mrs. Wiggins had given in to him and he'd been carried to Mrs. Payne's cottage.

What a fuss Mrs. Payne had made at the sight of him! He'd been put into her own bedchamber, on her enormous bed piled high with goose down mattresses. He'd never lain on a bed that big and soft in his life—four men might be comfortable in it. His pillows had been fluffed and tea and biscuits brought to him on a tray. Mrs. Payne was to sleep on the sofa in her sitting room and said she'd be at the ready to see to his every need.

It had all been exceedingly comfortable, until Rupert had been brought in. Now, the gruff old fellow was in the bed with him and Doctor Prentiss was asking him a slew of questions.

"How hard did you hit your head?" the doctor asked, holding a candle in front of his face and peering into his eyes.

"I don't rightly know," Rupert said. "I don't remember."

The doctor felt around Rupert's scalp. "My God, man," he said, "you've got three lumps—how many times did you fall down?"

"I don't remember," Rupert said.

"Well," Doctor Prentiss said, setting the candle down and rubbing his chin, "your pupils are even, but your lack of memory is a concern. You ought not to be moved for the time being. Stay as still as you can, head raised. I'll look in again on the morrow."

Doom quietly sighed. Now he was to share a bed, and Mrs. Payne's attentions, with gruff old Rupert. He had no idea how the man had managed to fall down so many times, but he found it very inconvenient.

FREDDY HAD BEEN at the rails next to Mr. Farthingale for the start of the race. He'd been exceedingly hopeful that their plan had succeeded when Lord Cabot's horse did not come to the start with the other horses. Even when he'd spotted the rider's colors coming out in the nick of time, he'd held out hope that he'd done enough to swing things their way.

It had seemed it would be so, right to the very end. It looked uncomfortably close, but Triple Jinx would prevail.

Until the horses hit the rise. Triple Jinx slowed and Bucephalus gained.

As he watched the disaster unfold, and watched the expression on his master's face at the sight of it, Freddy slowly backed up. His only hope now was to get away, to slip into the crowd, never to be seen again.

Mr. Farthingale would be ruined. Mr. Farthingale might just kill him over it.

The moneylending game had always been risky and now the bets ran against them.

He'd known the whole thing was too risky, even if Mr. Farthingale had not. Freddy had not liked the plan one bit. It was all well and good to lend funds to the swells so they might throw it away how they liked, but poisoning and drugging were something else altogether! And then, he was sure he'd broken that boy's arm. A boy no older than himself, probably just trying to make his way in the world.

He wondered if the boy had made it back to the stables, or if he languished in the woods somewhere. If he made it back, what story did he tell? Were men even now looking for someone of his description?

Worse, what if the boy lost his arm on account of it? Could he ever forgive himself for that? And what of Mrs. Lowell? What would that kind lady think of him when she heard the tale?

Freddy blushed as he imagined the good lady discovering there had never been a grocer named Mr. Cumberbald.

No, the game had been comfortable when they'd sat in London pushing papers around. He'd jumped at the chance to apprentice with Mr. Farthingale. He'd delighted in the idea that the two of them were very cool customers—never ruffled and always getting the best of any transaction. He'd not felt an ounce of pity for Mackery and had laughed when he thought of the fellow's surprise at being dunned in Italy under the nose of his contessa. *This*, though, was not the life for him.

Freddy had not, until that moment, been aware that he harbored any particular sensibilities. As it turned out, he did.

It was time to start anew, far from here. Far from anywhere Mr. Farthingale might be. He'd pick up some line of work that didn't involve breaking arms and poisoning horses.

But, before he slipped onto a ship to the Americas or wherever he decided to go, he would just have a look around that wood to be sure the young groom had gotten away. He might even leave a letter for Mrs. Lowell if he had time to write it.

He ducked and weaved through the crowd as Bucephalus crossed the finish. He was out of sight before Mr. Farthingale turned to look for him.

➤➤➤◄◄◄

"I HAVE WATCHED more horses run by me today than I ever care to again," Kitty said, laughing.

Penny had seen the carriage arrive with Kitty and her aunt and had pinched her cheeks and forced a smile for Kitty's inevitable arrival to her room.

"I am certain it was never your favored way to spend a day," Penny said as Kitty threw herself on the bed. "My aunt and my father were no doubt grateful for your company."

"I would not know," Kitty said, "as there was little time to converse with them. Lord Grayson was far too busy dominating the talk with nonsense."

Penny nodded, certain that Lord Grayson had made himself an enormous pest. "How did my father get on?" she asked, knowing well that his wins and his losses would affect him greatly.

"Two won their races, one came in third, and one is to go on the morrow, or so your father said. He has very high hopes for that one, though I pray he does not have need of my company again. But you, Penny," Kitty said, looking at her quizzically. "Your father said your horse would not race. I was sorry for that, I know you looked forward to it."

"Yes, well, my rider injured his arm and there could never be found a replacement on such short notice."

"That is a terrible shame. I pray it is not serious?"

"The doctor has been in and says it will mend in time," Penny said, not wishing to go into any detail about the nature of the injury.

"That is good news, in any event."

"But Kitty, I know you do not enjoy these activities and I find I have also lost interest just now. Would you care terribly if we were to go home?"

"Not at all, if you wish it," Kitty said. She took Penny's hand. "My dear friend, I think it is not only the races you wish to be parted from so eagerly. Am I right in thinking you would not mind seeing the back of Lord Cabot?"

Penny nodded. There was no need to apprise Kitty of all of the circumstance, but it was pointless to hide what her friend had already surmised. Though, she could not dismiss that it might be Kitty herself who would not wish to be off so soon. She had no interest in horses, but might she not have some small interest in Lord Cabot? An interest that might grow when he revealed himself a scholar? Kitty had laughed off the idea, but Penny well knew how easy it might be to succumb to the man's charms.

"We may put it off if you wish it," Penny said. "I would not for the world pull you away if, well…"

"Well what?" Kitty asked, appearing genuinely perplexed.

"Lord Cabot, Kitty. As you know, he has an interest and when he shows you that you are both more similar than you thought…and well, his person is attractive, there is no getting round that. I only say—"

"I beg you not to say, dearest Penny," Kitty said, laughing. "I can assure you that I have less than no interest in the ox head. He might recite Gilgamesh from memory and I would not be moved."

Penny did not see how Kitty would not be interested, but she could perceive that her friend was resolute against the idea. At least for now.

"I only hope my aunt is as agreeable to the scheme," Penny said. "And then, of course, my father."

Kitty rested her chin in her hand as she did when she thought something through. "We will divide our forces," she said. "*I* will speak with your aunt and *you* will speak with your father. By the end of it, we will have everybody convinced that we must be gone."

Penny was vastly relieved. "I was hoping we might set off on the morrow. There is still time, I think, to pack and alert the stable to have the carriages ready. Petit can see to the transport of Bella and Zephyrus when the races conclude. He will see that Doom is cared for and transported home carefully. I trust him as I trust myself."

"I will manage your aunt, and of course Mr. Petit will see to Doom. But, do not ask me to weigh in with an opinion on the horses. I have had far too much of horses this day."

"As I feel, surprisingly," Penny said. "I would rather skip the ball as well, but that would disappoint my father far too much. It is the one ball of the season he actually enjoys."

Kitty put hands on hips. "We will dress, we will dance, we will sleep, and then we will set out for Devon."

Penny smiled. It was so very like Kitty to attack a plan with such confidence. She paused as she recalled something that might put Kitty off the scheme.

"I must tell you though, Kitty, that I have done this trip before with my aunt. She has a particular route she would take that you may find burdensome. First a few days' stop in London, though it be out of our way, then to Bath, and then Devon. She has many friends in Bath so count on *at least* three days stop. Especially since Mr. Thornbridge intends to make his way there in a day or two. With all the zigs and zags, we shall be traveling for over a fortnight."

"I do not mind it at all," Kitty said with enthusiasm. "I quite enjoy viewing new scenery and I adore your house in Bath. In any case, the lure of Bath will likely encourage your aunt to acquiesce. How you shall persuade your father, on the other hand, I know not."

Penny smiled. "Do not fret on that score. I know exactly what to talk about that he never wishes talked about."

THE SUN WAS beginning to set as Freddy finally gave up searching the wood for Miss Darlington's groom. He wished to believe that the fellow had gotten to safety, but how could he be certain? He wished to believe the boy still had ownership of that arm, but how could he know? He was not at all comfortable with the idea that he might have to wonder about it forevermore.

His ideas about self-preservation told him he ought to get far away from Newmarket. Mr. Farthingale would be looking for him even now, especially as he'd relieved the man of the money he kept hidden in a cleverly sewn pocket inside a boot in his room at the tavern. It wasn't a fortune and had been risky to leave there, even in a locked room. But it had been even more risky to have it on one's person at the races.

Mr. Farthingale would know instantly that he'd taken it, and his fury would reach new heights. He'd be watching the road to London, hoping to come upon his feckless apprentice. What he would do if he found him, Freddy shuddered to think.

A ruined man with nothing to lose might be counted on to do

any outrage.

He could slip by Farthingale's net easily enough, of that he was confident. He might stay off the roads and keep to the fields and woods. After all, Mr. Farthingale could not be everywhere and so the chances of escape would run in his favor.

He just must see with his own eyes how the boy got on.

He set off across the farmer's field, in the direction of Mendbridge Cottage.

THOUGH DOOM HAD not been enthused to have Rupert as his bedmate, or to share Mrs. Payne with the fellow, laudanum and a good dinner had gone some way to soothing his irritation. Rupert had equally been made comfortable and was not half as gruff as he'd been when he arrived.

As the wind blew heavy outside and the soothing sounds of leaves and branches blowing drifted around them, they had a desultory conversation. They spoke low in the dark room. Though it was just after sunset, Mrs. Payne had ordered them both asleep and had taken the candle with her.

Doom supposed it was the laudanum talking, as he was not usually known as a chatterer, but he'd gone and told Rupert the whole of what had occurred that morning. How a lad named Freddy had attempted to poison Bella and then broken his arm when he was chased.

"The wretch," Rupert said of Freddy, "he ought to swing for it."

"I reckon so," Doom said, "though I don't know why he done it. Was he after Zephyrus? Bella was not even to race, why bother with her?"

"Maybe Zephyrus, maybe another," Rupert said. "I'll think a scoundrel such as that is none too quick in the mind. If he was, he'd be doin' an honest day's work."

Doom had not considered the idea that Freddy had not been after *either* of Miss Darlington's horses. Was the fellow really that stupid to have made such a vast mistake?

No. Freddy was not so stupid. If the fellow had made a mistake, it could only have been that he could not tell one horse from another. The two horses that looked most alike were…Bella and Bucephalus. They were so alike, that even Miss Darlington had once confused them. If one did not know to look for the five white hairs on her withers…

And then, Bucephalus had been in the other field, not conveniently in a stall labeled with Lord Cabot's name on it.

And here was Rupert, with a bang on the head and no memory of the race!

Had Freddy snuck up behind him and clobbered him?

"Do you happen to remember anybody hitting you over the head?" Doom asked.

Rupert was silent for some moments, the only sound the rushing wind outside. "No," he said, "I remember making my tea, then I remember Miss Darlington standing over me and tellin' me I won. First race I ever won without noticing."

The tea! Doom thought back to the vial in the pouch he'd recovered from the wood. The pouch Freddy had been so eager to get rid of. Maybe that brown substance was some sedative meant for the rider? Had it gone into Rupert's tea somehow?

But then, if Rupert had really been drugged, who had ridden Bucephalus?

Like a horse pounding across the finish line, it came to him.

Miss Darlington. Great blazes, Miss Darlington had ridden that horse. Nobody else could have stepped in and won so handily. *That's* why she'd been standing over Rupert when he awoke. *That's* why he couldn't remember riding at all.

Doom sat up, careful to hold his broken arm still between the splints. It was a remarkable conclusion, though he was certain he was right. He only did not know what to do with the information.

Perhaps he ought to just keep it to himself. Sometimes buttoned lips were better than flappin' lips.

Doom heard scratching at the window. A face appeared, staring at him.

It was Freddy.

CHAPTER FIFTEEN

P ENNY HAD DRESSED for the ball and gone down early, assured
that she would find her father in the drawing room. There
was a sideboard stocked with wines and port in that room, and
Lord Mendbridge was likely to be nearby it. It had always been
his habit to indulge in a glass before they set off for any kind of
party. He called it *mankind's great lubricant,* and said it made
people appear more pleasant and interesting than they actually
were.

She was sorry to have to discompose him while he engaged in
that comfortable habit, but she must gain her aim. She'd already
asked Petit to have the carriages ready at dawn. He would assume
Lord Mendbridge knew all about the plan.

"Penny!" her father said, surprised to see her down so early.
"Do not tell me you have decided to join me in a glass?"

"I have not," she said. "Though I would speak with you on a
particular matter."

Her father patted the seat next to him.

"I found myself very out of sorts today," she said.

Lord Mendbridge nodded sagely. "I do not doubt it. I've had
my own trials and tribulations when I could not run a horse. A
terrible blow to people like us."

"Indeed it was, though my note earlier did not go into particular detail. Someone attempted to poison Bella with deadly

nightshade. A grocer's boy, in fact, though who hired him I do not know. Doom chased the boy and that is how he injured his arm."

Seeing the look of dire concern in her father's expression, she hurried on. "Bella is well-recovered and Doom will heal right as rain according to the doctor."

"We ought to find the scoundrel, though," Lord Mendbridge said. "We ought to speak to the club about it. These things cannot be tolerated!" The lord paused, and said quieter, "Though what can the scoundrel have wanted with Bella? She was not even registered to race."

Penny did not wish her father to examine the situation too closely, lest he seize upon the idea that Bucephalus had been the real target and began wondering about the story of that horse's rider having a concussion.

"I think it pointless to pursue, Papa," she said hurriedly. "The boy will be long gone by now and we will never know his purpose. I think it best that we set our sights on prevention in future, more than anything else. Perhaps some burly guards for the stables?"

"Yes," Lord Mendbridge said, always happy to think of an action he might take. "The burliest, if I have anything to say about it."

"In any case," Penny said, now coming to the part that would alarm her father far more than deadly nightshade could ever do, "I find the entire situation has brought on some…womanly problems."

At the mention of womanly problems, Lord Mendbridge fairly leapt from his seat. Penny bit her lip to stop a smile, the poor man looked as if he feared catching one of those womanly problems. He might not have the first idea of what they were, but he could fear them all the same. She'd often wondered what on earth her mother had ever told him of it. Whatever it had been, she'd painted a terrifying picture.

"Say no more, child!" he said. "Whatever it is you wish, you must have it. We need not speak of it further!"

"Indeed, Father," Penny said, pressing on, "the only thing that will help at all is to be home. I am sure my aunt will not mind and Kitty most definitely does not. I thought to set off on the morrow."

"And you think," Lord Mendbridge said slowly, "that is the only solution?"

"Oh yes, I know it. My aunt will agree, I am sure."

"Then it is settled," Lord Mendbridge said. "We'll say no more about it."

"What is settled?" Lord Cabot asked.

Penny turned. When had he even come into the room? What was he doing, stealing into their drawing room like a panther?

Lord Mendbridge turned very red in the face. "Did you not hear, Cabot? I just *said* we will not say any more about it!"

✦≫≫✕≪≪✦

DOOM COULD BARELY believe his eyes. It might well be the laudanum playing tricks. There was no possibility that Freddy was at the window. In fact, he had fairly convinced himself of it until Rupert sat up and said, "Who is that? What does he do, peering in here like that?"

Doom was silent for a moment, not sure how he should answer. Had Freddy come to finish him off? Should he raise the alarm, or would that put Mrs. Payne in danger somehow?

His ideas that Freddy might have arrived with some nefarious purpose dwindled to nothing as he noted the boy's face. He was white as a sheet, shivering, and looked as if he'd seen a ghost.

Whatever his purpose for coming, Doom did not think this shell of a boy could overpower him through a window, broken arm or not.

"Sshhh," he whispered to Rupert, and slipped out of bed. He cracked the window, the sudden influx of cool night air blowing his hair back.

"What do ya do here, you villain?" Doom asked.

Freddy handed a small pouch through the window. Doom took it with his good hand. He could feel through the fabric that it was coin.

"That's all I got in the world," Freddy said. "I never did set out to break your arm, though I'm glad to see ya still got it. I never wanted to do nothin' to horses neither. Mr. Farthingale's got Lord Cabot tied up for three hundred guineas and he thought he'd make the horse lose and he bet against her to take an even bigger profit. He's a scoundrel and I left him. Tell Mrs. Lowell I be heartily sorry over my part of it and she bakes the best cakes I ever tasted."

Doom saw in an instant how it was. He'd seen it a hundred times on the streets of London. A boy desperate for a protector, for a roof and a bed and hot food, took up with anybody that'd have him. The boy then finds he's got to look the other way at any unsavory activities. Then the boy finds he's *doing* the unsavory activities. He'd almost been drawn into that kind of situation himself. George Semple, that old rogue, had fed him a mutton chop and a glass of ale, and promised more to come. If only Doom would perfect his skill as a pickpocket.

"So you was after Bucephalus and got Bella instead," he whispered.

"Yes, no, I don't know who I got," Freddy whispered back.

"Ya got the wrong horse, you numbskull."

"Is she all right, though?"

"Aye. Now what did ya do to old Rupert, there?" Doom asked, hooking a thumb over his shoulder.

Freddy stood on tiptoes and peered into the room, looking very surprised to see Rupert in the bed.

"Laudanum in his teacup afore he got there," Freddy whispered.

Rupert, who now struggled to sit up, said, "Well? Who is it? What does he want? Why don't he come in the front door like normal folk?"

"Take your money and be off with ya," Doom said, handing the pouch back to Freddy. "I won't tell nobody I seen you. Be more careful on who you decide to work for next time."

Freddy smiled and disappeared from view. Doom shut the window just as Mrs. Payne came bustling into the room.

"What's all this noise I'm a-hearin' when you're meant to be asleep? Doom, what do you do by the window instead of tucked under the blankets?"

"It blew open is all," Doom said smoothly.

"That dang window!" Mrs. Payne said. "It's done that to me on occasion and what with the wind blowin' I suppose it ain't no surprise. Back in bed with ya, I'll fasten her up tight."

"That's all it was," Doom said, staring at Rupert. "The wind."

"Course it was the wind, my little monkey," Mrs. Payne said in all good humor. "Don't be conjurin' your imagination and thinkin' up ghosts and ghouls a-tryin' to get in."

"Absolutely not," Doom said. "There was nobody at the window."

Rupert sank back on his pillow and stared at the rafters. "I really *ain't* right in the head. I coulda swore...what in blazes am I gonna imagine next?"

JARVIS HAD DRESSED Lord Cabot with particular care. He was not privy as to why this ball was more important than any other ball, but his master had made clear that it was. The lord had been so persnickety over his neckcloth that Jarvis wondered if he'd somehow woken up and discovered himself in Lord Grayson's employ.

He supposed it had something to do with it being at the club and hosting every well-known horseman in England.

Now, the valet had managed to get his lord on his way out

the door and he took himself down to the kitchens. Jarvis would rather not visit that unwelcome place, but he would not get tea otherwise. As usual, the seats around the table were taken and a lone chair was placed in a corner, as far from the fire as possible. Mrs. Lowell would not outright refuse him his tea, but it would somehow be lukewarm when it reached him.

The household regarded him sullenly. He sullenly regarded them back. Mrs. Lowell shoved a teacup at him.

Miss Darlington's maid, Dora, sniffed in his direction. She said, "We'll all be glad to see the last of him, is all I say."

Jarvis was perfectly aware that he was the *him* in question, though Lord Cabot was not scheduled to leave the house for another week. The mongrels had been hinting at their delight at never seeing him again ever since he'd arrived.

"The coach will be ready at six," Mr. Montrose said gravely. Jarvis supposed now even Montrose was to join in the battering of his person. Was this some broad hint that he and his lord should be *in* the said carriage?

"None too early, neither," Dora said. "A lady what's seen the true temperament of a particular gentleman don't want the acquaintance to linger. Once that terrible temperament is known, well…it's *known*."

Jarvis tightened his grip on his teacup. His true temperament, as she called it, was very good. Everybody said so. Except in this blasted house.

And since when was Dora to be known as a lady? She might be a washerwoman for all her manners!

"The worst of it is," a kitchen maid said, "what he said not even be true!"

"You are correct," Dora said. "The gentleman has shown himself to be terrible *and* wrong! He injured a lady who is so good and she still suffers over it! A lady what is an angel still cries over it! He showed his true colors and he ought to be very sorry for it!"

Jarvis pressed his lips together. He'd never been terrible and wrong in his life. As to injuring a *lady*? He rather thought not.

While Montrose raised his hand to caution Dora, Jarvis decided he'd had just about enough of these people. He drained his tea and stood. "I am not terrible or wrong and you are no lady! Much less an angel! Whatever I have said, it was well-earned and you may keep your injured feelings to yourself! I don't know who you think you've called a carriage for, but *I* will not be in it!"

Jarvis strode out, feeling a sense of great victory. It had been a vigorous defense against their spurious attacks. Oh, he had launched some scathing comments toward them before this moment, but *now* they felt the entire wrath of his true feelings!

Behind him, the kitchen maid said, "Why's the rube think we be talkin' about *him*?"

Jarvis continued walking. Let them try to backtrack if they would. Let them realize they'd gone too far and he'd cut them down to size. *He* knew they spoke of him, and he'd let *them* know he knew.

Rube, indeed.

THE SEASON BEFORE, Penny had been surprised by the club's ballroom. It was not more splendorous than other ballrooms she'd found herself in, in fact it was rather less so. It had taken her awhile to pinpoint why it seemed so different, until she had realized it was the manliness of it. A London ballroom was always the purview of the lady of the house. One could count on pale colors and airy lightness. This ballroom, with its dark-paneled walls and hint of tobacco and leather in the air, was all man. It felt as if one had tiptoed into a gentlemen's club. She supposed they had done just that, as the ballroom was, on any other day, the coffee room. It would be the scene of cards and bets and raucous male laughter. It was only on this one night of the year that the tables and chairs had been taken away and dancing would be the preferred activity.

Penny had been grateful that her aunt and Kitty had not delayed their departure from the house. She'd gone downstairs early to convince her father that she must be off on the morrow, and that had been speedily done. But then, Lord Cabot had come in at the end of the conversation and this had put her father out enormously. Penny was certain Lord Cabot had no notion of why he had been shouted at, but *she* did. Her father had deemed the matter settled. Lord Cabot had inquired over what had been settled. The notion of having to explain anything at all associated with womanly problems had pushed her dear father over the edge.

The drawing room had gone on tense and silent afterward and thankfully it did not go on long. Kitty had tripped in with her usual cheerfulness and complimented her father on one of his horses. That, and a generous glass of port, had gone a good way to soothing Lord Mendbridge's ruffled feathers.

Dear Kitty had also been successful in convincing her aunt that they should be off and away from Newmarket at first light. Mrs. Wellburton had been exceedingly cheerful over it as they rode in the carriage. It seemed she believed Penny to be put out about not being able to take part in the race, she was not at all sorry to go, and was happy to note that Mr. Thornbridge also planned to be in Bath so they would likely see him there. Her own interests were so thoroughly engaged in the scheme that she was as satisfied as she might have been had it been her own idea.

They had entered the club amidst half of Newmarket standing on the street and cheering their arrival. Unlike a London ball, where footmen would chase away any gawkers, it was a tradition for all and sundry to welcome those arriving to the club for the ball. Of course, leaving was another matter. At that point in the night many a man lounging in the street would be the worse for drink and *would* be chased off, lest they become too impertinent. For now, though, the crowd was of a happy temperament.

Penny handed over her cloak and had been given her card. Mrs. Wellburton was soon spotted by Mr. Thornbridge and he hurried to her. Penny and Kitty left their party still in the hall, as her father and Lord Cabot had been besieged with congratulations from admiring gentlemen. Penny sniffed over the idea. Lord Cabot had done nothing to earn such accolades. If the truth were known, it would be herself congratulated. Still, she supposed she must be grateful that the truth was *not* known.

Once she and Kitty entered the ballroom, they were near surrounded by hopeful gentlemen. Unlike a usual ball, where half the unattached men could be counted on to arrive late, most of the gentlemen were staying at the club and had only to walk downstairs. Penny knew from her father that the club considered it bad form to turn up tardy to it. Not even Lord Grayson was given leave to delay over some perceived imperfection in his neckcloth.

Her card filled rapidly, some by gentlemen she was acquainted with and some who had just arranged a hasty introduction. She must feel the compliment of it, and never more than when she had so recently wondered if she were careening into spinsterhood. Though, as seemed to be becoming usual, she could not say she was delighted with some of the gentlemen. Lord Grayson had taken the first and Lord Dalton had taken supper. At least Lord Burke was in the mix and would interrupt the dreariness.

Kitty was no less popular, though she had initially wondered if she ought not stay at home, as her parents had not been asked about this particular entertainment. Lord Mendbridge had scoffed at the notion. The ball was not to be over-large and he could personally vouch for the respectability and behavior of the club's members. The matter had been happily settled and Kitty had dressed.

Kitty's parents need not worry over even a hint of impropriety, Penny was certain. Though Kitty was sought after, by none more than the persistent Lord Grayson, she would not lose her head. Penny supposed Lord Cabot might choose the moment to gain his aim with Miss Dell, but he'd have a steep hill to climb to convince her he was not, in fact, an ox head. He might be exceedingly learned, but he had done far too fine a job at hiding it.

As Penny stood talking to various gentlemen, she kept one eye on the door. She knew very well she looked to see when the ox head would finally make his way in. She had fairly resigned herself to being an idiot. After all, she could not at once claim that she was full of good sense and also that she'd ridden his horse to victory that morning. She could not say that she was a sensible individual, and had also rescued a man who had been cruel to her and was now intent on securing her friend, either for love of her or her money. Those things were so diametrically opposed as to cause her logical mind to throw up its hands in despair of reason.

She was a fool, a Marianne Dashwood, and she well knew it. However, she would regain her composure and her spirits in Devon. That was what she must keep her thoughts on. This night might seem endless, but it would only last so many hours. At dawn, she would be off. She was determined to get into the coach and not look back. This nonsense must end.

Lord Cabot entered the ballroom. Penny's heart fluttered, as it did whenever he suddenly presented himself. She did not condemn herself over it, she was long past that, but only sympathized with her poor heart and assured it that the infirmity would not last.

He made straight for her and held out his hand. "Miss Darlington, if I might?"

She handed over her card. The last dance of the evening was free and she supposed he would be determined to take it, out of deference to her father. He need not, her father would be entirely incognizant of anything but the various conversations he would have with other men about the races.

Lord Cabot stared at her card, his expression showing his consternation. "Grayson for the first? Dalton for supper?"

Penny did not see how she would be expected to answer such comments, and so said nothing. Lord Cabot hastily put down his name in the last remaining spot. He stormed off in the direction of Lord Dalton.

DESPITE MRS. PAYNE insisting that they ought to be asleep, Doom and Rupert had convinced her that they could only begin to think about dozing off if they had tea and something to eat. As much as the lady put her faith in sleep as the great restorative, she could not be easy with the idea of anybody in her sphere of influence going hungry. She'd bustled about in her kitchen and brought in a large tray of tea, biscuits, cold ham, rolls, mustard, pickled beets, two large slices of cake, and her legendary fishpaste sandwiches.

Since then, Doom and Rupert had worked their way through everything edible, except for the beets, which neither of them could abide. Mrs. Payne's regular and thunderous snores drifted in from the parlor.

Doom had been at once this way and then the other way over whether to tell Rupert the truth of what had happened to him at the races. If it were himself, he'd desperately want to know it. On the other hand, Doom would never reveal anything that might hurt Miss Darlington.

He decided to test the waters.

"Rupert," he said, dusting the crumbs from his nightshirt, "now that you've had time to recover and think it over, have you managed to piece together what happened this morning?"

Rupert ate the last bite of cake with considerable relish and said, "I see flashes of scenes in my mind, they come on all sudden-like. Just a minute ago, I remembered that I was talkin' to the other fellas about zebras. I seen a sketch of 'em once in a book and I got it in my mind that I ought to ride them."

"At the Royal Menagerie?" Doom asked.

"No, Africa," Rupert said. "Though now that I'm thinkin' on it, I reckon it would take months to even get there."

"What else do you remember?" Doom asked casually.

"It's not so much what I remember or don't," Rupert said, "as it is things that don't add up. How is it I remember talkin' of zebras, but I don't remember an entire race? Not a shred of memory of saddlin' up Bucephalus or going out there or comin' back. One minute I'm ridin' zebras and the next Miss Darlington is standin' over me…."

Doom watched Rupert with interest. The fellow's expression was disconcerting, almost as if he'd received a great shock.

"That's it!" Rupert said. "I couldn't have rode that horse!"

Doom's hand tightened on his teacup. "Why do you say so?" he asked.

"On account of rememberin' Miss Darlington ordering me into my colors. I was just into them when the boys came in. *After* the race. If I'd tried to ride without the colors, I'd a been thrown off the turf. I can't suppose I had 'em on, then took 'em off, then put 'em back on again, all in the space of minutes now can I?"

Doom was beginning to think he'd have to tell Rupert the whole story. It might be the only way to convince the man not to go spouting off about not being in his colors until after the race.

"But," Rupert sputtered, "somebody rode her. If it weren't me, who was it? Why do they not claim it?"

Doom took in a deep breath. "Rupert," he said, "I'm gonna tell you the facts of the case, but you got to keep the information close. If it were known, it'd cause…a lot of problems."

Rupert set down his teacup and said, "Well?"

A half hour later, Doom had finished with the tale of how Rupert came to be congratulated for riding a horse he'd never ridden.

"But Miss Darlington?" Rupert whispered. "Why would she…"

Doom nodded sagely. Though the whole house was ranged against Lord Cabot, and it was supposed that Miss Darlington despised him, he had come to the only conclusion possible. There could only be one reason the lady had dared to ride for the lord.

"Love," Rupert said musingly. "It do strange things to people."

CHAPTER SIXTEEN

PENNY WAS EAGER to see the end of this ball. As she had expected, Lord Grayson had spent all of the first dance expounding on the charms of Miss Dell. His attentions were getting so particular that Penny had decided to caution Kitty once again when they had a moment alone. It was not that Penny thought for a moment that Kitty could be fooled by the consummate fool, it was that Lord Grayson's latest infatuation was always talked of. Society would insist on discussing whether or not the preferred young lady had pinned her hopes and what was to be the end of it. She suspected that gentlemen might even lay bets about it in their clubs and she would not like Kitty to find herself the subject of gossip.

After she'd gladly ended the first with Lord Grayson, Lord Burke was momentary reprieve. He was pleasant as ever, though more subdued than Penny was used to seeing him. Penny did not pry into what might trouble him, as one never knew how a gentleman's bets had fared at Newmarket.

Lord Dalton had been as genial a dinner partner as he was capable of being, she supposed. Though he had attempted to revisit the idea that Lord Cabot was soon to reveal himself the scholar to Miss Dell, Penny had abruptly changed the subject. She had no wish to keep herself apprised of Lord Cabot's schemes. Every mention of it felt a slap to herself. Lord Dalton, being a gentleman, if not a particularly genial one, turned the conversation to horses.

All of that had been got through and Penny felt she now approached the final fence after a long day in the saddle. She was almost back to the stable, but for the tedious minuet that must close the ball.

Penny well remembered it from last year, though Kitty had studied the steps sent out ahead of time as she had never danced it. The club liked to keep some of its habits peculiar and rooted in history and so would hold on to the dance as a mark of some distinction. That nobody cared much for the dance and it had fallen out of favor would only serve to cement its worthiness more fully into the club members' minds. There had once been some talk of it being distasteful in its French origins, but the club claimed the French had stolen it from the Italians and then the English had so much improved it as to *make* it English.

The dance had not been a particular favorite for Penny last year, but this year it would be downright agonizing. Last year, she had been squired about the floor by Mr. Haveleigh, a nondescript gentleman who had congratulated himself on his mastery of the steps. This year, though, she must face Lord Cabot.

Just this dance, Penny reminded herself. Then, she would be off. She would not see Lord Cabot for many months and by that time her heart would be rid of him completely.

"Miss Darlington," Lord Cabot said, holding out his hand.

She laid her glove atop it and allowed herself to be led, ignoring the heat that always emanated from the gentleman's hand.

They separated to take their places, the music struck up and Penny curtsied to Lord Cabot's bow. They began en effaçant l'épaulé in silence.

As they passed each other, Lord Cabot said, "Miss Darlington, I must speak."

"And so you are speaking, Lord Cabot," Penny said warily. There was an urgency to his tone that she did not like.

"I know all," he said.

Penny felt a tightening in her chest, despite the sedate nature of the dance. How could he know she had ridden Bucephalus? He could have only found out from Rupert. Why did not that groom leave well enough alone?

"Burke is not the right man!" Lord Cabot whispered furiously as they executed the arriere du coté droit.

Burke? Why on earth was he talking of Burke?

"I only say, Miss Darlington, that I realize I have not been in your good books, but that is no reason to, well what I mean is, we…after all—"

They separated as they made their turns. Penny could not work out what Lord Cabot was talking about, but praise God it did not appear to be anything connected with the race that morning.

They came back together and Lord Cabot went on. "What I say is, to be direct, I would ask for your hand."

Penny kept her steps moving in the right direction, though her legs felt as if they had filled with ice. Lord Cabot looked searchingly at her. He was in earnest.

Why should he be so? Months ago, her answer would have come from her lips gladly. But now?

"You do not answer," Lord Cabot said. "I only say we are suited. And…I love you. I really, really do. It was only that…I did not know it. Or realize it. Now I do."

They turned from one another and Penny advanced to her side. How could he say it? What new torture was this?

Though, how could she resist it?

Could she resist it?

She must resist. As wonderful as the idea seemed at this moment, this earnest man would not always be before her. His ardor would cool, and then she would see the real man. The man she had glimpsed at the Tudor ball.

Though, he loved her. Was that not wonderful? He did not love Kitty after all. He loved *her*. Would that not be enough for her? Could she not bear the insults and cruelty that would come her way from time to time? Had not many women borne an unjust or bad-tempered husband?

She supposed many had, but she could not. She knew it of herself. He would break her heart and never be able to put the pieces back together again. They would end miserable, because her own temperament could not stand up against his. She was too easily hurt and he was too easy *to* hurt.

"I know your pride was stung," Lord Cabot said, leading her around the circle, "unnecessarily so. The fault was all mine, it was stupid to say and not at all what I think."

He called his words unjust, and of course they had been. But there would only be more unjust words to come if she accepted him. He would always be sorry, but he would not be different. How could she lay her heart in his hands, always wondering when it was to be crushed?

If only he could account for the things he said in some man-ner that would explain them. Why could he not point to the circumstance being strange or unusual and not a part of his temperament? That *somehow*, it was not him. That it had been some kind of aberration!

He could not, though. He regretted it, he wished he did not say it, but he could not account for it, nor swear he would not do so again.

As they came to the final sequence of the dance, Penny said, "I thank you for the offer, but I must decline."

She made the final curtsy and hurried to find her aunt.

HENRY SAT IN the early dawn light staring at the cold fireplace. That was that, he supposed. The evening had not gone as planned, nothing had gone as planned. He had been intent on securing Miss Darlington for supper. He'd felt that would give him a good amount of time to lead up to his question. Then he'd been mobbed in the front hall and by the time he got into the ballroom all that was left him was the damned minuet.

He'd sought out Dalton and asked him to step aside, claim a headache or some such, so that he might take Miss Darlington's supper. His friend had only narrowed his eyes and said, "Not on your life."

How was one meant to get a proposal out during a minuet? Still, he'd tried. It had been badly done, he was sure of it.

The lady had declined.

He very much wished he could blame the nature of his delivery on her refusal, but he suspected not. She was determined to marry Burke.

How on God's earth had he ruined his chance for happiness with one bad-tempered outburst?

The sound of carriage wheels crunching the gravel below reached him. He lazily got up to see who could be arriving at that early hour, suspecting it was some drunken lord driving a phaeton who could not remember where his host's house was. Possibly, Yarrowdale—the fellow was renowned for getting lost and Henry knew him to be staying a mile down the road.

He pulled the curtain aside and peered down.

It was one of Mendbridge's carriages. And another promptly followed it.

Henry watched in consternation as Miss Darlington, Miss Dell and Mrs. Wellburton were helped into the first. Luggage and ladies' maids were got into the second. Two burly and well-armed coachmen and four footmen completed the entourage.

She was leaving! To where? Why? Nobody had said a thing about it. Did she know she was leaving when he'd spoken to her at the ball? Was she leaving on his account?

Perhaps Burke had requested it, sensing in Henry some competition.

Perhaps they went away in preparation for the banns to be read.

But surely, Mendbridge might have said something about it.

Was the departure what he and his daughter had spoken of in the drawing room the evening before? The thing that had been settled between them. Henry had casually asked what was settled and Mendbridge nearly took his head off.

Perhaps Mendbridge, himself, understood Henry's aim and wished to get his daughter away from the scene. The man preferred Burke.

No, he could not pretend to himself that Miss Darlington went against her will. She was a stalwart sort of girl and would not be meekly sent away if she did not wish it. Especially not sent away from the races.

The carriages had been loaded with remarkable alacrity. They set off.

Henry watched them disappear down the drive.

She was gone, out of his reach. The next time he saw her, she'd be married.

It was all up with him.

PENNY HAD BEEN grateful that they'd not got home until after three and had not had time for more than a few hours nap before it was time to set off. She had not slept at all and did not wish to speak at all. Fortunately, Kitty and Mrs. Wellburton were exhausted and dozed on and off so the coach went on quiet.

She'd almost said yes. Then, she had declined. Had she made a mistake? It was all such a muddle!

She could not forget that he'd said he loved her. She loved him, too. There was no point in denying that. For a while, she'd fooled herself that she loved only the idea she'd had of him, and did not love the man he really was.

Had that been true, he would not have affected her when he came to stay in her father's house. She certainly would not have ridden his horse. A lady does not put herself in peril for a man she *used* to love.

What did it matter, though? She had refused him. He would not ask again.

She supposed she had been right to refuse him. She really could not imagine what life would be like, married to a gentleman who was by turns charming and cruel.

At least she knew what she wanted, even if it was not to be particularly exciting. She would marry somebody safe. Somebody who never said a cross word. She might not end deliriously happy, but she could go forward without fear of being bruised.

She might consider Mr. Wallington. He'd always paid her marked attention. As marked, anyway, as he dared to. He was exceedingly retiring and spoke of the quiet comfort of his country library and his collection of dead butterflies. He'd had nothing at all to do with the war. Nobody was certain why, though there might be no end of reasons—he had a limp, was said to be a pacifist, and rumored to bruise easily. He would not enthrall her, but he would be no danger to her.

She must just set her mind to it. She must only dismiss thoughts of any other gentleman.

Penny paused. Poor Mr. Wallington was so retiring that she suspected she might have to propose to herself. And then, there was her father. How was the slight and near-silent Mr. Wallington to approach her father? She supposed she'd have to do that, too. Of course, she had never seen the gentleman on horseback. He would be one of those who only rode in carriages. As a result, his calves would be horribly thin.

She must stop thinking of gentlemen's legs! Or a particular gentleman's legs!

Penny heaved a sigh.

Or eyes that crinkled at the corners. Or pleasing height and broad shoulders. Or lovely chestnut hair. Or a particular timbre of voice.

After all, could she not entertain herself with children? Could she not make her children her life's work?

Penny grimaced as she thought of the means of actually *getting* children from Mr. Wallington.

"Oh bother!" she said to herself.

⟫⟩✕⟨⟪

JARVIS WAS NOT certain what to do with his master. The day was not half over and so far none of it was as it should be.

For one thing, much to his surprise, the carriage Montrose had mentioned the evening before *had* actually arrived at six. He'd been certain it had been some low taunt to himself, but he'd watched from a hall window as the ladies of the house departed.

He'd not been the least sorry to see Dora and her bold talk leave his vicinity, though he was somewhat muddled over the idea that he'd been wrong about the carriage coming at all. He'd since gathered that the ladies set off for Lord Mendbridge's estate in Devon.

Then, there was his master to consider. The night before, he'd refused to be undressed and Jarvis heard him moving around the room until well after seven that morning. They had been supposed to set off for the races at nine, and Mendbridge had left in good time. However, when Jarvis had entered his lord's room to dress him, he'd found him asleep in his clothes. After Lord Cabot opened his eyes, he'd practically thrown Jarvis from the room and said, "The races can go to the devil."

What did it all mean? He might think, under usual circumstances, that his lord suffered in the head from too jolly a time the night before. But to send the races to the devil? That was unheard of.

No matter, it was past eleven and he could hear his lord had risen. He hurried in with the basin of water that he'd been reheating all morning.

One of the first things Jarvis had ever learned about being a valet was to pretend that nothing at all was amiss, even if everything was amiss. That knowledge, he thought, would come in handy just now.

"My lord," he said, just as he said it every morning.

His lord sat on the side of the bed. "That's it, Jarvis. It's all up."

Jarvis momentarily froze. That kind of talk could only mean one thing. His lord had lost heavily at the races. So heavily that they were entirely out of funds.

But how could it be? His horse had won! Good Lord, he must have bet on another race and lost spectacularly.

Jarvis collected himself and said, "Your father is sure to step into the breach, my lord."

"My father?" Lord Cabot asked. "How is my father to convince a lady who has declined me to change her mind?"

Jarvis set the basin of water down, more lost than ever. "A lady?" he asked.

"Miss Darlington. She's declined. Oh, come on, you know all about it. I insulted her, remember? Well, as it turns out, she has no intention of ever forgetting about it."

"I am surprised, my lord," Jarvis said, the last evening's conversation racing through his mind with incredible speed.

"So was I," Lord Cabot said.

Jarvis had not known his master intended on securing Miss Darlington. Of course, he'd realized Lord Cabot liked the lady and was put out about not being forgiven over some ill-chosen words. But this new development put the conversation in the servant's hall in an entirely new light.

The valet staggered ever so slightly and gripped the bedpost to steady himself. If the announcement of the coach that was to come at six had never been about himself, then had anything they'd said been about himself? My God. When he'd left them, he heard one of them say, "Why does the rube think we're talking about *him*?"

What if it had not been about him at all? What if they had

been speaking about Lord Cabot and Miss Darlington? It was Miss Darlington who was to leave at six. Therefore, what if it had not been Dora who had been mortally offended by himself, but it had been Miss Darlington offended by Lord Cabot.

What had Dora said exactly? A lady that has seen the true temperament of a gentleman…once that terrible temperament is known, it's *known*.

She spoke of temperament. Of permanence. Not ill-chosen words, not a verbal scuffle, not a transient disagreement, not a silly argument. Temperament. *That's* what she said.

"Oh dear," he said softly.

Lord Cabot looked up, annoyed. "What are you oh-dearing about, Jarvis?"

"I believe, my lord, that the words you spoke to Miss Darlington, the ones you regret, might have been taken to be less an aberration and more a revelation of your temperament. If I am right, Miss Darlington believes that those words you spoke showed her who you are. Who you *really* are. At least, that is what I can gather from the servants' talk."

Lord Cabot stared at his valet for a long and uncomfortable minute. Just as Jarvis was beginning to think that he'd taken too much of a liberty, that one ought to let the lords and ladies sort things out for themselves, his master threw himself prone on the bed.

Lord Cabot stared at the ceiling and said, "My God! She thinks she's glimpsed the real man! She thinks me cruel at heart and only wearing a polite veneer for society's sake. She thinks I wore a mask and let it slip for a moment! No wonder she prefers Burke."

"But she could be made to see otherwise?" Jarvis said hopefully.

Before Lord Cabot could answer, there was a soft knock at the door. Jarvis hurried to answer it, and to send away whoever it was. No doubt it was the diabolical Peg insisting she must tidy the room.

A footman stood at the door holding out a letter. "Just arrived and marked urgent," he said as he handed it over.

AFTER A LONG day of ruminating, Penny was relieved to see that they had arrived to Bishop's Stortford. As Lord Mendbridge was a frequent visitor of the George, they were assured they would be afforded the best rooms available. In truth, Penny was not so certain the rooms had *been* available. They had been led into a dining room and served tea and it was nearly an hour before they were shown up. Maids were hurrying out as they came in and Penny saw one carrying a large portmanteau down the corridor.

She would have felt very sorry for whoever they had displaced, if she had the strength for it. As it was, all she wished to do was sleep. Whether or not sleep would find her, she did not know. But, she must at least pretend that it did. Mrs. Wellburton and Kitty had both expressed their concern that they did not think she'd slept a wink since yesterday.

They were right. She had not. Her thoughts and feelings had veered every which way, and they had left behind a dark heaviness she could not seem to lift from her shoulders.

It was as if the world had grayed and color had fled. Perhaps that was what happened when one became an adult. Truly an adult, not the silly girl that she had been, dreaming of romance.

The grown-up world was not as colorful, but perhaps it would be better for its clearer outlines.

"Do rest, Penny," Kitty said. "Your aunt and I will take in a walk to stretch our legs, but you must rest. You are awfully pale. Dora will stay by you and get you anything you need."

Penny had nodded, not at all sorry that those two pairs of astute eyes would cease to examine her. She laid herself down and closed her eyes, listening to their chatter about which direction to go and what sort of shawl would be best, and where that shawl might be located amongst their trunks.

Finally, Penny heard the door close behind them.

"Oh Dora," she said quietly, "I hope and pray I have not made a mistake."

"A mistake, miss? Have you changed your mind over what you fancy to wear on the morrow? Don't fret over it, I can root through the other trunks easily enough."

"Not with clothes," Penny said. "With my life."

As Dora was not a deep nor philosophical individual, Penny did not expect an answer to that particular statement. Nor did she get one.

HENRY GRABBED THE letter from his valet's hands. At the mention of it marked urgent, he'd had one thought. Had Miss Darlington's carriage overturned or had she encountered some other trouble on the road?

As soon as he thought it, his logical mind pointed out that such news would be sent to Lord Mendbridge, not to the houseguest who had recently been declined. When he saw the handwriting, he felt even more foolish.

He handed the letter unopened back to Jarvis. "It is from my grandmother," he said, lying back down on the bed and closing his eyes. "She thinks everything she says is urgent."

Jarvis had taken the letter. He said, "I suspect word of your accident has reached her and she is worried over your health."

Henry nearly smiled over the idea. "Jarvis, the dowager does not fret. It is far more likely that she has written that she orders me to stay alive, as she would find my death inconvenient."

As his valet remained standing with the letter in hand, Henry said, "Open it and read it to me."

Jarvis nodded and unfolded the paper. He cleared his throat.

"Cabot, take this letter as a direct order to recover from your foolish riding accident. I have been told the cause was a fox. It has long been a tradition in England to kill foxes, not be killed by them. If you have any sense at all, you are already on your feet so we'll say no more about it."

"Told you," Henry said.

"There's more, my lord," Jarvis said.

Henry waved for his valet to continue.

"As you are staying in Mendbridge's house, I will presume you have groveled your way back into his daughter's good graces. If you have not, I advise some soul searching to discover why. A man's character is revealed in a day, but in steady actions and consistent discourse."

Jarvis paused, then he said, "She signs it, 'your vaguely unhappy grandmother.'"

Henry sat up. For once, his grandmother had said something useful. A man's character was not shown in a day! It was shown in a hundred days or a thousand days.

He slumped. Why did Miss Darlington not see that? She had known him for so many days and it had only been one day that he'd not conducted himself as he should.

Why could she not dismiss that *one* day?

Because she thought she'd glimpsed his temperament and she was frightened. How did he not realize that before? A lady put herself and her future, the quality of her life, her comfort, her very happiness, into her husband's hands. An unhappy man might stay at his club and take a mistress. An unhappy man might arrange things so he hardly noticed he inhabited an unhappy marriage. A woman could not do so.

His intemperance in that moment, at that blasted Tudor ball, had the effect of showing Miss Darlington what she could expect for her future. Of course she was not willing to put herself in his hands.

She was not right in her assessment, he knew that. But he did not see any way to repair the situation.

They were meant for each other, but it would never be. All for one day.

CHAPTER SEVENTEEN

I N BETWEEN MRS. Payne's fussing and bringing plates in and taking them back out again, Doom and Rupert had talked over the situation backwards and forwards.

It was like moving round pieces of a puzzle. If they were to tell Lord Cabot that Mr. Farthingale had attempted to poison his horse, did that not lead to the fact that Bella had been poisoned instead? Did that not then lead to the idea that Miss Darlington must have some knowledge of what had occurred? Though if they were not to tell him of it, then the lord would still think he owed whatever he'd borrowed from the scoundrel. Lord Cabot would end up paying the man who'd tried to kill his horse.

If they were to mention that Rupert had been drugged, that then led to the question of who had ridden Lord Cabot's horse? Miss Darlington had, they both knew it. Did Lord Cabot already know it?

After all, she was in love with the lord, so the lord must be in love with the lady. At least, that was their reasoning.

But then, Doom had pointed out that Dora had said Miss Darlington had once admired the lord, but did no longer. They'd had a falling out.

They'd been going round in circles when Jarvis came into the room. As neither Doom nor Rupert were on the friendliest terms with the lord's valet, they looked at him skeptically.

"And what brings you out of your fine surroundings to this low end of the property?" Rupert asked.

"Never mind your insults, Rupert," Jarvis said. "Lord Cabot will be here in less than a quarter hour to inquire after your health. I came ahead to ensure that you do not make yourself ornery. As it is your natural stance, I thought you might make some effort to overcome it."

"Why should he be anything other than what he is?" Doom asked. His defiance on behalf of his friend was well-received by Rupert, as evidenced by his vigorous nodding.

The valet appeared incensed and came closer to the bed. In a low voice, he said, "Your master has not had a very good twenty-four hours. His hopes on a particular matter have been dashed and that is all you need to know about it."

"He won at the races," Rupert pointed out.

"And we happen to know he don't owe Farthingale a far-thing." Doom leaned back against the pillow, unsure if he was amused by the similarity of *Farthingale* and *farthing*, or alarmed that he'd brought up the idea at all.

Jarvis sniffed. "Naturally, low born persons can only imagine that money must be the most important thing in the world. Cultured individuals perceive that there are other things of higher value. Love and honor, being examples for you to consider."

Doom looked at Rupert. Rupert looked at Doom.

"Miss Darlington," Doom said softly.

Jarvis went an interesting shade of pale. "Say no more! I'll have no more talk of...how could you even know...that's enough!"

Doom crossed his arms. "That *is* enough, I'd say."

From outside the doors, Doom heard Mrs. Payne say, "Lord Cabot! Goodness, here you are. Yes, come in, love. I'll take you to him."

The three men inside the room stared at one another. Jarvis put his finger to his lips. Doom shook his head.

Lord Cabot was in the room in a moment.

The lord seemed surprised to see his valet there, but Jarvis mumbled something about checking on the invalids and hurried out.

Doom prepared to tell the lord the most remarkable story he'd ever hear.

DOOM HAD FINISHED his tale and Lord Cabot had stood silent for some moments. Glancing at Rupert, Doom wondered if he'd committed some kind of effrontery. He'd told the truth, but that didn't mean a lord wouldn't be affronted by it. They were a prickly species, as far as he could figure.

Lord Cabot began to laugh. Then, he abruptly stopped. "Wait," he said. "I must be certain. Rupert, do you believe what this fellow has just said?"

Rupert nodded. "Aye, I do. And if you're thinkin' of kickin' up a fuss about me missin' the race, you might want to consider all the scrapes I done rescued you from since you were knee high."

Lord Cabot blinked at his groom. "A fuss? Are you joking, man? Miss Darlington rode my horse!"

"We know it," Rupert said gravely.

"Don't you see?" Lord Cabot asked. "She loves me. She must do."

"We know that too," Doom said.

"My God, that brave, brave girl…" Cabot said, wonderment in his voice.

"Question is," Doom said boldly, "what you gonna do about it?"

"Hush, boy," Rupert said. He shrugged his shoulders and said, "The young fellow don't mean to be so forward."

"I do," Doom said, never liking to be told he was not to be something. "I only say, it's a steep hill he's got to climb. *All* the servants are against him."

Lord Cabot appeared exceedingly amused. "What care I for a thousand servants against me if Miss Darlington is not? Rupert, stay here until you can travel, Mendbridge's people will see to you. As for me, I am going to give Mendbridge the what-for about his darling Burke and then I am off!"

"Who is Burke?" Doom asked. He was not answered, as Lord Cabot was already out the door.

A HALF HOUR later, Henry pushed through the crowd at Newmarket, making his way to Lord Mendbridge's stand. He found his host surrounded by various friends who had worked their way into his private seats. The mood appeared exceedingly jolly and so Henry assumed Mendbridge had prevailed with his horse.

"Cabot!" Mendbridge called upon spotting him. "I wondered when you would turn up. You've missed the whole thing—Jupiter won it handily."

Henry approached the foot of the stand. "Excellent, yes, very good," he said. "Lord Mendbridge, I have come on a vital matter."

Mendbridge peered down at him, as did all the other fellows in the stand.

"Yes?" Mendbridge asked.

"The thing is, well, the truth of the matter is…Burke will not do! I am sorry but he simply will not!"

Lord Mendbridge drew his brows together and said, "Eh? Burke will not do what?"

Henry breathed out a sigh of relief. He'd been worried that Mendbridge would be absolutely set on Burke.

He bowed and said, "I understand you perfectly, sir! I will set off at once!"

Henry left Lord Mendbridge staring at his coat tails as they flapped behind him.

It would not be an hour later when Lord Dalton and Lord Grayson arrived to Mendbridge's stand. Dalton inquired where Cabot was. Upon hearing that he'd taken himself off to somewhere after insisting Burke would not do, Dalton turned to Grayson.

Grayson said, "Do we try to stop him?"

Lord Dalton, so rarely used to defeat but becoming more accustomed to it by the season, sighed and said, "We'll never catch him."

FREDDY HAD DODGED and weaved all the way to London. Mr. Farthingale had been on his heels, but never really had the chance to catch him. After all, the gentleman was not prepared to sleep in fields and haylofts. Therefore, Freddy had surmised his old master would stick to the usual roads and stop at the usual inns. He'd have good dinners and sleep in a bed.

For himself, Freddy had taken a more direct route over hill and dale. He packed up enough food in a rucksack and he drank from streams along the way. He hitched rides on carts when he happened on a convenient stretch of road and went on foot through fields and forests. He traveled night and day with barely an hour to sleep here and there. He used the sun and the stars to guide him south. By the time he arrived to the outskirts of London, he was satisfied that he'd left Farthingale far behind.

He'd initially thought of going to America. But on reflection, he realized he'd never afford the passage. He'd have to indenture himself for a year or more. He had no wish to indebt himself to anyone, having just shaken off one scoundrel.

There was, though, a particular scoundrel he had decided to see. A certain Mr. Mackery who just now lived with an old contessa in Italy. But first, he must get to Farthingale's office and find Mackery's notes.

PENNY'S CARRIAGE ARRIVED to London in good time. Time, however, had not been on the town staff's side. As they had no notion that any of the family would be arriving, Penny had a momentary glimpse of how they lived when nobody was about. As evidenced by the open book and half-glass of port on her father's desk in the library, the senior town footman considered himself very senior indeed when Montrose was not residence. They all had a look of terror on their faces and ran this way and that to destroy all notions of impropriety. It was the first thing that had made Penny laugh in days.

She, Kitty and Mrs. Wellburton would not trouble them long. They would stay over a day to complete some shopping and then be gone. Mrs. Wellburton would usually prefer a stop of three or four days, but her aunt had become more and more eager to get to Bath.

While Mrs. Wellburton ticked off the names of all the ladies she was interested in calling on in that town, Penny was certain she was most interested in seeing Mr. Thornbridge. He was a great proponent of the waters and kept a house on the Paragon just as they did. In truth, Penny's father did not own the house but rented it and she was certain her aunt had been the instigator. Lord Mendbridge had little use for Bath or its waters. Mr. Thornbridge remained devoted to the town, though it was not what it had been. Penny was all but certain her aunt was not as enthused about the waters as she was about Mr. Thornbridge residing conveniently nearby.

Mrs. Wellburton would not go so far as to send word to the gentleman that she would soon arrive, but then there was little need. Bath society was small enough in these days that word of their arrival would circulate instantly. If that were not sufficient, Mr. Thornbridge would certainly see the activity of the house being opened for them. She was sure he would call at the first opportunity.

Penny looked about her London bedchamber thinking it almost seemed foreign to her. It had been the scene of so many happy days! All those happy days until the last unhappy day.

She fondly remembered the excitement of getting ready for a ball, certain that Lord Cabot would attend. How her insides had fluttered and the air felt electric, like the moment before a lightning strike in summer. How intoxicating it had been when he had secured her for supper and they could hardly stop speaking to one another, only reluctantly turning to their other sides occasionally for decency's sake. How wonderful it had been to come home and describe to Dora what the ladies wore and how dashing the gentlemen were. Secretly, and silently, she would review to herself how dashing a particular gentleman had been.

It had all been a lovely dream.

"Goodness, Penny," Kitty said, "are you well? Why do you stand as still as a statue in the middle of the room?"

Penny turned, forcing herself to smile. "Daydreaming is all," she said, making an attempt at cheerfulness.

Kitty crossed the room and took Penny by the hand. "You are deeply unhappy, my friend. I've known it since we set off. Did something happen at the ball?"

Penny looked away. She really did not want to explain what had happened. She could not imagine saying the words. Worse than that, she did not wish for anybody to pity her, especially not Kitty.

"I think the ox head has upset you again," Kitty said. "I am beginning to thoroughly dislike the gentleman."

Penny turned back to her friend, determined to regain her spirits. "Never mind it, Kitty. We are off to Bath tomorrow. You know how we both have a fondness for Mr. Wraith's shop and I have quite a bit of money with me. I shall bury us in new fabrics and ribbons."

Kitty smiled, having a particular weakness for Mr. Wraith's ribbon selection. "Then we may call on Mrs. Yardley when we return home. She has all the newest circulars and we will make designs and have fittings."

"With plenty of tea and biscuits," Penny promised.

Kitty squeezed her hand. "You will be better in time, from whatever ails you. You'll see."

Penny hoped Kitty was right.

HENRY HAD CHANGED horses more times than he could remember as he made his way to Devon. He made excellent time, but what he could not understand was how he had failed to overtake Miss Darlington's party. He'd stopped and asked in the usual places and had tracked them as far as the George. They had seemed to vanish since then.

It was not ideal. Part of his plan had been to catch up to them in some dramatic fashion as evidence of his devotion. He'd intended to gallop alongside her coach like a regular Dick Turpin and, rather than demand her purse, he would state his case.

As he had lost full confidence in his oratory skills after the terrible minuet proposal, he'd spent a good deal of time rehearsing everything he could possibly think of to induce her to accept him. If all went perfectly, she'd order her coach to stop. And then, well, he'd figure out how to proceed from there.

As they could not possibly be ahead of him, he had somehow passed by them. Now, he would be left to cool his heels in some nearby inn in Devon until he got word they'd arrived. He'd visit the house and attempt to get some idea when they were expected. Miss Darlington would be apprised of his inquiries and instantly surmise that he'd set off after them. That would have to do by way of dramatic gestures.

While he'd been composing his case, he'd had ample time to think of how he could convince Miss Darlington that he was not the man she'd witnessed at the Tudor ball. That, very uncomfortably, had led to an examination of who he *had* been that night. Petulant over Ashbridge, and alarmed for himself and his own feelings. To reject both of those things, he'd conducted himself like a spoilt child being denied a piece of cake.

He'd let loose with those juvenile feelings, depending on Miss

Darlington's good nature to carry them through it. He had not taken into account a lady's situation.

In truth, he did not think he had ever really taken into account a lady's situation.

His friends routinely joked about determined debutantes and their steely-eyed mamas. It had been a great jest. None of them had closely examined what was at stake for those women. If a man did not marry, he was perennially a desirable bachelor until he hobbled with gout. If a lady did not marry quickly, she was put on a shelf. Worse, if she did not have some means of support, she became a burden to her family or hired herself out as a companion. A female pressed to make a choice in a few number of years must be careful. Very careful, else she end up wishing she'd become a dowager's companion after all. The ghastly situation had always been there for all to see, and yet somehow he had not consciously thought of it. He had since paid a great price for the information.

No matter, he would rectify Miss Darlington's fears. He must. After all, she must love him. She'd risked so much to take his horse across the finish. As it happened, she would not even have known how much had been at stake. She would not have known that he had bet heavily and had been in deep with Farthingale.

Farthingale might be finished now, but he had not been then. Miss Darlington could not have known all the ins and outs of the plot against him.

What she *had* known was his love of the races and his care for his horses. She had understood the importance of the day to him, as no other lady could.

She loved him, but she was afraid of him. What a situation! Still, he thought smiling to himself, she *did* love him. There were, from time to time, niggling ideas that suggested there might have been another cause for the lady riding his horse that he could not yet fathom. He pushed them away with energy. Now was no time to lollygag and wonder.

He had come to the lane that led to the Mendbridge estate.

He spurred his horse on to the front doors and leapt down. It was not a moment after he banged on the door than a very old footman answered it.

The man looked at him bewildered. "Sir?"

"I know the family is not at home at this moment," Henry said, "at least I assume not. What I would like to know is when Miss Darlington is expected."

The footman looked confused by the request. Henry said, "Excuse me, you'll want to know who I am. Lord Cabot, a friend of Lord Mendbridge."

The footman nodded slowly. "I expect they'll get here in a fortnight or so."

"A fortnight!" Henry nearly shouted. Seeing he had frightened the man, as evidenced by him staggering back, he lowered his tone.

"I do not understand," he said. "At Newmarket, I understood they had set off for Devon?"

The footman nodded. "If I knowed Mrs. Wellburton, which I *have* knowed these many years, she took her own particular route."

"What route!" Henry cried.

The footman rubbed his chin. "Well, she do favor a stop in London, I think I know that much."

Henry stared at the man. The old fellow might be senile, or they might have gone to London, or they might arrive here tomorrow, or they might have gone somewhere else altogether.

"But you think London," Henry said.

"Aye, I think it," the footman repeated.

"To London I go, then," Henry muttered.

As he mounted his horse, the footman called to him. "Shall I tell them you called, Lord Babbitt?"

"Cabot!" he shouted. "It's Lord Cabot!"

THOUGH IT HAD often been their habit to stop overnight at Froxfield on the way to Bath, it had been agreed that they would forgo it this time. Mrs. Wellburton was a friend of a family who lived there, and often thought it an obligation to stop. Penny was not sorry to skip it, the lady of the house was severely ostentatious and the house was run on a strict timetable. She found she was forever staring at a clock when she was there, lest she arrive late to anything the lady had arranged.

In any case, the road to Bath had been so vastly improved of late that they all agreed they might set off early and be in Bath for a late dinner as long as no calamities were met with on the road.

Penny could not help but note the eagerness with which Mrs. Wellburton took up the idea. Her aunt was impatient to get to Bath, and she was sure, impatient to see Mr. Thornbridge.

Did the gentleman not see her aunt's fondness for him? They really were well suited and Penny did not see why he did not get on with it. They were not young, but they were not so old that they might not enjoy a good number of years together. Why did they waste the time they had?

Though they had all presumed they would get to Bath in good time, Penny once more realized how foolish it was to ever expect a trip to go smoothly. There was invariably something that caused a delay—a broken wheel, a lame horse, a passenger who felt ill and needed to get out and walk for a while.

On this particular trip, one of the springs on the carriage had broken and it had taken hours to repair. There had been some talk of finding a local inn and setting off again in the morning, but Mrs. Wellburton was convinced they ought not to. The lady claimed that one could not rest easy at an inn one was not familiar with. Penny did not know if that was a real fear or not, but they went forward all the same.

It had been after ten o'clock when they finally arrived. Fortunately, the landlord of the house was an organized and patient gentleman and had seen to their comfort. The rooms were ready, the staff was ready, and there had been a sideboard left with meat and drink.

They had eaten in near silence and gone to bed.

The next day dawned fine, at least as fine as one could hope for through the smog of Bath. Penny had breakfasted and then occupied herself in her room, leaving Kitty the time to lounge around with her books before they went out shopping.

She finally went downstairs out of boredom. She paused at the drawing room doors as she distinctly heard Mr. Thornbridge's voice. Penny smiled. The gentleman had wasted no time in making his way over.

"You deny me outright, then?" Mr. Thornbridge said.

"Believe me, I do not wish to," Mrs. Wellburton answered.

"Then why—"

"I cannot leave until Penny is settled. Even if I were willing to do so before, I fear something troubles her now. My brother is a dear of a man but he is not suited to raising daughters."

"I see," Mr. Thornbridge said, in as sad a tone as ever Penny had heard.

"I hope you *do* see, Mr. Thornbridge," Mrs. Wellburton said. "I must not throw over my obligations."

"I understand you, madam. Now, I think everything that can be said just now has been said. I thank you for your consideration and I will take my leave."

CHAPTER EIGHTEEN

As Mr. Thornbridge took his leave from her aunt, Penny ran from the door and made her way to the back garden. She wound through the rather unkempt rows of flowers, dashing a tear from her cheek.

He had asked! Mr. Thornbridge had finally asked her aunt for her hand. Mrs. Wellburton had refused him—on *her* account! Her dear aunt, who she was certain was in love with Mr. Thornbridge, had turned him away. They were well-suited. They could be happy, she was sure of it.

None of that was to be because Penny Darlington was troubled.

She had ruined her own happiness, and now she had ruined her aunt's chances too.

And why? Because she was afraid somebody might hurt her feelings?

Penny stumbled to the old stone bench in the back of the garden. It was inconveniently covered in green lichen, but she had no care for her dress at that moment.

Her family had always surrounded her in a soft cocoon. They had recognized early that she fell on the sensitive side of things and buffered her against all that might upset her. She had known nothing but kindness in Devon. Of course, it had not been possible to protect her so well in London. And then the first time someone had really hurt her feelings, she had all but disintegrated.

She, Penny Darlington, driver of a Hooper High Flyer. Daring rider of the winner of the thousand guinea stakes. She had felt an insult and blown apart like a dandelion clock in a breeze.

How was she to go on so? Could any marriage, regardless of the amiability of the gentleman, entirely escape a row or two? Even her father, who had loved Penny's mother so dearly, sometimes spoke of the time his wife nearly left. He'd come in late to his own dinner party, having been on a fox hunt and making a subsequent ill-advised stop at a tavern.

Recriminations had followed, generally along the lines of horses and foxes being more important than his wife. Lord Mendbridge laughingly recounted his grave error in mentioning that dinner guests might wait but foxes never would. He'd thought it an exceedingly clever turn of phrase in that moment, until he noticed his wife's lady's maid packing up her things for an extended visit to her mother.

The rift had been patched up via a profuse apology, a spectacular diamond tiara, and a new rule in the house that there was never to be a fox hunt on a day they hosted a dinner.

Penny Darlington would not have even been born if that argument had not been patched up.

Penny put her hands to her cheeks. What a goose she was! After all, what was the worst thing that could possibly happen if someone she loved made her cry?

She would cry, that was all.

Then, at some later point, she would stop crying. Her mother had cried over that dinner party. No, really she had cried because she thought her husband loved his fox hunt more that he did herself. And then, she had stopped crying and got on with it.

Her mother did not die over it and neither would Penny.

She sighed. It was all well and good to come to the realization now, but it was far too late. Lord Cabot would not come back for a second trouncing, and she suspected Mr. Thornbridge would not either. At least, he would not venture it until Penny was married and no longer a burden to her aunt.

Perhaps that was the right course, then. She must marry somebody suitable and pretend to be happy about it. At least that would give her aunt a chance at *real* happiness.

While she was at it, she would seek to toughen herself up a bit. She was exceedingly daring on the back of a horse. She must find a way to be daring with her feelings too.

HENRY HAD MADE his way to London as fast as he had made his way to Devon—riding hard and changing horses often. He was determined to catch Miss Darlington there and did not wish to risk having her set off and missing her on the road again.

He'd jumped off his horse, handed the reins to a boy, and bounded up the steps. After a good pounding, a footman Henry recognized from prior calls opened the door.

"I would like to see Miss Darlington," he said. "I know it is not her at-home day, but it is urgent. Lord Mendbridge knows all about it."

The footman's brows had been slowly coming together on his forehead as Henry spoke. Another footman tittered somewhere in the hall behind the fellow.

"I'm sorry, Lord Cabot," the footman said, "Miss Darlington is not at home."

"Oh, I know she'd say so," Henry said, "but I must insist all the same. She'll change her mind if I am afforded time to speak."

Now the footman looked really confused. "No, my lord," he said hurriedly, "I mean she is *really* not at home. She is not here."

"Where then?" Henry said. "Has she gone riding in the park? I could catch up to her there, I suppose."

"She's gone to Bath, my lord," the footman said.

"Bath!" Henry cried. "Why? Why has she gone to Bath?"

"Well," the footman said slowly, "they came from Newmarket on their way to Devon."

"Yes, I know," Henry said, suppressing the urge to throttle the fellow. "But what has Bath got to do with it?"

"It's Mrs. Wellburton's particular route," the footman said.

"What kind of route is that!" Henry shouted. "Who goes from Newmarket to London to Bath to Devon?"

"Mrs. Wellburton, my lord," the footman said, backing up.

Henry turned and jogged down the steps. Mrs. Wellburton was a madwoman, and he was going to Bath.

THE DAY HAD been agonizing for Penny. She'd had to put on a bright face for Kitty and then Mrs. Wellburton had to put on a bright face for them both. The only individual with an authentic bright face was Kitty.

It had been planned that Penny and Kitty would shop and then they would escort Mrs. Wellburton to the pump room, but her aunt had decided she did not wish to go after all. In fact, Mrs. Wellburton suggested they cut the visit short and leave for Devon in two days' time, as so many of her friends were not in residence.

Kitty believed what she was told, but Penny did not. Her aunt did not want to encounter Mr. Thornbridge again under what could only be extremely awkward circumstances.

Penny had thought she would not disclose that she had overheard the proposal, and Mrs. Wellburton's reason for declining, but then she began to waver. Perhaps it would be best to confess her eavesdropping and convince her aunt that there was no cause to refuse Mr. Thornbridge on her account. Her father was well able to escort her to London next season and Kitty would be there too.

Penny had waited until they had all gone above stairs and enough time had passed that she could count on Kitty being engrossed in a book and oblivious to any sounds in the hall. She tiptoed to her aunt's door and softly knocked.

"Enter," Mrs. Wellburton said.

Penny came in and her aunt said, "Goodness, I thought it must be my maid forgotten something. Can you not sleep?"

Penny sat down on the cozy velvet sofa next to her aunt. "Not a wink," she said. "I must say this all to you quickly or I shall never say it all. I heard Mr. Thornbridge's proposal and your refusal. I did not mean to eavesdrop, but you must not do it! I am perfectly fine and I could not go on thinking I had ruined your happiness too."

At the mention of the proposal, a faint pink bloomed on Mrs. Wellburton's cheeks. She was silent for a moment and Penny feared she was angry to find her niece had been listening at doorways.

"You just said, my happiness *too*," Mrs. Wellburton said. "That is precisely what I have feared. Tell me, Penny, how it is that you think you have ruined your own happiness?"

Penny had not anticipated the conversation going in that particular direction. Still, with her dear aunt holding her hand and looking into her eyes, she could not dissemble.

After she had done pouring out the tale of Lord Cabot—everything from his marked interest, to his insult, to his proposal during the minuet, only leaving out that she had ridden his horse—Penny sat back exhausted. It was not an unhappy exhaustion, though. It had felt good to put everything into words.

"Good God, girl," Mrs. Wellburton said, laughing, "you *have* made a mess of it."

Penny did not see why her aunt should find the whole thing amusing. In fact, she felt a little stung by her aunt's reaction. A lot stung, if she were to be honest. She had a great urge to run from the room. Instead, she remembered her recent vow to toughen herself up.

"Yes, I admit it," Penny said. "I have made a wretched mess of things."

"Well, do not look so forlorn over it," Mrs. Wellburton said. "It is true, I have not favored Lord Cabot. I did not think he took the flirtation seriously, but perhaps I only measured him by his father's yardstick. I must have, else he would not have proposed to anybody until he was forty. What I have never taken Lord Cabot for, though, is an easily put off gentleman. If he is in earnest, he will try again."

Penny was cheered by her aunt's words. Not because they were true, she knew they were not, but because of the effort her aunt took in attempting to assuage her feelings.

"But do you think the same of Mr. Thornbridge?" Penny asked. "You must not turn him down again! You must not or I will be so unhappy!"

"Well, I cannot say what Mr. Thornbridge will do," Mrs. Wellburton said. "He has not the energy and pigheadedness of youth."

"But if he does, Aunt," Penny pressed on, "you will not say no."

"As your father says, we will clear that fence if we come to it."

HENRY ARRIVED TO Bath in the middle of the night. He had no house there, nor any friend who might be in residence. He'd finally found an inn on the outskirts of town that would take him in, and that only because of the quality of his horse and his autocratic manner. He'd been traveling so long without his valet that his appearance was a rumpled and unprepossessing mess.

He'd cleaned up as best he could, though it was not particularly up to anybody's standards. Jarvis would have had apoplexy over the state of his coat, and downright died at the sight of his neckcloth. Disheveled or no, he would see Miss Darlington this morning.

It had not taken long to ask around and find out where she stayed, though a few people he'd asked had said nothing and only hurried away from him. He was certain they thought him some mad sort of gentleman intent on carrying the lady off for nefarious purposes.

Finally, he banged on the third front door in as many days in his quest to overtake Miss Darlington.

PENNY, KITTY AND Mrs. Wellburton were in the drawing room. Mrs. Wellburton made a great show of attending to her sewing, Kitty was absorbed in a book, and Penny gazed round the room, settling on nothing.

She sat up at the loud banging on the door. Could Mr. Thornbridge have gathered his courage and come back for another run at it? Whoever it was, they had arrived with vigor.

From out in hall, Penny heard Lord Cabot say, loudly, "I must insist on seeing Miss Darlington this instant!"

Mrs. Wellburton's head snapped up from her sewing. Penny was frozen where she sat.

He had come!

Why had he come?

Her aunt rose and nearly ran to Kitty's side. She pulled her up and away from her book. "I must show you something in my room, Kitty. Now."

"Now?" Kitty said, her face all wonder.

"Right now, come."

Mrs. Wellburton hauled Kitty from the room. In the hall, Penny heard her aunt say, "Good morning, Lord Cabot. My niece is in the drawing room. Miss Dell and I shall return presently."

Penny smoothed her dress, she patted her hair, she fussed with the ribbon at her waist. What should she do? Where should she put herself? How should she receive him? She didn't know what to do!

Before she could give in to an almost overwhelming urge to run, Lord Cabot strode into the room. He bowed.

Penny rose and curtsied. Then she peered at him. He was an absolute mess, what had happened to him?

"Miss Darlington," he said approaching, "I apologize for my appearance, but I have been to Devon, and then London, and now Bath, in search of you!"

"You did not know my aunt's particular route," Penny said, in lieu of saying anything of sense.

"I did not, but I know it now," Lord Cabot said.

"Yes," Penny said. "She likes to stop in London. And then stop in Bath."

"As I understand it," Lord Cabot said. "Surely, you must know why I've ridden over half of England to catch up to you?"

Penny sank down on the sofa. She hoped she knew, but she could not say so.

"First," Lord Cabot said, striding back and forth across the carpet, "I must outline all the reasons you should throw over your fears. One, I was all in a jumble at the Tudor ball because of Ashbridge and well, because of you. I had not yet sorted out my feelings, though they were laying there right in front of me and I sought to deny them. I was an imbecile, as you very well know."

Lord Cabot had reached the bookshelf and turned, walking briskly back again. "Second," he said, "I now realize what you are afraid of. You worry that I am a beast and have been hiding it all this time. It is not true! Yes, I was a beast on that occasion, but I am not usually. In fact, I would go so far as to say hardly ever."

The lord reached the door and swung around to continue his pacing. "Third, I am willing to write the following into a marriage contract: Should I ever insult Lady Cabot, I will stand in the middle of the street and shout that I am a beast that does not deserve her. You see? I am willing to go *that far*."

Penny suddenly said, "But you see, I am not afraid of you hurting my feelings anymore!"

"My God," Lord Cabot said, stopping in his tracks. "It cannot be true. You cannot love Burke. Would he shout in the street? Would he go *that far*?" Lord Cabot stared at the far wall. "I do not think he would."

Penny was entirely lost. "What does Lord Burke have to do with it?"

"Does he have nothing to do with it?" Lord Cabot asked, turning to face her. "But then, why should you no longer fear I could affect your feelings?"

"I did not say you could not affect my feelings," Penny said. "I said I am no longer afraid of you hurting them. You *would*, you know. Sooner or later."

Lord Cabot appeared irate over the suggestion. "I would not! I swear it! Your feelings shall be as a delicate china cup in my hands! I will never even put a chip in them!"

"No," Penny said, laughing, "You are wrong. I am certain you will chip them. You will come late for dinner, and I will call the carriage, and you will apologize and buy me a tiara. Then we will carry on."

Lord Cabot rushed to her side. "Do you accept then? I can buy you a tiara today if it makes the slightest difference."

"I do accept," Penny said, "but delay the tiara. You will need it someday."

"Miss Darling," Lord Cabot said, grasping her hands. "I mean, Miss Darlington."

"Leave it at Miss Darling," Penny said. "Or just Penny when we have a row."

Lord Cabot lifted her chin and kissed her softly. "Very well, Miss Darling."

They stayed in that position a shocking amount of time. So shocking that after nearly an hour Penny distinctly heard Kitty out in the hall. "Hadn't we better go in, Mrs. Wellburton," she said loudly.

They did not come in, though. Mrs. Wellburton knew when to stay away.

It was well that Kitty was kept away. Penny and Lord Cabot, or Henry as she knew him now, had very much to speak of.

"I must tell you something very shocking," Penny said between kisses. "And you must promise not to be angry with anybody involved."

"I swear," Lord Cabot said.

"It was not Rupert that rode Bucephalus. It was I."

"Yes, I know it," he said.

"You know it?" Penny asked.

"Of course I know it. What else could have given me the courage to ride for days across England in pursuit of you? I realized you must love me if you rode my horse."

"That is a very bold assumption, my lord."

"But I was right and we shall not have a row about it. Now, I must tell *you* something shocking. You have no idea the scope of the service you did me. I am ashamed to say I'd got myself involved with a moneylender."

"Yes, I know it," Penny said.

"How—"

"Lord Grayson," Penny said. "He was in a pique over the idea that you pursued Miss Dell."

"Miss Dell?" Cabot said laughing. "I was thought to favor Miss Dell and you were thought to favor Burke?"

"Burke?" Penny asked. "Where would you get such an idea?"

"Lord Dalton," Cabot said ruefully. "I should have never believed a word of it. But you know, you *were* laughing with Burke that first night at dinner. Quite a lot, I thought. Too much, I also thought."

Penny was pleased to note a hint of possessiveness in his tone, though she could not ignore her own past tinges of green.

"Lord Dalton told me that you were a great scholar and would reveal it to Miss Dell to secure her favor."

"A scholar?" Lord Cabot said laughing. "You never did believe that."

"As it happened…but you're not?"

"God, no. Shall we even have a library at home?"

"We will have a small section for equine genealogies and such," Penny said, "and then the rest for Kitty to read when she comes."

"Very good notion. And, perhaps one of our children will be a very great reader."

Penny laughed merrily over the idea. "One never knows, I suppose."

"In any case, whatever our wrong-headed ideas have been, it has all come right in the end," Cabot said. "Our path going forward is remarkably smooth—I spoke to your father before I left Newmarket and he was approving of the match."

"Was he?" Penny asked.

"Oh, yes. Very."

Lord Cabot had entwined his arm around her waist and pulled her so close she could barely breathe. She did not mind it at all.

Though, a very sudden and urgent thought came to her. "Mr. Thornbridge!" she cried. "We must fix Mr. Thornbridge!"

After apprising her fiancé of what she meant by fixing Mr. Thornbridge, they speedily set off to find the gentleman. That both Mrs. Wellburton and Kitty were surprised to see them fly out the door was to be expected. Especially poor Kitty, as all she heard was, "We are engaged! We shall not be gone an hour!"

PENNY AND LORD Cabot were true to their word. They'd found Mr. Thornbridge at home and Penny had speedily apprised him of the current circumstances. Mr. Thornbridge had mused over the idea that he might wait until a suitable time had expired after his first proposal. Perhaps he would allow the lady's thoughts to settle before a rapprochement. He was still talking when Penny ordered a footman to get the gentleman's coat and walking stick.

He was back at the house not many more minutes after that, and the situation was resolved to everybody's satisfaction. Mrs. Wellburton might have blushed like a schoolgirl and Mr.

Thornbridge might have stumbled over his words, but the end of it was they would marry.

LORD MENDBRIDGE LOOKED upon the recently concluded race week with satisfaction. He'd not won every match up, but he'd won enough of them. Poor Penny had not been able to race her horse at all, but she was young and there would be other races. All in all, it was a job well done.

The town had begun to clear out and he hosted some of the remaining gentlemen of the club for a last evening's celebration.

They had concluded a very good dinner and just passed round the port when Montrose bustled in with a letter. He handed it to his lord and said, "From Miss Darlington in Bath, my lord. It appears as if she's written in a hurry and it has been sent by private courier."

Lord Mendbridge looked at the scrawl on the outside of the letter. Montrose was right, it was badly written. His daughter had very neat handwriting as a usual thing, this was near illegible.

"I hope nothing has gone wrong," he said quietly.

Montrose nodded. Though Lord Mendbridge had spoken quietly, the men round the table grew silent. Nobody liked to be nearby when a letter came so urgently. A special courier who was unexpected generally brought bad news.

Lord Mendbridge tore it open and scanned its contents. A smile spread over his features.

"Gentlemen, I suppose you will be the first to know. My sister marries a certain Mr. Thornbridge. You may have met him while he was here. A pleasant enough fellow, though he doesn't know a thing about horses."

Lord Mendbridge read on to the second page. The paper fluttered to the table.

"Lord Cabot has asked for the hand of my daughter!" the lord said, his surprise evident.

Both Lord Grayson and Lord Dalton stared at one another from across the table. In unison, they said, "Of course he has!"

They likely said it louder than they meant to, and perhaps Dalton said it with more than a tinge of disgust.

"And, she has accepted him," Lord Mendbridge said.

"Of course she has," Lord Dalton muttered.

"Eh, Dalton?" Lord Mendbridge said. "You knew it was in the works? Cabot never said a word to me, although my daughter is convinced that he has. She writes, I know you have already given your hearty approval."

Lord Mendbridge paused, staring at the paintings of his beloved horses that lined the wall. "Penny is to marry. Well, I suppose Cabot's got a fine enough stable."

⟫⟫⟫⟫⟪⟪⟪⟪

LORD CABOT HAD found a tailor as soon as he could and had suitable clothes made. It was well that he did, as he could not very well spend every waking moment at Miss Darlington's house, or escorting Miss Darlington round the town, as disheveled as he had been on the day he'd first arrived.

It had been decided between them that they would forgo a wedding trip. Neither of them were remotely interested in wandering around the continent, only to return and bore their friends with tales of this or that museum.

Rather, they would take Cabot's soon-to-be freed funds and Penny's not inconsiderable dowry and remake his country house in Dorset. It was not so far from Lord Mendbridge's estate that they could not go back and forth easily. Further, it had the recommendation of already beginning with good-sized stables. It was the stables, it surprised nobody, where their efforts would be concentrated. They had a plan of becoming the preeminent horse breeders in England.

If a lord looked for a particularly fine horse, they wished everyone to say, "You had better go and see Lord and Lady Cabot."

They would go to London during the season, of course. But not for the entire season. They would make more of an effort to attend the races, wherever they might be held. They were, after all, horse people.

Kitty eventually came round to the idea that Penny was to marry Lord Cabot. Though, it had come as a shock. The first thing she'd said about it was, "But I thought you did not like him!"

Penny had laughed and said, "I loved him. You see, that was the problem."

Kitty would eventually warm to him and delight in reminding him that they had once called him the ox head, on account of his having a horse named Bucephalus.

⇻⟫⟩⟩⟨⟨⟨⇺

FREDDY WAS ABLE to retrieve Mackery's notes and take them to the gentleman in Italy. He'd had a vague idea that he'd trade them for a career as a valet or some such employment. As it turned out, the contessa's son took a shine to him and Freddy would end up managing that family's finances. He found he liked the Italian sun and he liked their way of going on. Gone were the stiff manners of England, and in were the passions of the continent. One might be forgiven anything if only one were loved, and he was very much loved for his talent for figures. He also had a great fondness for the food and where once he had been slight, he ended on the more portly side of things.

Both Rupert and Doom followed Penny to her new house and Doom would eventually become the stablemaster after Rupert retired. He always kept an eye out for some unfortunate youth who might be molded into something. This led to no end of situations and scrapes and irate neighbors who needed to be soothed. After all, it was no simple trick to take a hardened boy from the street and turn him into something sensible. But, it had been done for him, and so, he would press on with the idea. He kept the name Doom, though, and never went back to using Daniel. He found the name inspired a proper amount of fear in anybody young and recently employed, which was always helpful.

Mr. Farthingale found himself ruined. He'd counted on Mackery's notes to pull him through, but discovered them gone. He instantly understood what had happened and knew there was little point in chasing Freddy to Italy. Rather, he gathered up what he could and sold what he could and sailed to America. This ended up far better than he had hoped, as such a bunch of rubes he had never dreamed of encountering. Had he known that his English manners would paint him as some kind of duke to the society of the environs of Cincinnati, or *Queen of the West*, as the Americans hilariously called the town, he'd have emigrated years before. He started a gentlemen's club in the English manner and ended very comfortably in his own house. He'd become the arbiter of all fashion and manners to people who wouldn't know the proper way of going on if it hit them over the head. To his surprise, he developed a fondness for his new people and eventually married one.

As for Jarvis, he would never admit to indulging in a short period of lording it over Mendbridge's servants when it was discovered that Miss Darlington had accepted his master. He might not *admit* it, but he *did* it. And gladly too. When he was relocated to Dorset with the new Lady Cabot and her maid, Dora paid dearly for all of her prior insults. Those were happy days— his chair closest to the fire, his tea hot, and not an end of meat in sight. He and Dora would eventually come to an uneasy truce after having to live in close quarters, but not before their squabbles had almost unhinged Lord Cabot's butler.

The dowager sent a letter upon hearing that her grandson

had engaged himself to Lord Mendbridge's daughter. It was the usual scolding, but Henry was pleased to see it signed, *Your more sanguine grandmother.*

Lord Cabot did, from time to time, find himself on the road shouting, "I am a beast and do not deserve Lady Cabot." That only changed when he had to shout that he did not deserve her grace. In truth, Penny thought he got off rather easily for his occasional bruising of feelings and she was not sorry for it. For one, she did her own bruising on occasion. For another, they spent most of the time in the country, so very few people ever heard him shout it. In any case, she had three lovely tiaras and had learned a vital lesson—her feelings, whatever they might be, would not kill her.

That was something she'd have to explain more than once to her daughters, as they were veritable copies of her and cried if they were even looked at askance. She did not surround them in a cocoon as she had been, as she wished to prepare them for the wider world and the knowledge that they could withstand anything. On the other hand, she was often amused, as her poor lord could never comprehend why somebody was always weeping somewhere in the house.

Weep they would, for now. But when they went to London for their own seasons and met their own Lord Cabot, there would be far less drama and angst about it.

At least, she hoped so.

The End

About the Author

By the time I was eleven, my Irish Nana and I had formed a book club of sorts. On a timetable only known to herself, Nana would grab her blackthorn walking stick and steam down to the local Woolworth's. There, she would buy the latest Barbara Cartland romance, hurry home to read it accompanied by viciously strong wine, (Wild Irish Rose, if you're wondering) and then pass the book on to me. Though I was not particularly interested in real boys yet, I was *very* interested in the gentlemen in those stories—daring, bold, and often enraging and unaccountable. After my Barbara Cartland phase, I went on to Georgette Heyer, Jane Austen and so many other gifted authors blessed with the ability to bring the Georgian and Regency eras to life.

I would like nothing more than to time travel back to the Regency (and time travel back to my twenties as long as we're going somewhere) to take my chances at a ball. Who would take the first? Who would escort me into supper? What sort of meaningful looks would be exchanged? I would hope, having made the trip, to encounter a gentleman who would give me a very hard time. He ought to be vexatious in the extreme, and *worth* every vexation, to make the journey worthwhile.

I most likely won't be able to work out the time travel gambit, so I will content myself with writing stories of adventure and romance in my beloved time period. There are lives to be created, marvelous gowns to wear, jewels to don, instant attractions that inevitably come with a difficulty, and hearts to break before putting them back together again. In traditional Regency fashion, my stories are clean—the action happens in a drawing room, rather than a bedroom.

As I muse over what will happen next to my H and h, and wish I were there with them, I will occasionally remind myself that it's also nice to have a microwave, Netflix, cheese popcorn, and steaming hot showers.

Come see me on Facebook! @KateArcherAuthor